Perfect Crime

A COLOMBE BASTARO MYSTERY

BOOK TWO

NINO S. THEVENY

SÉBASTIEN THEVENY

TRANSLATED BY

JACQUIE BRIDONNEAU

SELF-PUBLISHED

Disclaimer

Formatted with Vellum

My daughter, Luce,
My most beautiful daughter!
No contest!"

"Oh, tu seras jamais la reine du bal
Vers qui se tournent les yeux éblouis
Pour que tu sois belle, il faudra que tu le deviennes
Puisque tu n'es pas née jolie »

(Jean-Jacques Goldman, *C'est ta chance* [It's up to you]

— Prologue —

THOUSANDS OF MEMORIES

Biscarrosse, March 2020

"I'll get it!" shouted my girlfriend when she saw the mailman opening our mailbox at the end of the driveway.

I met Colombe nearly four years ago, while I was in the historical center of Nice and she'd become my intern.

Since then, I had been spellbound by her and our love story grew until we found it normal to live together. We started out with me still in Paris and Colombe in Nice, where she was finishing up her university degree and I was making sure my career was taking off. Then thanks to what I'd been able to save from the money Lucie Lacassagne gave me when her husband Charles[*] passed away, I had a serious down payment allowing me to purchase that little house in the pine forest, not far from Lake Biscarrosse, which was where we'd fallen in love when we'd gone there on vacation.

Colombe went back into the living room, holding up the package she'd been expecting.

"It's here!" she said triumphantly, joining me on the couch where I was finishing up an article for *New Business in France*, the magazine that I worked for remotely.

"Let's go! Unwrap it, I can't wait!"

She ripped the envelope open, and we admired the long awaited grail, full of shiny and brilliant colors: the photo book of the week we'd spent in Guadeloupe end of February, beginning of March 2020, right before the beginning of lockdown. We were so lucky to have been able to spend a week on the island right before France rolled up its carpet and shut its doors because of Covid 19, and nearly got stuck in the Caribbean, something that we really wouldn't have complained about though.

A fantastic vacation, in a bungalow in the little town of Deshaies, and we'd come back to France with

---

* *French Riviera, One too many brothers*, Nino S. Theveny, 2021

think. All those people dying in such a short time, like statistically speaking, it's impossible!"

"The law of series, maybe?" I tried.

"Like, 'tough luck, losers?' I don't think so. But still, that story is terrifying me. Especially when you discover who died, it makes me shiver. Honey, I'm scared."

"What are you scared of?"

"Um, I don't know... afraid that well be the next ones on the list..."

"But come on, what list are you talking about? You're not making any sense."

"I sure would prefer that this would just be a delusion of my overactive imagination, but once again, all those coincidences... We were there too, at the same time they were!"

"So what? We don't even know them, except that we were on vacation with them in the same place during the same week. It's a fluke. Just as if you told me: *Mr. so-and-so died, and another guy too who was on the same plane that we took...* You really think the five hundred other passengers on that plane are in danger of dying? That's crazy, just fiction, that's what I'm saying!"

Colombe thought that over, tense.

"But still, I have to understand that crazy story. I'm going to investigate it. For my own peace of mind."

"Or not!" I replied ironically.

But I knew that now that Colombe had that idea in her cute little head, she would hold on to it until she'd clarified that case. I was far from imagining where that crazy story would be taking us...

"Let's look at the photos again," she proposed. "That'll help us remember everything, you know when you see the images we'll reminisce back on what happened, little things that maybe we weren't even paying attention to while we were there. The common denominator of these deaths seems evident to me: our week in Guadeloupe! We must have missed something."

"Sweetie, you're getting worried about nothing."

"Jerome, please. You know about my notorious intuitions..."

"That I do. Okay! What do you want to do?" I abdicated.

"We're going to go through the photo album and my notebook, look at the photos, reread what I wrote. As if we were reliving our week of vacation. I'm sure that we'll discover a tiny detail that we missed. To understand the origin of those deaths, the why, when, who, and above all, the how..."

an internal question as boiling hot as was the mouth of the Soufriere volcano. And an enigmatic sentence, that she said, almost to herself, lost in her thoughts.

"Jerome... I think we were close to dying there..."

"What are you talking about?" I replied, surprised.

Colombe was now white as a sheet, trembling. She put the photo album back down, got up suddenly and walked into the office. She came back with her laptop, its browser opened to her inbox.

"You remember the email that I got back in response to one of mine, a couple of days ago?"

I went through it.

"Of course I do."

"Have a look at this."

She logged into her Facebook account, searched for two friends in the profiles, clicked on the results and turned the screen towards me.

"Well? What do you think of that?"

While reading through the latest posts on those profiles, my face crumbled. After the last word, I could only stammer.

"That's completely crazy... How could that be possible?"

"It's too exceptional to be a mere coincidence. Just

great memories, having met friendly people, had memorable cocktails and all we wanted to do was come back as soon as possible.

We knew though that our souvenirs would fade as time flew by, becoming just a few images, fragrances or emotions. That's why Colombe had spent so many hours sorting hundreds of photos, putting them in chronological order, comparing them with the pages of notes she'd taken so she wouldn't forget the names of the places or sites and we wouldn't get mixed up later on when thinking back on our stay. That mass of images had been transformed into a hundred-page book of photos that we avidly were going through, sitting on the sofa in our living room.

Page after page, we relived *Gwada*, as they called it there.

A thousand and one memories, a thousand and one colors. Images, words, laughter, questions.

She had chosen dozens of photos of our group when we climbed to the top of Soufriere Hills volcano at the end of that glossy papered book. Especially one where we were proudly posing in front of the volcano with its green cone topped with sulfurous smelling fumaroles expulsed by the craters.

And Colombe finally stopped on a curious photo, frowning, a sign that she was thinking something over,

I had no other choice than to defer to Colombe's determination.

We sat back down on the sofa, with the photo album and notebook on our knees. The title she'd given the book was written on the first page:

"Welcome to Gwada!"

Part one

WELCOME TO GWADA!

Pointe à Pitre. Two weeks earlier.

CHAPTER 1
Maracudja

THOUGH WE WERE STILL in France, as soon as we stepped off the plane we immediately felt it was a far cry from being in Europe. We were wearing our winter coats and the scorching heat of the Caribbean air hit us as soon as they opened the doors. We'd stuffed summer clothes into our suitcases and hoped that they wouldn't be lost someplace in the meanders of the airports, having had that happen to us during a previous trip to New York. So when going through the tunnel linking the plane to the airport, we were already sweating in our winter coats, though it was night.

We heard voices coming from the airport, probably people anxiously waiting to welcome their friends or families. We went through the automatic doors leading to the arrivals hall and saw a group of women dressed in bright Creole colored clothing, wearing hats and fancy hairdos, singing their hearts out with lively songs. No doubt about it, we'd arrived and were immediately immersed in the welcoming environment of Pointe à Pitre. I could feel right off the bat that we'd be having an exceptional vacation. I was far from thinking at what point the word "exceptional" would be using its literal meaning, "constituting the nature of an exception."

At the wheel of our Peugeot 208 rental car, white, like most rentals here, we were disappointed that we couldn't see the scenery because it was too dark. Almost an hour later, thanks to my smartphone's GPS, we drove into the "Bougainvillea Domain," on the hill-sides of Deshaies. It was dark and there weren't many lights on, and no one seemed to be expecting us when I stopped my car in the parking lot, across from a row of palm trees with gigantic leaves. Yet the owner, someone named Severine, had been irreproachable and reactive, ever since we'd reserved here a few months ago. Colombe finally decided to call her, and she appeared nearly instantly in the path between two bungalows, something they called 'Ti'Caz" in Creole here.

She was a thirty-some year-old lady with a complicated chignon topped with West Indian braids. She was wearing a type of puffed up sarouel and a top with thin straps supporting her generous forms. She held out her hand while smiling at us.

"Welcome to Gwada!" she said. "Did you have a good trip?"

"Thanks. We're just happy to have arrived."

"I'd imagine you must be tired. Just follow me, I'll show you your bungalow."

She preceded us through the lush vegetation here, and I had to admit that I had no idea what most of the trees or bushes were, up to our cozy bungalow that we'd be staying in. I could make out others, some with their lights out, others still lit up. There was a languid lady on the front porch of one of them, wearing a brightly colored sarong, reading in a wide rattan chair. As we passed her she stopped reading and looked at us, nodding to welcome us here.

"How many bungalows do you have?" I asked.

"We've got seven," Severine replied proudly. "And that's not counting ours, which is on the top of this lot, behind the pool. I'll show you around tomorrow if you'd like."

"Thanks, that would be great. Are you full?" asked Colombe.

"Nearly so. You just saw Nathalie, who arrived yesterday. There will still be people arriving tomorrow night, and after that, if you want of course, I'll be able to propose a few group trips. I've got lots of choice addresses and things to do and see."

"Great!"

"In the meanwhile though, you're probably more interested in a good night's sleep. With the time difference, it must be three in the morning for you, I'd imagine that you're a bit tired?" joked our hostess when she walked into our bungalow.

I nodded, and I'm sure the bags under my eyes also showed how exhausted I was.

"This is so beautiful," said Colombe rhapsodically. "That's the kitchen?"

"That's right. Here most of the kitchens open to the outside. They're a part of the patio. That's because it's nice all year around in Gwada."

"Is 'Gwada' a nickname for Guadeloupe?"

"It's actually the name in creole for it. You'll see, it's fun to discover Creole names. I'll let you be surprised by them. But in the meanwhile, welcome to Maracudja!"

"Is that Creole too?"

"It is, that means passionfruit. I hope it will be the symbol of your stay here with us," said Severine, winking. "Is this your honeymoon?"

"No, we're not married," smiled Colombe.

"Sorry, that's none of my business," added our hostess.

She showed us around, explained how to turn on the air conditioning, advised us to make sure the mosquito net was in place so we wouldn't be eaten up by the mosquitoes and yen-yens by the end of the week.

"Yen-yens?"

"They're miniscule, little insects that look like mosquitoes and bite you nonstop. It'll take you over a week to get used to them."

"Thanks for the tip! We'll be careful."

When she'd finished showing us around, Severine wished us an excellent first night here and went outside onto the patio-kitchen.

"See you tomorrow morning? I'll stop by and tell you what to do and see here on the island. Unless you want to join us? I've already got a little program for my guests here. You can tell me if you're tempted by it."

"Not too early I hope," I warned her. "We're so exhausted I'm sure we'll be sleeping in tomorrow morning."

"Jerome don't be sure of it. It is Jerome, isn't it?"

"It is. But why?" I asked, astonished.

"Because with the time difference, I'd bet you

anything that you'll be all rested up by five or six in the morning!"

"Bets are on!" I laughed in response.

"Here we go to bed early and wake up early, like the sun. Good night!"

I FLOPPED down on the king-sized bed with its open mosquito net, each part of it rolled around one of the four wooden posts, and joining on top to make a canopy that made me thing of baldachin beds back in the day, like those I'd imagined featuring in novels from the eighteenth century, like *Les Liaisons Dangereuses*, the original 1782 epistolary novel by Choderlos de Laclos, where the word "love" is treated as a four-letter word.

"Marquise de Merteuil," I chuckled to Colombe, "would you honor me by lying at my sides on this humble yet comfortable bed?"

"My dear Vicomte de Valmont," she answered, "I will only lie with you after you have washed and groomed yourself. Or in other words, my dear, you stink!"

With that scathing response, I swallowed my desires of lust and headed to the shower, trying one more time though. You never know...

"Would you care to join me under a refreshing tropical shower?"

"As this shower isn't as large as the ones in the Negresco, and because I'm really tired, I'll let you enjoy it with a bit of privacy."

Colombe and I loved to play verbally just like Laclos's libertines did in his books. But tonight, she had no intention of following me to the shower.

Half an hour later, we pulled the mosquito net out, the air conditioning was purring and the birds were chirping away in the Caribbean night. It wasn't even eleven o'clock in Deshaies and we were already sleeping like logs.

CHAPTER 2
Reciting them by heart

Aren't they cute, Severine thought to herself as she walked out of the Maracudja bungalow. They seem so deeply in love those two, and passion fruit fits them like a glove, she continued.

She walked back to her own bungalow, though it wasn't really what you could call a bungalow. Contrary to what she rented out to tourists, her house wasn't completely made out of wood, it also was made from stones. A colonial type of house, a harmonious one, that showed without the shadow of a doute, that business must have been good. Such a huge lot, seven bungalows, her own home, a pool with a bar next to it, overflowing yet perfectly maintained vegetation, Severine could be proud of her investment and of herself. She'd just turned thirty-three and was already her own boss. She congratulated herself on the choices she'd made, so young, to get there.

She also went straight to her shower. With the humidity in this part of the world, it was impossible for someone to go to bed without a quick trip to the bathroom. She had no one else left to greet tonight. Nathalie was already installed, the two young ones also and tomorrow would be a busy day for her, with staggered arrivals. She was expecting four more tourists and had to finish up preparing the bungalows and arranging a few other things with friends with whom she lived to work on the island. It's always a good thing to be surrounded by a little team of loyal people, often "metros", meaning people who originally came here on vacation, for a summer job, or longer and who then caught the island virus up to a point where they couldn't even think of living elsewhere than here. Severine was one of them.

Cooled down, wearing a large light towel around her, the young lady looked at herself in the mirror above the bathroom sink. That face, those features, those lines, she had gotten used to them, though it had taken time, nearly ten years. She often confused dates, memories also faded away. Then they came back, left again, just like the waves on Grande Anse Beach, not too far, waves you could sometimes hear when the nocturnal birds stopped chirping out their concerts.

She put some natural face cream on, one she'd made herself, from products found right here on the island, like that coconut oil that was omnipresent and not expensive. Then, before going to bed, she went into the office and sat down in front of an opening – could you call that a window as it didn't have any glass but just a shutter that you opened vertically and propped up using a wooden stick?

From there she could see the coast down below and the Caribbean Sea that twinkled from the light of the rising moon. She nearly had no need to turn on the lamp on her desk to read the pages of the notebook she took out of one of her drawers, the one that she could lock. And that she unlocked with a key that she wore on a chain around her neck like an exotic piece of jewelry.

She often needed to be alone in the evening, her own time, during which she would read through pages of that worn notebook, patinated by years gone by and by how often she'd rubbed her fingers on it, manipulating it. The pages also had seen better days, and you could feel how often they had been turned and rubbed. Some words seemed to have been half wiped out or diluted perhaps by fingers that were greasy, or even tears, why not? These notebooks, her diaries, were places where she noted her joys, her heartaches, pains, fantasies, desires, interrogations and of course, her hopes.

Severine read inattentively through several pages, old ones, amongst the first ones she'd written. She could have recited the first ones by heart, she'd read and reread them so often, year after year, with mixed feelings each time. Then she skipped several pages until she reached a blank one. And there weren't too many blank ones left in her hundred or so page diary. She'd either have to decide not to continue or buy a new one. Would that be the end of her story or the beginning of a new one?

While she was reading, once again she was surprised to see how much her handwriting had changed over the years. What a difference there was between ten years ago and today! It apparently has been verified that people's handwriting does change, even when they're adults. Severine found a huge gap between that of the student, always in a hurry, and the calm adult she now was. And sometimes handwriting can even change in one year, depending on the person's emotional state. Whether you were relaxed and zen or all worked up, it was crazy how it could change.

The young lady quit thinking about those purely graphological thoughts so she could concentrate on what she wanted to write tonight, on her cream-colored paper. She picked up her wooden pen, the one that her mother had given her when she was just a child. She liked the way it felt when she held it, the way the ballpoint delicately slid over the paper without having to press too hard, the feeling that she had when holding it between her thumb and index finger; in a nutshell, she liked using a pen to write.

With her tight and hurried handwriting, she blackened nearly two pages, as if driven by a sudden urgency that she couldn't explain. It was her heart rather than her head that dictated those words to her, and they seemed to appear nearly autonomously on the blank pages in her diary. Oh, it was not great literature, far from the novel that she'd always wanted to write! Just thoughts, emotions, mental images transformed into words and sometimes delusions that, when she reread them, seemed totally inept to her, such as those she was undoubtedly writing that night.

Ten minutes later, she heard a low groan coming from the neighboring room, immediately followed by a voice with its characteristic Creole accent.

"My doudou? You coming to bed or you waiting till I'm sleeping?"

"Coming, my little kitty cat!"

Eusebius, the little kitty cat in question, was much more like a huge lion. Severine sighed when closing her dear diary, put it back into the drawer, locked it, and joined her doudou under the mosquito net.

CHAPTER 3
Heaven on Earth

Our hostess was right. At five thirty in the morning, light was already coming in from the frames of the doors and windows in our bungalow, and we were awake. Just as Severine had predicted, both Colombe and I were completely alert and hungry… for each other! The tropical atmosphere? Beginning of our vacation? The exotic Caribbean? Whatever the cause was, as soon as we woke up, we had a bit of naughty and delightful fun before getting up, though we were careful not to make too much noise as we were afraid that the walls in our wooden bungalow wouldn't cover our sighing and panting. After that matinal sequence, we were both damp and fulfilled.

Shortly after we were sitting outside on the patio, a cup of coffee in our hands, choosing from the selection of huge Danish pastries we found in a wicker basket that the owner must have discreetly placed there while we were sleeping. I was afraid to imagine that she had surprised us in our early morning acrobatics session.

When I saw Severine a few seconds later, I didn't dare ask her when she'd delivered the Danish pastries...

"Thanks for breakfast!" I simply said.

"Did you sleep well?" she asked with a large knowing smile.

"Like babies!" Colombe confirmed. "You were right, we're not even tired."

"Great! Is this a good time to talk? I know it's early, but you know about the early bird, right? I brought you a map of the island. Is it okay if I explain a couple of important things to you, give you some advice and useful tips, things not to be missed, all that? After that I'll tell you what I organized myself, with a group of trusted friends, for those who are staying with me during the week. If you want, you can join us, we'll be happy to include you. It's up to you."

While circling names, things to see, and the best ways to get there on the map of Guadeloupe, Severine told us more about this island she'd adopted. She explained that she'd fallen in love with it the first time she vacationed here and that she'd moved here nine years ago. There were so many things to see, she said enthusiastically. Like heaven on earth in every nook and cranny. She explained that it was impossible to get lost as there was only one road that snaked through Basse-Terre, in a half-butterfly itinerary, and on Grand-Terre it was just as simple. Between the two of them, Pointe à Pitre was like the butterfly's "thorax." She advised us to take the Route de la Traversée to go there, which cut through the middle, rather than risking traffic jams on the coastal road. Colombe was taking notes as she spoke so she wouldn't forget anything. We could already see that our one-week vacation would be too short to see everything and were already regretting not having taken two weeks.

"So, that's about what you should do before going back to France, but you'll have your head full of images and your heart full of memories. Like I said, of course you can go out on your own, but if you want to join our little group, that's also fine. I've already planning an outing in Sofaïa, a boat trip in the mangrove, scuba diving in Malendure, another outing in the sea to go whale watching, and of course, climbing the Soufriere Hills volcano," Severine said, counting the activities on her fingers. "Think it over! Have a good day, I've got to finish preparing my bungalows."

Our hostess sure knew how to sell her island. You could tell she really wanted us to appreciate our stay here, whether it was at her place or generally speaking on the island. Her eyes sparkled when she was describing Gwada. And there was a never-ending smile on her lips, making you want to be friends with her immediately. Yet, something was bothering me with that smile. Maybe it was that scar above her top lip that made it a bit off kilter? While discreetly observing Severine's mouth, I couldn't help but wonder what accident she had had, one that opposed the pleasantness of the rest of her face to the indelible physical wound on it.

We thanked her for her advice, and she disappeared in a rustling of her sarouel, just like an unexpected and powerful tropical storm.

We spent our first day at Gwada just the two of us, as lovebirds. We put our swimsuits on – Colombe's drove me absolutely crazy – and rushed down to the nearest beach, anxious to try out that Caribbean water that had been taunting us since we'd arrived. Used to going skiing during winter vacations, us French metropolitans were licking our chops in advance, just thinking of swimming in the warm and welcoming sea and working on our tans. Petite-Anse Beach, just over a mile away, was perfect. A beach in a tiny cove, a couple of palm trees to shelter us from the sun, clear water with colorful schools of fish that we could admire with the masks and scuba diving equipment we'd purchased, an idyllic decor for us as a couple.

For lunch, it was local food only, and we enjoyed hot accras, a type of fritter, dipped in what they called "dog sauce," though no dogs were (luckily) used, for our first course, and then a delicious chicken Colombo with a rum-based beverage.

In the afternoon, while most people were busy napping, we visited Deshaies, with its little port, a tiny Main Street and its botanical gardens, where the guide-books told us that Coluche, a famous French humorist and actor, used to live about thirty years ago. But that was ages ago, something that didn't end well and that the locals had chosen to forget.

At the end of the afternoon we came back to our resort, having enjoyed our day out and having decided to spend the rest of the afternoon at the poolside. That was where we met the other people staying in the bungalows.

Not the best memory that we had of our stay...

WITH OUR TOWELS around our shoulders, we went to Severine's pool, which was open from seven in the morning till six at night. And we were sure we'd be using it.

There already was one person there, lying on a sunbed, with a straw hat on her head, rolled up in a thin sarong, with a pencil in her hand, probably doing a crossword puzzle. She must have been a bit north of fifty, her sarong masking a body that many younger women would have loved to have. She looked quite stiff and arrogant, making me think she was a young widow from the high-class districts in Paris, though I had no idea why I thought that.

She only seemed to notice us when we greeted her.

"Ah! Hello," she said, nearly jumping.

But that was it. I imagined she must be Nathalie, the tourist who'd arrived the day before us.

We didn't want to bother her and splashed around a good twenty minutes in the pool, keeping an eye on her and making sure we didn't get her wet with our aquatic games and discrete hugs under the water. Without paying any attention to us at all, she continued doing her crossword puzzles, looking up from the paper every once in a while.

When I got out of the pool, I walked behind her sunbed, looking at what she'd been so busy doing, my natural curiosity having won over good etiquette and decency. She wasn't doing any crossword puzzles.

She wasn't holding a magazine of summer games on her knees, but rather a Canson drawing paper notebook, and I had to admit that the drawing she'd been working on wasn't bad at all.

She'd been drawing the landscape that we had been admiring from the pool. The lush tropical vegetation, sheeting on the roofs of the bungalows, and far away, the coast, a sailboat, then the horizon.

That lady was a really good artist!

What surprised me the most though was the silhouette that was in the foreground. A young lady who was half immersed in the pool and who looked just like my dear Colombe...

But maybe I was imagining things, seeing my darling's face all over, including in the drawing that an unknown person was doing?

IN THE WHOLE time we spent at the pool, the lady didn't get up from her sunbed, as if indifferent to the heat, and when we left the pool a bit before six, she still was there. We wanted to take a shower and change before joining Severine at her welcome cocktail-dinner that she was hosting for our group, here at the bar by the pool.

When we were walking up to our bungalow, we

ran across our young hostess, escorting a new guest to his bungalow, a young man about thirtyish, surfer style with muscles and a Crest toothpaste smile. Certainly someone that women would see as candy for their eyes, something that Colombe's look made me understand, with a twinge of jealousy...

CHAPTER 4

Biguine music

We could hear the music in our Maracudja cabin, announcing the beginnings of the festivities taking place at the bar next to the pool. We couldn't wait to meet the other tourists that week, those who would be our neighbors for a couple of days. I thought our hostess's idea was an excellent one: having all the occupants of the bungalows get together right at the beginning of the week to make friends.

And it was even truer that with rum and tropical cocktails, we'd all be uninhibited! Often alcoholic beverages make your tongue loosen up and give you courage.

We weren't the last ones to arrive, but almost. When we reached the bar, with a row of colored and perfumed glasses on it, we found our brief acquaintances of the day, the artist and the good-looking kid, as well as two other people, a young lady and a young man. We'd soon learn that they were a couple.

Standing behind the bar was a tall and muscular guy who seemed to have been born here in Guadeloupe, with dark skin and long dreadlocks held together by a big rubber band, who was preparing the cocktails. I thought he was one of Severine's employees and nearly made a mistake before Severine introduced him to us.

"Jerome, Colombe, this is Eusebius, my husband. And Eusebius, this is the couple of lovebirds I told you about from Bordeaux."

He held out his hand.

"Pleased to meet you! And welcome to our resort. What can I get you? A coconut punch, planteur, ti'punch, rum, a mojito?

"What's the least alcoholic one?" asked Colombe.

"Well, on all of them, you have to pace yourself. Why don't you start with the planteur, it's full of lots of fresh fruit that was picked right here on the island."

"You sold me on that!"

I followed the barman's advice and picked up a glass with attractive bronze tints.

The hi-fi behind the bar was playing some biguine music. A rhythm making you want to join in, shake your hips for women or shoulders for men. Some did it discreetly, others more frankly, like Eusebius behind his bar, naturally aroused by the notes.

We were thus eight for the moment, walking around by the pool or bar, each of us a bit shy to start talking to the others. Luckily, Severine, a perfect hostess, introduced everyone as a new person was arriving, a handsome fifty- or so-year old man with carefully brushed gray hair, a salesman's smile and a slim silhouette.

"Ah!" the hostess exclaimed. "You were the only one missing, Jacques."

"Sorry," he apologized.

"No big deal! We're on vacation, aren't we? And like it said in the Bible, 'the last will be first.'"

"Didn't Celine Dion say that?" asked one of the men.

"Or maybe Jean-Jacques Goldman," Severine said smiling. "The festivities can start. I don't need to introduce myself: Severine. And like I told you, I'll be here to brighten up your stay here and can't wait until you take part in the program I drew up for you. But more about that later. Right now, I'd like to introduce my husband, Eusebius."

"At your service!" he said, bowing, while rolling his

arms around comically, like the aristocrats did back in the Renaissance days.

Everyone laughed, and our two hosts both seemed to be the life of the party. They instinctively knew how to make people trust them.

"Then, after that, we've got – if I get everything right and don't get you mixed up, correct me if I'm wrong – this cute little couple, Jerome and Colombe, such and original first name, I'll never forget it."

Colombe smiled at everyone, and I raised my hand and waved.

"And here's Nathalie."

Natalie, the artist we saw at the pool, discreetly raised her glass.

"And as I'm gallant, I'm continuing with the ladies. Let's all welcome Naima, who's got a smile as wide as the Champs-Elysées."

And she confirmed this by showing us a row of white teeth that her copper-colored complexion made even more evident.

"And now turning to the men, here's Jacques, that everyone knows. And Bruce, who makes me think of the actor Jean Dujardin, when he's playing a surfer, of course! And finally, here's Gregoire..."

"Gregory," the man who looked like a tough guy

and was wearing his cap backwards, like Eminem, said to her.

"Excuse me, Gregory! I guess I won't get an A on my final exam," joked Severine. "So that's everyone who'll be here this week. All that's left to do now is to raise your glasses to toast your vacation and hope it'll be the best one so far in your life! But for me, I don't doubt that once you're experienced Gwada, all you'll want to do is to come back! Here's to a great vacation!"

She raised her glass as did we all.

"By the way, has anyone been to Guadeloupe before?"

People were shaking their heads, only Nathalie responded.

"I came to the Caribbean twice, but it was in the Dominican Republic and in Martinique. Not so far, after all."

"But not as nice," crowed Eusebius, defending his island.

"Quite the chauvinist," said the artist.

"Just proud of Guadeloupe where I was born!"

And he tinted his glass against Nathalie's glass of planteur punch, so as to terminate any possible verbal hostilities in a good mood.

. . .

Little by little everyone relaxed, got to know the others with the kind assistance of Severine and Eusebius who both flitted around exchanging a few words, getting to know us and telling us how they'd imagined and created their touristic haven, one that was perfectly integrated into the landscape, totally in harmony with Mother Nature. One that you could call an "environmentally friendly complex."

We took advantage of being there to greet the artist we'd seen that afternoon, who seemed to be a bit more approachable than before at the poolside.

"It's Nathalie, isn't it?" I asked, raising my glass of planteur punch. "You're an artist? Though I wasn't spying on you, I saw you drawing and believe me, you're good!"

"Thank you! It's true that I love arts, and I like to draw. When there's a nice landscape, of course it's something that inspires you."

She finished her sentence and looked longingly at Colombe, taking a long sip from her iridescent cocktail.

"I like beautiful things," she said with a wry smile.

I could see my girlfriend blushing. Colombe didn't like to be at the center of things and was actually quite shy, especially with someone she barely knew, who was staring at her head to feet.

"Perhaps your job involves drawing things?" I asked to spare Colombe and her latent uneasiness.

"You could say that. I work in plastic arts."

"Great! I've always admired people who are artistically gifted. And more precisely? Drawing, painting, sculpture, engraving?"

"All of that actually."

I could see that my conversation didn't really interest her and apologized.

"Excuse me, I'm a journalist, so you must understand, I've got the bad habit of asking a lot of questions, doing interviews. I'm curious about everyone and everything!"

"Sometimes, Jerome, curiosity can be very unwise..." Nathalie said, accompanying her sentence with an ambiguous wink and heading towards the bar with a brief, "Excuse me."

Colombe walked up to me.

"She sure isn't Miss Congeniality!"

"You're right, and something about the way she looked at us made me uncomfortable."

We had to speak up to hear as the music in the hi-fi behind the bar was blasting away *Party Rock Anthem*, the unofficial hymn of the LMFAO:

Party rock is in the house tonight
Everybody just have a good time (yeah)

A RHYTHMIC SONG making Eusebius sway quite naturally, Creole style, sparking looks of admiration from the women there, at least that was my take on it.

As the artist had dropped us like a pair of dirty socks there next to the poolside, we walked up to Naima, who was enjoying an accra fritter that she'd dipped into some Creole sauce.

"Those accras look delicious!" said Colombe.

"They are!"

The young lady, with delicate Maghrebin features would undoubtedly please Nathalie, who said she appreciated physical beauty. A copper-colored complexion, almond shaped eyes, thin lips, wavy black shoulder-length hair, a twenty-first century Cleopatra!

Naima seemed much friendlier than our precedent inculcator. She must have been about as old as Colombe, roughly thirty. She told us she was from Strasbourg, in the northeastern part of France where she worked in a home for the disabled. She loved her job, a noble task that she described passionately, helping those who didn't have much, those left behind, those that life hadn't favored right from the beginning. The young lady seemed to have exceptional empathy, making me think she was a good person, in the moral sense of that term. Or to put it in other words, Naima was as beautiful inside as out.

Then after LMFAO, it was Zouk Machine belting out their immortal tube in Creole, *Maldon*. The trio of ladies born in Guadeloupe, made all the new arrivals here on vacation want to dance!

Nétwayé, baléyé, astiké
Kaz la toujou penpan
Ba'w manjé, baw lanmou
E pou vou an kafey an chantan...

PLUS THE COCKTAILS that Eusebius had prepared helped everyone warm up, except for Nathalie who seemed more reserved. Maybe she was just too shy to easily become a part of a group?

On the other hand, Naima and Bruce were dancing a zouk that neither of them actually mastered, making it quite comical.

Jacques and Gregory were talking, elbows on the

bar, one of them laughing out loud at the jokes that must have been good, that his neighbor was telling him. I said jokes, even though I didn't actually hear what they were saying.

It was nearly midnight when Severine turned down the music.

"My friends! I don't wanna be a party pooper here, but tomorrow if you guys want to see some whales, let me remind you that you have to be at the landing dock at seven sharp! It's only a five-minute drive from here. Let me assure you that it's worth getting up early. Does everyone want to see the whales and the orcas?"

Everyone shouted out a loud "yes" and raised their glasses.

"Fantastic! What about you, Colombe and Jerome? Will you be coming with us?"

We'd already made our decision that afternoon and the good atmosphere at the welcome party made us think we'd made the right decision.

"We will" I exclaimed joyfully.

"Well, it sure looks like a good week then," our hostess concluded. "See you all then at a quarter to seven in the parking lot, we'll all go together in our van.

. . .

AT ABOUT ONE in the morning, Colombe and I were in bed surrounded by our mosquito net.

"Most of them seem to be nice," my sweetie summed it up while yawning.

"Yeah... except for that antisocial Nathalie, the others seem like lots of fun. Gregory, the loudmouth who looks like a rap singer, Jacques the old but still handsome guy, Naima, that beautiful lady from Northwest Africa, Bruce, that blond wannabe surfer and our great hosts! Looks like we struck out fine!"

"What about us? What do you think they call us?"

"Lovebirds?" I whispered holding Colombe with evident intensions that could be imagined in neon lights on my forehead.

"My lovebird who stinks of rum... I'm going to say good night! The alarm goes off in five hours.

I switched off my brain and my desires and slept like a log.

CHAPTER 5

All the contempt they had

"WHAT A GREAT PARTY SWEETIE!" said Eusebius enthusiastically was he flopped into their bed. "You were fantastic, as usual."

"You too, honey. Your cocktails and music were just right."

"Coming to bed?" honey wanted to know.

"Give me ten, I've still got stuff to put away."

"Need any help?"

"No, it's okay. I won't be long."

Severine kissed her hubby on the forehead and walked into the kitchen. She finished emptying the dishwasher, put the clean dishes in the cupboard, put some leftovers into their Tupperware containers and put them in the fridge, and then washed her hands.

But before joining her husband, with his ethereal snoring, she went into her office. She suddenly wanted to reread a couple of pages of her diary and maybe write a few lines in it. *Ten minutes max*, she said to herself.

But ended up spending over an hour.

Sunday, March 19, 2012.

I've made my decision, this is where I want to spend the rest of my life. At least my second life, because my first one is over, finished, finito! I can't stand that one anymore, it made me suffer too much. It's over, I'm leaving. I already left on the day I bought my plane ticket for Guadeloupe, almost two years ago. A one-way Paris - Pointe à Pitre. For my return trip I still hadn't decided when I was at the check-in counter. What a lie! Of course I'd already decided. I'd decided to leave metropolitan France, to put as much distance as possible between me and... my past. Between me and... what I was before. Because I'm no longer the same person. Before, I had the impression that I *wasn't really me, whereas today, I know that I am. I feel good in my skin, my body, freer in my head.*

Here, in Gwada, in the midst of Mother Nature's beauties, its relaxed life, the calm philosophy the natives have, the way they never judge other people. Everyone is how they are, and everyone can be respectable. I feel that I'm respected, that no one judges me by the way I look. In metropolitan France it was quite the opposite. I could see all the contempt they had about... my difference.

Since then, I was lucky to have met Eusebius, someone else who luckily didn't judge me by my appearance, my body. Though he, and I have to admit it, is someone who's really a hunk! You just gotta see his ebony body when he's nude and sweating above me, his muscular pecs and tense biceps, straining like bows ready to shoot their arrows of love into me.

We're a funny couple, him and me. Beauty and the Beast, or would Beast and the Beauty be more accurate?

I wonder what people think of our couple.

Or actually not, that's stuff I don't care about anymore. Those types of questions were okay for the person I was before. Now I couldn't care less... I think.

I remember back in 2010, my crucial year, my vintage one. As soon as I'd set foot on the Guadeloupean ground, I felt as if I was at home. Welcome to Gwada! the island seemed to be whispering to me, as welcoming as its inhabitants. At first I said I'd go back when I was tired of it here, when I wanted to. But I never did.

A few months later, I moved in with Eusebius and then we discovered the ad for this lot in Deshaies. It was love at first sight, we quickly signed and began to work. It's far from being finished, but what a great project! In a couple of months, a year at the most, we'll be ready to open our first bungalows and host our first tourists.

I'm alive again!

Severine closed her diary, a tear fell onto her cheek, as often was the case when she reread her recollections. She glanced at the clock on the wall above her desk. Two in the morning. Her honey was snoring like a Cessna engine. In less than four hours, the alarm clock would be ringing, and outside the hummingbirds would be waking up.

She and her new group of vacationers would be beginning a fun-filled week.

CHAPTER 6

The black depths

THE WARBLING of the hummingbirds woke me up before the alarm on Colombe's phone rang. Getting woken up by birds rather than by the stridulations of a high-tech device, and that to boot in a tropical environment like Bougainvillea Domain was enough to convince me that I'd be having a magnificent day.

"Get up, rum sack!" I shouted out to my bed partner.

I felt like a tease, wide awake, bright and early to start the day, which, looking through the light coming in through the slits in the shutters, was going to be hot and sunny.

As a response, an avenging pillow hit me right in the middle of my face.

. . .

At six forty-five sharp, we joined the group in Severine's van. She was already behind the wheel. Nathalie was seated next to her and responded to our greeting by an inaudible murmur and an imperceptible movement of her chin. Her sunglasses prevented me from seeing if her eyes were wide open or still heavy from last night's planteur punches.

The others were in the back of the vehicle: Naima, surrounded by Bruce and Gregory. We sat in the central seat with Jacques.

"Everyone here?" asked the driver. "Well, ready to rumble then."

"Eusebius isn't coming with us?" asked Jacques.

"No. He saw whales all the time when he was a kid, plus there's work to be done here. You have no idea how fast things grow around here."

The trip to the little Baille-Argent fishing port just south of Deshaies only did take about five minutes. The boat belonging to the little association that organized our outing was already there, with two people – a young Guadeloupean guy and a red-headed girl – who were busy filling up the boat and preparing the equipment needed to listen to and find where the whales were in the ocean.

"Welcome aboard!" the young lady said. "I hope

you're all fine. My name is Vanessa, and this is Toussaint, our pilot.

"Hi everyone," he said.

The young lady gathered up our shoes and backpacks and put them into a watertight plastic barrel, which she then locked in a safe in the stern of the boat.

"Does anyone feel they'll be needing a life jacket?"

"I do!"

Those were the first and who knows, maybe the last words of the day for Nathalie.

"Severine, you're not coming with us?" asked Jacques.

"I've been out there dozens of times and have observed loads of whales. Though it's magnificent, I have better things to do. But Toussaint and Vanessa will take good care of you."

The pilot turned the key, and the outboard began to purr. Vanessa unhooked the ropes on the deck. She leaped into the boat just like a mountain goat as it was slowly making its way from the pontoon. I've always admired the know-how and dexterity that seamen have. That incidentally made me think of the Lacassagne children, their sailboat, and their unfortunate tragedy on the sea off of Nice in the summer of 1986. I shook off that image that did nothing to reassure me.

Besides our group from the Bougainvillea complex,

there was also a couple of Germans with two children, both blond and pleasantly plump, but with large smiles.

"Do you understand French?" the young lady asked them. "If not, I can translate into English, if that's better."

"*Nein, nein*, no need. I understand," said the father.

Once we crossed the channel, the pilot sped up, the bow of the boat raised itself, whipping through the small waves.

So there were twelve of us on the boat, including Toussaint and his crew member. Sitting on four benches on each side, some people were hanging on for dear life, whereas others were swaying with the boat, going with the flow, whether they had sea legs or not. As for me, I was holding on though Colombe often stood up to see if there was a dorsal fin surfacing someplace.

After half an hour at top speed, the pilot slowed the boat down and then turned the outboard off.

"Did you see something?" asked Naima excitedly, with a hand as a visor over her hope filled eyes, looking out over the horizon.

"Just a minute, Miss," smiled Toussaint, getting up.

He grabbed a long pole with some round metallic thingy at the end of it. Sort of like a metal detector that some people take with them on beaches to look for hypothetical lost jewels or coins, but that was about twice as big.

"What the heck is that?" asked Gregory.

The pilot burst out laughing.

"One of my big ears! More seriously though, it's an electronic sonar that allows me to listen underwater. With that, I can hear whales singing for miles."

Turning talk into action, Toussaint plunged the pole into the water, connected some listening device to it then told everyone not to make any noise. Then he put headphones on and closed his eyes.

We all surrounded him, subjugated. What did he hear in his big ears? Whales singing or maybe mermaids? All we could hear was the soothing sound of water lapping against the boat's hull.

Nathalie was the only one who didn't move closer to the pilot. She was isolated at the far end of the boat and had taken out her inseparable drawing notebook. For the entire time that he was listening to what was going on in the deep waters, her pencil never stopped moving. It visibly was a sure and inspired gesture. What was she drawing? The boat? The waves? One of us? I would have paid a lot to spy over her shoulder, but finally I was more intrigued by what the pilot was doing.

Toussaint winced, made a face and shook his head sideways.

"I'm not hearing anything right now. We'll go out another two or three miles."

He put his equipment away and started the boat up again.

Nathalie put her drawing book below her life jacket, where it wouldn't get wet, and any peeping eyes couldn't see it.

"Days go by but they're all different," Vanessa said apologetically. "That's nature, you can never be sure of anything. With yesterday's group, we didn't see anything for four hours but the day before, we saw lots of dolphins and whales. I hope they'll 'bite' today. Here we go again."

We all sat back down, hanging on so no one would fall, both in the boat or overboard. The wind had picked up a bit and the waves were starting to white-cap, forcing the boat to slice its way through them. Saltwater spray splashed on us intermittently, without however cooling us down, it was so hot out.

Ten minutes later Toussaint tried his listening device once again. Then he called out to his crew member.

"Vanessa, can you turn on the loudspeaker please?"

The young lady quickly did it.

"Toussaint heard something," she explained. "Listen up, you're gonna hear the whales singing!"

It's hard to describe that moment of intense communion with nature. I'd already listened to a CD of whales' songs, a type of "music" that was supposed to relax or destress you. But I realized that day on that boat off the port of Deshaies, that it had nothing to do with a real experience.

"That's strange, almost like clicking your tongue against your palate," said Jacques, astonished.

"Because those aren't whales," Toussaint explained. "What you're hearing there are sounds that a pod of Globicephala emit."

"What's that?" Gregory asked, probably never used a word with as many syllables as that.

"It's a Latin word composed of '*globus*' meaning a round ball, and the Greek word *kephale* meaning 'head,'" Bruce told us. "Or in other words, an animal with a big head!"

"To be more precise," explained Vanessa, "a Globicephala, also called a pilot whale, is a type of dolphin without a snout, with a very developed frontal melon."

"Ah! "Okay I get it," laughed Gregory. "A dolphin with a big head."

"Shh," Naima said, inviting him to shut up. "Just listen. Maybe you two could understand each other, you and them?"

We allowed ourselves to be rocked by the acoustics Toussaint's device captured. It was fantastic!

"Head west," the pilot brusquely said. "Let's go."

The motor hummed again. We were all excited, impatient to meet the group of dolphins that seemed to be calling out to us. Each of us, including Nathalie, were keeping their eyes glued to the bow of the boat.

Suddenly Toussaint turned off the gas and the motor stopped, letting the boat drift. The pilot held his hand out to the starboard side, our eyes following it without needing to say a single word.

A dozen little fins were cutting through the waves right at the top. Each of us rushed to our phones and put them in video or photo mode to immortalize that instant, our eyes twinkling just like those of little kids in front of the Christmas tree. Nathalie though, took her drawing book out again, subjugated by those novel subjects.

The group of delphinids progressed slowly, coming closer to our boat. Some of them let themselves be carried by the waves and others dove for a couple of seconds and we then saw them come up thirty or so feet farther. Finally all of them were there, against our hull, driven by their natural curiosity. We could nearly have touched them just by putting our hands out, but no one dared that sacrilege.

Jacques, a man who thought of everything, had prepared his submersible camera, which was screwed onto a type of selfies stick, and he put it in the water.

"What a great idea!" Vanessa said to him. "You'll have fantastic videos."

Toussaint explained to us that some of the dolphins, the male ones, especially, were eighteen feet long and they surrounded the boat or swam under it going from port to starboard.

Gregory chose that moment to try to be funny and scare Naima.

"And do you think it's possible that these eighteen-feet fish could capsize the boat?"

"Are you crazy saying things like that? I already was pretty scared, but now... thanks for nothing!"

"Oh excuse me, excuse me a thousand times my lady!"

"Come on Greg, just shut up," said Bruce, interposing his muscular body between them.

"There's nothing to be afraid of," Toussaint said. "These are not aggressive animals. Quite the opposite, they love escorting boats. Of course, you don't want to attack them because here, we're only seeing a part of their group, but at the bottom of the sea I think there must be about thirty of them, according to what I heard earlier. And I must say that faced with a colony like that, if you get them stirred up, we wouldn't be the winners here..."

I wasn't sure that his precision would relieve Naima's fears, but she furiously turned her back to Gregory. As for him, he put his cap on backwards and started filming them again.

The time we spent with the dolphins lasted about twenty minutes, but it seemed like twenty seconds to us with their bewitching show. Then when they'd satisfied their curiosity, one by one they disappeared back into the depths of the sea.

We continued for about an hour without seeing any other fish, our calm only interrupted by the tireless Gregory.

"Hey, Naima! Look, I think there's a shark over there!"

"Why don't you dive in and see for yourself?"

"Come on, you never saw *Jaws*?"

"No, maybe just your father's jaws drooling!"

"I thought there weren't any sharks in the waters surrounding Guadeloupe," said Jacques, astonished.

"Of course there are," Toussaint explained. "But not big white sharks like you see in those American movies. On the other hand, we often see lemon-sharks, nurse sharks, and tiger sharks, but globally, they're inoffensive."

That was enough to calm Gregory down and he didn't say another word until the boat was solidly attached to the pontoon in the Baille-Argent Port. Especially as his complexion had shifted little by little to becoming livid and he'd thrown up twice. That nauseous freshwater sailor was no longer trying to be a clown!

Severine, with a wide smile on her face, was waiting for us at the landing.

"Well, guys? You like it? Did you see any little fishies?"

In the van that took us back to Bougainvillea Domain, everyone had their word to say both about the fish we saw and about Gregory, the little trouble-maker in our group. We could feel that there was a type of alchemy that was drawing some of the members of the group together, something that had begun the night before during the cocktail at the pool, then strengthened by the outing we just had at sea. I suspected that Severine's idea was to generate that alchemy through the activities she'd organized during the week and mentally thanked her for having invited us. Nonetheless, I internally thought philosophically that at the origin, the word 'alchemy' designated an occult science, one that was born in secret chemical techniques and mystical speculations.

Sometimes the alchemy between people could be tight, creative, one that would generate great and beautiful things, but other times… passionate, frictional or destructive.

Which of those facets would dominate after our week in Gwada? I couldn't wait to find out.

CHAPTER 7

Perish...with pleasure!

WHILE HER GUESTS of the week were out in the peaceful Caribbean Sea looking for whales or dolphins, Severine didn't have the time to relax until they came back from Baille-Argent Port.

She had better things to do. She still had a bit of shopping to do at the local grocers to finish up the Creole meal she had been planning on serving them for lunch. They'd certainly be famished when they got back because though looking at dolphins nourished the eyes and heart, not much made its way to their stomachs.

When she came back with her arms full of goodies, she found Eusebius weeding the paths of their domain.

"How are you, honey?"

"Great! "Hey, did you remember to distribute that macerated rum we prepared to our guests?"

"Shoot, no, I completely forgot about it! I'll do it right now. I'm sure they'll love our little homemade cocktail with its fruit and spices. What do you think?"

"I think our rum is delicious!"

"I could even add, to die for, but to perish with pleasure!"

The couple laughed together.

Severine dropped off her groceries, picked up a basket in which she put as many bottles of their homemade cocktail as there were bungalows, and hurried off to distribute them. The tourists would be delighted to discover that surprise in their refrigerators. As each kitchen overlooked a patio, she didn't have to use her keys to get in. Here, everyone trusted each other. Even Severine's and Eusebius's bungalow was rarely locked. The only secret place, the one that was locked and protected, was the drawer in her desk where she put her diaries.

The hostess went from bungalow to bungalow, opening the fridges, putting the plastic bottles in them, in which slices of ginger, pods of vanilla and other exotic fruits with their gourmet colors floated in a very promising looking yellowish-orange rum. She always had fun seeing what was in her guests' refrigerators. That often tipped her off on how they'd behave. For instance, Gregory's fridge was completely different from Nathalie's and Jacques' had nothing to do with Naima's. And what to say about Bruce's, filled with facial creams that had to be refrigerated?

Though she had no intention of rummaging around, something in Nathalie's bungalow made her pay attention. Below a cutting board on the countertop, she saw a corner of a piece of paper that wasn't covered. The hostess tried to convince herself it was none of her business, but curiosity got the best of her. Maybe she shouldn't have, she'd be regretting that later on...

She delicately pulled the paper, discovering inch after inch, a crayon drawing, nearly finished, representative of a feminine character. At first though, it was hard to see who it was. But still?

Perhaps a self-portrait? Did the artist want to betray in that sketch, a type of unhappiness, spleen, self-hatred? Severine, who liked art, suddenly thought of *Scream*, the self-portrait that Edvard Munch did. It was frightening, perhaps the reflection of his perturbed emotional state?

Could it be Naima? No, the little Moroccan lady was much to pretty to be caricatured like that.

But when she looked at it closer, she focused on the facial features of the character. What if...?

Was she a victim of her overflowing imagination?

Was she sufficiently objective to draw true conclusions?

The fact was that Severine curiously recognized herself in the lady's drawing. She had to admit that Nathalie was a very good artist, and using essential minute details, someone able to embrace the essence of those she was portraying.

But those minute details... like that overly plump silhouette or that light fabric surrounding her legs, making you think of a sensual and light sarong.

Of course, it still was an unfinished sketch. Yet, that face, the irregularities in its eyes, around its mouth. Yes, without the shadow of a doubt, an irregular mouth. Not very symmetrical, a bit off kilter, imprecise. *Like me*, thought Severine melancholically. *I'm off kilter, imprecise, asymmetrical.*

She had a furious desire to rip the drawing up, reduce it to confetti. Her fingers clutched the edges of the sheet of drawing paper, clenched by dark feelings. Then reason took over, she let the drawing go and put it back below the cutting board, making sure one corner of it still could be seen, just like when she'd found it. She certainly didn't want her guest to realize that she'd looked at it. Especially as when she'd find that bottle of macerated rum in her refrigerator door, Nathalie would know that either Eusebius or Severine had been there. Who else otherwise? It only could have been them.

The hostess left Nathalie's bungalow with one more bottle to drop off in her basket. That one was for Bruce, that good-looking kid with his Donald Trump colored hair, as she liked to say to herself in secret. She loved giving her tourists nicknames, it was like a mental game for her.

She looked at her watch, saying she'd better shake a leg. She still had to finish making lunch before coming to pick up the one-day sailors at Baille-Argent Port.

CHAPTER 8

Could lead to drowning

"Is it always nice out here?" Gregory asked, his mouth still full of a deliciously golden and crispy accra fritter.

"Almost," replied Eusebius, from the other end of the table. "That's why once you've set foot here on the island, you never want to leave. Right, darling?"

Severine nodded.

"Completely right," she added. "We often say that it's nice here year around, never colder than 72°, that's why us Guadeloupeans live half-naked nearly all the time!"

"Sure sounds like a good idea to me," Bruce said, suddenly interested.

"There are actually two seasons in the Caribbean. The dry season, that we also call Lent, that lasts roughly from December to April and then the wet or winter season for the rest of the year. You know that our water temperature is rarely less than 70°?"

"Cool! What about surfing?" continued Bruce. "You got any good spots here?"

"Sure do! You can get good rides next to the Moule, or Saint-François, or the black sand beach at Bananier, all that's on the Atlantic coast, so the waves are good there. Do you surf?"

"When you're named Bruce, even if you're not from Hawaii, you're obliged to surf, aren't you? Seriously though, yes, that's one of my hobbies. But I'm no champion surfer!"

"Well, if you want, I can introduce you to one of my friends who'll take you to the best spots around here. You'll love it."

"Great, thanks!" said the blond enthusiastically, once again enjoying a mouthful of conche and mango salad on a filo pastry sheet. "Delish! Severine, you made that?"

"Yes I did! I learned how to cook Creole style you know."

"It really is delicious," agreed Nathalie, speaking for once.

One after another we praised the specialties that

our hostess had prepared for us and she nearly blushed, though it was hidden by her tanned skin.

"Thank you, you're too nice. It's just something you get used to doing. But we're not going to spend hours talking about my cooking. Let's get down to business."

"The meal *was* serious business," added Jacques gallantly.

"Jacques, I said stop! That's enough. So, for the rest of the program today, we've got the afternoon to spend together, and Eusebius and I thought of having you discover Acomat Falls."

We all looked at her. I thought I'd read about that place in a guidebook but couldn't remember what it was.

"It's a waterfall?" I asked.

"A lot more than that, my friend!" replied Eusebius, as enthusiastic as usual when describing the treasures of his island. "A lot more than that! Of course, it's a nice waterfall, that comes from a spring in the mountains. But more than that, it's a place where a lot of people dive from."

"Dive?"

"Yup, diving from the rocks overlooking the natural pool formed by the waterfall waters."

"Is it high?" asked Naima.

"There are different places you can dive in from, you'll see. Something for everyone, from a beginner to an accomplished diver. You wanna go diving?"

Murmurs came from the table. Bruce was the first one to validate the idea, followed closely by Gregory who couldn't wait, then by Naima, more conservative. Jacques declined, as did Colombe, and Nathalie didn't answer.

"I'll decide when I get there," I hesitated.

"Don't worry," added Severine. "The place is totally magnificent and those who don't want to jump or dive in can just dip their toes in the cool pond water. Something that feels so good. Ready?"

The project was approved, the meal finished, and departure time agreed upon.

~

THE VAN DROVE along the coastal road towards Pointe-Noire, which was called *Pwentnwa* in Creole. I loved the way that native language simplifies words. Like people say, *in Creole, you write what you pronounce*. Schoolchildren must have loved that!

When we got out of the village, Eusebius turned, leaving the coast. The road, snaking around towards the uplands, only led to this well-known waterfall and got narrower and narrower the closer we got. Chickens were running to and fro in liberty on the cracked road while others were in cages on the roadsides.

"Wild chickens here are a real plague. There are so many of them in the mountains that sometimes we have to control the population by hunting them down."

Eusebius had us get out of the van before parking it as well as he could on the roadside, near the place where we'd then hike to Acomat Falls.

But that was where, at the bottom of a bridge where the path began, we saw an old weatherbeaten sign, written by Pointe-Noire's Town Hall.

BEWARE!

Bathing is strictly prohibited during heavy rain.

Worried, we all looked up to make sure there weren't any rain clouds in the sky.

1. You may be surprised by shallow water.

We'll keep an eye out, I thought to myself.

2. Presence of an aspiration phenomenon to the bottom in the pond that could lead to drowning.

What the heck? Not too reassuring. I was already less enthusiastic.

3. Diving and jumping are strictly prohibited. Presence of sharp rocks at the bottom of the pool.

"Um... Eusebius? You're sure of what you're doing?" asked Jacques, panicked.

"Don't worry, Jacques, this isn't rainy season."

And he began to laugh loudly. His laughter was contagious, and we all went downhill with our guide. The narrow trail, with its steep slopes wound around huge roots that we used as built-in stairs. Sometimes you had to hold onto one of them to jump to the next one. We went past other tourists and locals coming up from the waterfall.

"It's pretty steep going down but it's not too long, we're almost there," said Eusebius to reassure us.

And we could hear people talking and laughing down below. In the midst of the conversations we suddenly heard the noise of someone diving, followed by a salve of applause and admirative whistles.

"Is there a show or something?" Naima wanted to know.

"For a show, there sure is one, just wait and see."

And it was. Right when I reached the clear river water running between the polished stones, my eyes were attracted to the left. There, I distinguished a man who had just begun his dive, from a height of at least thirty feet according to my estimation. He seemed to have dove off backwards to make a front loop before being swallowed up by the pond, with an impressive spray of water.

"Wow, did you see that?"

"He's no beginner, that's for sure."

"That guy is nuts! I thought that diving was prohibited because of the sharp rocks at the bottom?"

"Actually," Eusebius reassured us, "the sign we saw at the top is obsolete. The town hall put it up years ago after we had a rockslide. Since then, they've cleared the pond out and we can dive again."

"You just gotta trust, right?" said Nathalie ironically.

"That's right," repeated Severine. "So? Who thinks they can do the same thing?"

"Easy peasy," Gregory said triumphantly.

"Maybe," Bruce continued.

"I'll try," Naima dared.

"Not for me," said Jacques.

"Go ahead if you want," murmured Colombe.

"Why not?" I hesitated. "But not from that high. What about you, Eusebius?"

"I often go diving here. I love it."

"And I often watch him, trembling," admitted Severine. "What about you, Nathalie?"

"You gotta be kidding!"

Around the pond there were about thirty people either standing or sitting on the rocks, all looking out towards the natural diving boards above the water in the hole with its glassy surface below. Here, right next to the waves, it was beautifully cool. To reach the edge of the pool, you first had to cross the ford of the river, jumping from rock to rock, holding hands with the others to cross a few difficult passages. We finally all sat down on a large flat rock that overlooked the pond, ideally seated to admire those brave and intrepid divers. We all stripped down to our bathing suits, except of course and unsurprisingly for Nathalie, who sat a bit farther on from us, her drawing book on her knees, pencils in her hand. Her artist's eyes must have been soaking in the diver's show.

Then two groups naturally formed: the intrepid ones, with Eusebius, Gregory, Bruce, Naima, and to a lesser extent, myself, and the admirative ones, with Colombe, Severine, Jacques and Nathalie.

The intrepid ones went into the water to reach the natural diving boards. I just climbed up to the first level, about five feet above the pool, whereas the others climbed up to the next one, about ten or twelve feet. The rest of our group encouraged us at the bottom with whistles, chanting our names, clapping their hands.

It was one thing to admire the divers but a completely different one to be in your swimsuit with dozens of people looking at you, waiting for you to perform. I must say I did have the jitters. Already when I was at our municipal pool, I wasn't the greatest diver, but here, without being able to see the bottom, remembering the warning signs at the entrance, my legs wavered, my calves twittered, and my stomach growled. But I couldn't step down now. I closed my eyes, filled my lungs with air and jumped off, feet first, straight as the letter I, into the pool, hoping I wouldn't hit one of those huge fish that I imagined swimming below the surface of the water.

The first thing I felt was the air around me while jumping in, a jump that seemed interminable to me. Then the biting sensation of the water, an invigorating whiplash, especially as the pool was cool. Then the impression of sinking, my eyes obstinately closed, hoping I wasn't going to hit the rocky bottom. Under water, it was completely silent, a troubling and nearly intoxicating feeling, and I had the impression of having survived a harrowing trial. I finally began to kick and use my hands, my body came back up, my head was out of the water, and I opened my eyes. The first thing I saw was Colombe, looking down at me, with admiratively brilliant eyes for her brave lover. I swam up to her and stole a kiss.

"Who's next?" I shouted out, liberated, to Naima, Bruce, and Gregory.

As for Eusebius, he'd climbed up to the highest diving spot, the one that must have been thirty feet high, next to an older man with a grayish beard that contrasted with his black skin, bald, sitting on the rock with his eyes closed, waiting until it was his turn, perhaps also concentrated on his upcoming dive.

"Come on, Naima!" Severine said, encouraging her to come.

But the young lady hesitated, tensed up on the edge of the natural diving board, with Gregory behind her, but I could see he was looking at her strangely, something in his eyes bothered me, a type of malignant glint. I couldn't make out what they were saying to each other from where I was, but I could tell he was talking to her. Probably teasing her, like on the boat this morning. Those two would be having a cat versus dog week.

Right next to them, Bruce positioned himself, his arms outstretched, and his legs ready to pounce. He looked out below to make sure no one was in the pool as well as above him, in case another diver was ready. The coast was clear though, he bent his knees and jumped into the air, in a perfect dive, going into the water with barely a splash. Applause followed his dive though it quickly died out, followed by a worrying silence. Bruce hadn't come up.

"Shit, what the hell is he doing?"

"Where is he?"

"Anyone see him come up?"

Seconds went by, there wasn't a ripple in the pond, no more turmoil, no more bubbles, a too perfect calm.

Around the pool everyone started to murmur, spectators leaned down to try to see what was happening.

"Someone's gotta go in to see if he's down there," said one of them.

A man jumped in, with goggles on.

Each second seemed like an hour. Though it was hard to estimate how long Bruce had been underwater, it was something that seemed unusually long.

A blond head suddenly popped up like a jack-in-the-box. Bruce had reappeared, a huge smile on his face, like a salmon swimming upstream.

"You asshole!" shouted Gregory from his promontory.

"You scared us!" added Naima.

"Hey, relax guys," Bruce said with a laugh. "We're on vacation, we're here to have fun, aren't we?"

He visibly was the only one who'd found that funny.

Nathalie, who hadn't taken part in that agitation, was still furiously drawing, probably inspired by those young clowns showing off. A type of strange rivalry seemed to be driving Bruce and Gregory, probably with the goal of impressing Naima. At least that was my take.

And on the rock they'd dive from, Gregory was right behind Naima, trying to grab her by the waist – hoping to dive in with her? But the young lady resisted, slapping the young man's hands so he'd remove them.

She finally just jumped into the pool, not trying to impress anyone, just to get rid of him.

Then Gregory walked to the edge, excessively sticking his chest out, playing the macho man, comically rolling his arms and shoulders.

"Well, are you coming or going?"

"Don't wait for an invitation!"

"You gonna chicken out?"

That last one must have hit home, and Gregory, probably scared, finally dove in with a poorly controlled dive that ended up in a huge belly flop. When he came out of the water, his chest had the color of a boiled crayfish. Which of course made Naima and Bruce laugh hilariously.

"Okay, I slipped, that's all," he tried to explain.

"Watch the pros," said Severine, pointing at Eusebius who was getting ready.

His dive was clearly better than the previous one. Eusebius plunged face first, rolling to do a stretched-leg Salto jump and penetrated into the water with his arms above his head. When he came up, the public clapped with intensity and passion.

The following hour passed in a friendly atmosphere, some of us jumping or diving again, Nathalie drawing, others just as spectators. Colombe and I had left the group, following the riverbed upstream in a refreshing walk.

We got back to Bougainvillea Domain about five that evening.

"Free time tonight!" said Severine and Eusebius, abandoning us.

CHAPTER 9

To bury the hatchet

Opening the fridge to try to find some salami to accompany our before dinner drink, I found a plastic bottle with a tempting liquid and slices of fruit floating in it. There was a little label with a handwritten note on the bottleneck.

Cheers to our guests this week. Severine and Eusebius.

"Isn't that nice? Look, sweetie. It looks like a bottle of macerated rum."

"Open it up so we can smell it."

You certainly could tell this booze was homemade. We could smell wafts of vanilla and ginger when we opened the bottle. I poured each of us a glass.

"Here's to our dream vacation, honey."

"Here's to us!"

Right then we saw a shadow moving along the

path next to our bungalow, preceded by the characteristic noise of someone walking on gravel. The sun had already set, and the light was fading quickly. I thought I recognized a masculine silhouette that looked like Gregory, but when I saw his baseball cap on backwards, I was sure of it. He scurried out to Naima's bungalow, which was about thirty or forty feet from ours, a bit down below. The advantage of this complex of bungalows was that no one really overlooked anyone else, though everything was linked together by graveled paths that all led to the shared areas where the pool, bar, and washing machines were located.

"I sure know who's going to be happy," grinned Colombe. "Someone's best friend is arriving."

"For sure! That Greg though is pretty creepy. He found someone to pick on this week, in my humble opinion."

"Poor Naima! Maybe they'll make up around a glass of macerated rum, if of course, our hosts dropped one off at their place too."

"You never know, vacations make people close!"

Her wet hair in a towel, Naima rushed out of

the bathroom to pick up her phone that was vibrating furiously on the coffee table.

"Hey, my little angel, how you doing? What time is it in France? Ah, okay, you took time to call me, thanks. I just got out of the shower. Yes, it's really nice here. Did you get my pictures of the dolphins? Right, it was incredible."

With her phone stuck between her ear and shoulder, the young lady was hopping around trying to get into her panties and a pair of shorts.

"This afternoon we went to Acomat Falls, really nice too, I'll tell you about it. Yes, I'll send you pictures every day. Yes, we'll call each other every day too, promise."

She heard someone walking on the patio, followed by discreet knocks on her wooden door.

"Wait a sec, someone's knocking."

She saw Gregory, someone that she mentally called Dickface, from the window.

"Someone's here, I gotta go, I'll call you back, okay? Yes, it's a man. No, of course not, I'm not going to flirt with him. Anyway you know that... Well, you know! Take care, my love. I'll call you back."

Shaking her head, she hung up.

"Coming, just a minute!" she shouted.

She threw her towel down, ran to the closet to get a

top that she put on without even bothering with a bra. Anyway, her little firm breasts preferred freedom, a guarantee of tonicity, according to what she'd read in some girly magazine.

She opened the door and there was Gregory, holding up a bottle as if it were a trophy.

"To bury the hatchet!" said the young man with a smile.

"You decided to wreck my evenings too?"

"I can try."

"Well, let me tell you, you're doing a good job of it."

"That was in my fridge, maybe we can try it together? Nothing like a bit of rum to calm things down, don't you think?"

"Nothing ventured, nothing gained," Naima conceded, attracted by the suggestion of an exotic cocktail.

She thus invited him to sit down at the coffee table with its two wooden benches on the patio, went to the kitchen and came back with two glasses, some nibbles and sweet potato chips.

"Here's to peace!" Gregory attempted.

"And let's hope that this will be the case for the remainder of the week," said the young lady.

"I'll think about it," joked the young man. "But,

when you think of it, it would be too bad not to take advantage of this week, don't you agree? We could have a good time for next to nothing."

"Meaning?"

"Well, knowing that this week here didn't cost us much – at least that was the case for me, I don't know about you..."

"Oh? You scored that 'extraordinary deal' too?" asked Naima, cutting him off.

"Of course I did! I'm not exactly rolling in dough, so I didn't hesitate for a single second what I got their email."

"Me neither, I admit."

"That's why I'm saying that it would be ridiculous not to enjoy ourselves, seeing this is like a junket. See what I'm getting at?"

"I certainly do, Greg. But don't kid yourself about me. You seem like a nice guy, someone who likes having a good time, even though sometimes you're a bit thick. But I just want you to know, it won't go any farther between us, we'll just be friends on vacation. I'm not interested. Was I clear enough for your thick head?"

"You were," Gregory conceded.

They clinked glasses to seal their deal and spent over an hour talking about this and that, the best way actually to calm things down between them as they both had strong personalities.

While Gregory was serving a third glass of rum, they heard someone walking on the path behind their bungalow. They recognized Bruce's silhouette, though they had no idea if he'd seen them together. Bruce seemed to be going to Jacques's place, which was right next to Naima's bungalow.

"This sure is good rum!" said Jacques, who was wearing slacks and a flannel shirt, a both practical and elegant outfit.

"I totally agree," approved Bruce, who was just wearing bermudas and a tank top showing off his pumped muscles.

Those two very different men, both in age and appearance, had nonetheless discovered commonalities, passions they shared. That was what they were talking about in their impromptu cocktail. They both loved sports cars, elegant Italian or German cars, at least theoretically. Jacques didn't hide his pride in the Porsche 911 Targa he'd purchased just a few months ago. He showed Bruce photos of it, just like others show off photos of their kids. He described the dynamic four hundred and fifty horsepower engine, the three point six seconds it took to reach 65 miles per hour and its top speed of 189 mph on a racetrack.

"What a monster!" Bruce acknowledged, subjugated. "That must have set you back a couple of bucks..."

"About a hundred and fifty thousand, without the options..."

"I guess it's not for me then. Even in my dreams."

"What kind of car do you have?"

"You really wanna know?"

"Of course. Things like that interest me."

"So, as I could never afford a jewel like yours, I bought a used Volkswagen combi, big enough for my surfboards, to sleep in when I'm on the road, go to all the European beaches without having to pay for hotels."

"That's true, it's another lifestyle. I've got the freedom to buy what I want, and you've got the freedom to go where you want."

"Jacques, what kind of work do you do to have money like that?"

"I work in finance. A trader. A pretty good job."

"I guess so."

"What about you?"

"I'm a freelancer in web marketing. A pretty cool

job that allows me to go where I want, when I want and to work as much as I want. I don't earn enough yet to buy a Targa, but who knows, maybe someday."

"You know the proverb that everything comes to he who waits, young man!" concluded Jacques, holding up his glass.

Then they heard someone walking next to the bungalow, accompanied by a joyfully whistled Creole melody. It was Eusebius, a big smile on his face.

"Cheers, my friends!"

"Thanks for the rum," Jacques said appreciatively. "Would you like some?"

"Well, you know if I stopped at each bungalow to have a drink with each guest, at the end of the evening I wouldn't even be able to find my way back! Plus, someone's expecting me. Nathalie's refrigerator broke down, I have to see what the problem is."

"Okay, hope she won't talk the legs off you," joked Bruce.

"Ah! Ah! That's true, she's not Miss Talkative... Have a nice evening! Ah! I almost forgot, Jacques...

"Yes?"

"Here everyone calls everyone else by their first names."

"Gotcha!"

ABOUT A HUNDRED FEET FARTHER, behind a hedge of bougainvillea trees which was what the domain was named after, Eusebius had arrived at the foot of the three steps leading to Nathalie's bungalow. She was languidly lying in the hammock that swayed from two wooden girders on the porch.

"Knock, knock, knock," the host imitated pretending he was at a real door.

"Ah! Eusebius! I didn't hear you coming. I must have dozed off."

"That's no big deal, Nathalie. That's what vacations are for, right?"

"Well, I still didn't hear you coming."

Eusebius thought Nathalie had a pasty voice. When he looked in, he saw the bottle of rum whose level had decreased by at least fifty per cent on the coffee table and well imagined how she'd spent the last hour.

"You got a problem with your fridge?"

The fifty- or so-year old lady tried to get out of the hammock but couldn't.

"Just have a look at it. Anyway, I don't know a thing about electrical appliances."

Eusebius noted that she'd succeeded in

pronouncing the last two words without too much difficulty despite the fact that her tongue must weigh a ton in her mouth. Actually she held her liquor pretty well, he thought. He opened the refrigerator, the light didn't come on. Yet, he heard the familiar purring that it still was running. It wasn't really cold, that was true, but when he found the thermostat, he saw that that it was set at one. He pushed it up to four.

"It's working now! It was just set at the minimum. I jacked it up to the max. We'll see tomorrow morning, but in my opinion, I think that everything will be alright. On the other hand, I have to replace the lightbulb."

"Oh, that's why I thought it wasn't working. Sorry to have bothered you for nothing, Eusebius."

"No problem! That's why I'm here, you know. Like I said the other day, you gotta problem, just call Eusebius! I'll be right back with a new light bulb. I'll be back immediately."

And in less than ten minutes, he was. Nathalie had managed to get out of the hammock and was sitting on the wooden bench, a glass in her hand. There were about ten sheets of paper on the coffee table, all of them full of drawings.

"Got it! It'll just take me a minute and then I'll leave."

"No hurry," said Nathalie. "Quite the opposite."

She raised her glass in his direction and took a sip.

"Your rum is delish! Thanks so much. It's not too cold, but thanks anyway."

Is that alcohol that's talking or her?" wondered Eusebius while changing the lightbulb. Anyway she was unrecognizable compared to her behavior during that day.

"There you go! Let there be light! as the saying goes."

"Thanks so much, Eusebius. Would you... have a moment... to have a drink with me?"

"Um, Severine's waiting for me for supper."

"Come on, just one. I feel a little alone, me and my rum. Could you get a glass from the kitchen?"

"Okay, just one then."

He washed his hands in the kitchen and came back out.

Nathalie tapped the cushion on the bench where she was sitting.

"You can sit here."

He hesitated, but didn't want to vex his guest.

She poured him a tall glass, and topped hers up, probably so they'd both have the same amount. Eusebius noticed that her hand holding the bottle was wavering slightly, the bottleneck touching the glass, nearly spilling it on her drawings.

"You're really talented," he said. "You drew all that here?"

"I did, I was inspired by the scenery, the climate, this heat, all this humidity.

The last syllable of the last word seemed to take forever in Nathalie's mouth. Was it the alcohol or just the way she spoke?

"May I?"

"Please do."

Eusebius picked up a few sheets, admiring them. He recognized Acomat Falls, the Globicephala, and some of that week's guests. And maybe himself on the drawing he was holding with his fingertips.

"This one looks like me."

Nathalie smiled at him boldly.

"Could be, but I wanted to ask you something."

"Yes?"

"No, wait, let's have a drink together first!"

They clinked glasses and drank silently.

"So, what did you want to ask me?"

The woman's eyes sparkled in an ambiguous twinkle.

"Well, it's a bit daring, but it's vacation, right. And on vacation, you can do whatever you want."

"Maybe not everything," he stammered.

"I really can't quite get you, Eusebius."

"Get me?"

"Yes, draw you. I don't know, there must be something, a little detail, I'm missing. A spark I missed, the wrong angle someplace. Everyone's not a tame subject, you know. You, you're like a wild animal, you've got something that's elusive. Maybe it's because you're... you're too handsome... I mean in the esthetic meaning of the word, don't get any false ideas."

"Ah! You scared me there, I thought you were trying to flirt with me for a second."

"No, I don't do that, she whispered. "But more seriously, I'm attracted by your body, and I'd really like..."

Nathalie's hand maliciously rubbed Eusebius's athletic thigh.

"To?"

"Um, it would be so great... if you could pose for me."

He delicately, hoping not to hurt her, pushed Nathalie's hand away back to the cushion on the bench.

"You mean, like in a Fine Arts school?"

"I mean, not wearing any clothing, like the first

man on the first day. That first perfect man that God esthetically created."

Eusebius laughed nervously.

"Nude?" he managed to say.

"Like Adam... a black Adam. You know, as opposed to what most people think, Adam was black! You could be my Gwada Adam!" Nathalie said enthusiastically.

Eusebius having finished his glass, got up.

"Okay, I'll think it over. But in the meanwhile, I have to be going. Severine's expecting me."

"Just think about it," stammered the slightly intoxicated lady was he was walking away.

CHAPTER 10

Why not let myself be tempted?

"EVERYTHING OKAY, HUN?"

"Fine, sweetie!"

"It sure took you long enough. Dinner's cold. You had some problems with Nathalie's fridge?"

"No, it was just a burned-out lightbulb. But she thought it was on the fritz. But she was like seeing double, if you know what I mean."

"She sampled our macerated rum?"

"Sure did. They'd become new best friends! And you wouldn't say that just by looking at her, but she's one thirsty lady!"

Severine gave him a knowing smile.

"Are you hungry?"

"Famished!"

They sat down at their patio, reheated the accras

that they dipped in dog sauce while contemplating the stars.

When Eusebius went to brush his teeth, his wife entered her little office, following a ritual she'd established several years ago.

EUSEBIUS, the West Indian with dreadlocks, was enjoying his shower. He appreciated the feeling of his hands delicately rubbing his soap-covered brown skin. At the same time he massaged his muscles; biceps, pecs, trapezius muscles and quadriceps, each of them enjoying a pleasant palpation. While massaging himself, his thoughts by analogy led him to think back on that ambiguous conversation he'd had just a while ago with their artist guest for the week. Nathalie, besides her embarrassingly drunken state, had troubled him with the proposal she'd made to him. Actually quite a pleasant uneasiness.

Posing nude for her? Quite a ludicrous idea, but after all, why not, he thought. It was true that Eusebius was quite the hunk, though he refused to admit it. Up until now, he hadn't paid much attention at all to his body image. As was the case with many men in the West Indian area, he had been spoiled by lucky fairies when he was in the cradle, and they'd given him a naturally muscular and slim body. After that some manual work and swimming that honed those innate dispositions.

So why not? Was he shy? He didn't think so. When he was a teen, he'd often swum in the buff with his friends for a midnight dip. And God had gifted him with attributes he could legitimately be proud of. But still, it was a whole different story to pose alone and nude for a woman, during the day, compared to diving into the water during the night with a bunch of extroverted teens. If he did it, it would just be as a favor for Nathalie, that was it, he convinced himself. Just a simple relationship between an artist and her model.

That was it.

EACH TIME she opened her diary, she was troubled by its odor. It was the fragrance of souvenirs, joyful fragrances of her youth mixed in with a whiff of sadness. A smell that she needed, that she searched for each evening in the yellowed pages of her diary, an object she'd never let go of for any reason.

That evening, while Eusebius was taking a long and languid shower, she wanted to recall her very first souvenir, the very first page she'd written with a still hesitant child's writing, using round and carefully shaped letters, a schoolgirl's writing.

MONDAY, December 15, 2003.

Dear Diary,

I need you. No one understands me. No one loves me, at least that's what I think.

How come? What did I do wrong? I hate myself when I look in the mirror.

Today I want to die. But I don't know how.

That's why I decided to write and do something for myself.

Today, in class, I'm in fifth grade, I was never so ashamed in my life. Because of my teacher, the one I call the Bitch!

She wanted all of us to draw someone in class. We could choose whoever we wanted.

As some of my classmates couldn't decide, the Bitch had a great idea. She said it was a great idea, not me.

She pointed at me and told me to come

to the front of the class, to sit down on a stool and not to move anymore.

She said I'd be a great model, and it would be easy to draw me because I was... a little different.

Everyone in class laughed but I didn't laugh at all.

I wanted to run away but I couldn't.

I wanted to cry but that would have made the Bitch too happy.

So I just closed my eyes so I wouldn't see the other kids who were squinting and trying to draw me.

I closed my eyes so I wouldn't see the teacher's smile. I knew that she would be grinning with her rotten idea.

I want to die and I (...)

With a quick movement, exasperated by what she'd read and reread, Severine closed the diary of that little girl that everyone had mocked, her teacher and all the other schoolmates in her class. Though she wouldn't really call her schoolmates 'friends,' to designate the group of students who had rushed through that gaping opening that the unscrupulous Bitch had put in place.

What had that little girl done to deserve to be treated like that by her teacher and schoolmates in primary school? Undoubtedly nothing.

Had she been brave enough to talk about it to her parents, perhaps they would have known what to do, complain and have the teacher fired, or change schools for that little girl in Auxerre who had attended the same school since kindergarten.

But she hadn't dared to express her shame, her disgust of others and of herself, ever since she'd become aware of what she represented.

So that little girl from Auxerre kept it all inside. She'd found a notebook and had decided to write her wrath and hatred. Maybe the day would come sometime when she'd be brave enough to face the world surrounding her rather than closing up like an oyster. For now though, she wanted to convince herself that she was an oyster with a pearl inside it, though she was the only one who knew about the existence of that little mother-of-pearl sphere sparkling in her heart.

SEVERINE WIPED a tear from the corner of her eye and put the diary back in the locked drawer.

That night, she wasn't strong enough to write a new chapter and joined Eusebius in bed.

CHAPTER 11

A safe outing

LIKE MOST OF US, I was really excited about today's outing. Eusebius had just driven us to Malendure Bay, one of Guadeloupe's most popular beaches, because it was located in a protected area. The Cousteau Natural Reserve, named after the famous scientific explorer and environmentalist, was opening its arms to us. Not far from the shore we could see the two Pigeon Islets, and we were heading towards them in our little boat with our diving instructor.

"Jean-Pierre and I have been friends for nearly fifteen years," our host told us when introducing him.

We were surrounding a fifty- or so-year old man, originally from France, with ruddy Gwada sun kissed skin, wrinkled up like an old apple, but with permanent smile wrinkles.

"Hi everyone. It's great to see you this morning and I'd like to thank Eusebius for having brought you here today. I hope I won't disappoint you. But I'm sure that won't be the case. Right over there," he said, pointing to the stretch of water that separated the beach from the islets, "it's chock full of natural wonders."

"We can even see sea turtles here?" Colombe asked enthusiastically.

"SURE CAN, Miss! All you gotta do is swim out thirty or forty feet with your goggles and scuba diving equipment or even hold your breath and dive and you'll see one or several turtles. So just imagine what I'll show you if you go diving with an oxygen bottle! Speaking of which, has anyone already gone diving?"

Everyone shook their heads from right to left.

"Okay then, what I'll do is get you all on the boat and then I'll explain what we'll be doing."

One after another, we boarded Jean-Pierre's little skiff on which he'd already loaded all the equipment: oxygen bottles, pressure regulators, goggles, wetsuits, and fins. Naima was the first one onboard, followed by Gregory and Bruce, then Jacques, Colombe and me, and Nathalie who was now the shadow of Eusebius's shadow, and finally our diving instructor.

Severine once again said she wouldn't join us because she had shopping to do, but we knew that with Eusebius and Jean-Pierre, we'd be taken care of. JP told us which wetsuits to take, and we put them on with a lot of difficulty, as no one was used to wearing something as tight as that.

"Hey, Naima, that tight black suit looks great on you."

It unsurprisingly was Gregory who'd said that, a bit too loudly for it to have been discreet. The young lady rolled her eyes, hitting him on the shoulder. Ever since the beginning those two could have done standup together, I thought maliciously.

"Nathalie, you're not going to put your wetsuit on?" asked Jean-Pierre. "Isn't it the right size?"

"I'm not really at ease with the idea of diving. But if that doesn't bother anyone, I'd still like to go on this outing to go swimming around the islets."

"That doesn't bother anyone at all! To each his own. In that case, I'd advise you to wait until I've dropped the anchor next to the pool."

"A pool?"

"Yup, it's a natural pool though, one that's sheltered between the small islet and the big one, you'll see, it's like heaven. You could always take these goggles and snorkel if you want to put your head into the water and admire the superb fish."

"Plus that could inspire you for your drawings!" added Naima.

"But you won't be able to touch the commander's head..."

"Meaning?"

"One of the highlights here. We always take our divers above Commander Cousteau's bust, but it's almost thirty feet down. A pleasant anecdote!"

"All right! You'll greet him for me then."

Eusebius said he'd stay with her, something she accepted discreetly.

JEAN-PIERRE TOOK us out to the spot called "Corral Gardens," dropped the anchor and then began to instruct us on how to dive in shallow water as well as how to breath using the pressure regulator and oxygen bottle. After making sure we'd all understood, he concluded.

"So my friends, to sum this all up... Above all, don't worry, this is a safe outing, but you have to comply with a few rules. We'll be in the water for about forty-five minutes and won't go any deeper than thirty feet. That means we won't have to apply any decompression stops, it's an easy dive. We'll stay in a group, and I'll always be above you, watching you. As we only can communicate visually, just remember these two very simple signs: when you put your thumb and index finger together and raise the other three fingers, what does that mean?"

"Everything's okay," replied Gregory, like a teacher's pet.

"Congratulations, young man. But when you raise your thumb like this, towards the surface?"

"That means you've got a problem, like 'Help, I gotta go up to the surface!'"

"Well explained. Everyone got that? Ready?"

Jean-Pierre checked our equipment one last time, our wetsuits and the capacities of our oxygen bottles on our backs. And then it was the huge leap... backwards, obviously. Reminding me of that old joke: Why do scuba divers dive backwards and not forward? Because otherwise they'd dive headfirst into the boat! I know, it's idiotic, but that has always made me laugh.

The first impression I had was that I was sinking to the bottom, weighed down by the bottles. Then I quickly recovered, got my balance back and felt lighter, like I was floating between the bottom I could see and the top of the water, where the sun was twinkling.

Taking Colombe's hand, I began to try my hand at fin swimming. Jacques was busy filming us and the undersea with his submersible camera. Behind us, the trio of Naima and her two "pilot fish," Gregory and Bruce, were swimming at our speed too. Above us, the reassuring shadow of our diving instructor guided us, pointing at a school of fish here, some remarkable coral over there, and a bit farther on a pile of rugged rocks stemming from the volcanic formation of these little islets.

We were swimming in clear, peaceful waters, Cousteau's universe that he called "the world of silence." Around us, everything seemed to be floating like in a dream. The magic was suddenly complete when we discovered the majestic and slow silhouette of a sea turtle swimming about ten feet in front of us. A splendid specimen about three feet long, swimming in a slow dance above the algae-filled seabed, one that it nibbled on from time to time. We watched the beautiful lady enjoy her picnic and I had the intimate feeling that I'd experienced an instant of eternity. Jean-Pierre had told us not to try to touch them, nor scare them by trying to get too near. We were in their home, not ours. We were just simple visitors and had to respect them.

We swam for several minutes above its shell,

keeping in rhythm with the animal. After that, it either had noticed us or had finished its little snack, and it began to swim more energetically and quickly swam away from us, leaving us only with its moving souvenir.

Then our group was soon above Commander Cousteau's bust. He was there, right below us, on a concrete slab, with his irremovable red cap on his head. Well actually it was no longer red, as the stone statue was now covered with greenish looking algae and bits of corral. That didn't stop us from posing one after the other next to Cousteau, imitating his gesture meaning "Everything's fine," with our thumbs and index finger in a circle like Jean-Pierre taught us.

Our instructor then made a gesture saying we'd be going back up to the boat. Time had flown by like the movement of a bird's wing, or a turtle's fin and reluctantly we all began to go to the surface.

That was when it happened.

Naima, suddenly panicked, began to gesticulate, vigorously shaking her head, pedaling in a disorganized way with her feet, her hands on her pressure regulator.

Bruce and Gregory signaled to Jean-Pierre that they needed help and in seconds he swam to the trio, seeing that the men were designating Naima by raising their thumbs to the surface. The professional monitor put his arms around the young lady and swam vertically up to the surface.

For Naima, those thirty feet must have seemed like thirty miles. I swam up with her and saw that her eyes were closed. Her legs were just kicking limply. Jean-Pierre, an experienced diving instructor, quickly understood the problem, spit his own pressure regulator out and jammed it into her mouth. Either her oxygen bottles had emptied abnormally, or something was stuck in them.

Naima's face came to the surface, and she finally could breathe in fresh air, swelling up her lungs which caused her to cough and spit.

We weren't far from the boat, where I saw Nathalie, still leaning over her drawing pad, just wearing a light sarong that barely covered her bikini. Across from her, Eusebius seemed to be posing, looking out over the sea, standing at the bow like a figurehead. When he saw what was going on, he dove in and joined Naima with just a few strokes, to help Jean-Pierre swim her up to the skiff.

A few moments later, Naima was already less pale. At the end of the day, everything was fine, a technical incident luckily controlled by the instructor with the help of the whole group.

THAT EVENING, Jean-Pierre carefully examined the equipment that the young lady had used and found with stupor that the collar leading to the pressure regulator was cracked. He would have sworn he'd conscientiously checked and double-checked everything before the outing. But accidents could happen at any time, he convinced himself. In cases like that he remembered the truism that said, "Fifteen minutes before he died, he was still alive!" He transposed it into today's incident, "Fifteen minutes before it was cracked, the collar was still intact!" and fell asleep peacefully, relieved to have avoided a tragedy that would have been his fault.

CHAPTER 12

A suspicion of doubt

WHILE NAIMA and the rest of the group were out diving and then recovering from it, Severine was busy with quite something else. She'd left Bougainvillea Domain right after her husband and the group, first in the same direction, taking the sole coastal road towards the south of Basse-Terre. When she was on the heights above Malendure Bay, she briefly looked out over Pigeon Islets and recognized Jean-Pierre's boat that was anchored near the islands. Had she had binoculars with her, and more time, she would have realized that the only two people on the boat were her husband who was wearing his swimsuit posing in front of Nathalie's gourmet and expert eyes. Would she have appreciated that? Not too sure of that.

She continued on the same road for several miles,

along the coast until Basse-Terre, where she turned inland, towards the mountains. When she'd gone through Saint-Claude, all that was left was to continue this interminable road, one that wove from right to left in hairpin curves and that ended up at the departure parking lot for those hiking up to Soufriere Hills volcano.

Severine, a facetious hostess who was full of energy, only had one goal that week: to make sure her guests had a good time. That was why she'd decided to prepare a little surprise for them, one that they undoubtedly would never forget, any of them.

And she had a bit of preparation to do. For everyone to have a great time, she had a few details to put in place first, ones that required a lot of precision.

So that's what she did that day, alone on the sides of that famous volcano whose stinky smelling fumaroles regularly emanated from the crater. That day it was cloudy, and you couldn't see the peak, yet it was still quite warm. Severine dearly hoped it wouldn't be the case on the day she'd be going with them during the ascension. Soufriere Hills volcano wasn't the same thing when it was cloudy or when it was nice out. But before that, she had to go there alone.

She luckily was able to park right next to the departure point of the trail leading up to it, which allowed her to not have to carry the load that she'd put into the trunk of her SUV for five or six hundred feet. It wasn't that it was heavy, it was just quite cumbersome. But that was what she needed to have the final result she was expecting. She took her job as a *G.O.*, a Club Med invention meaning *Gentle Organizer*, very seriously. She wanted the week to be a fantastic one for everyone, up to the last detail.

That required a couple of hours and when she got back to her SUV, perspiring heavily, she felt both lighter and heavier. Little by little she began to worry, unless it was a suspicion of doubt. Would her idea work? Would the alchemy take place? All that was left to do was to try it out, and that would be done by the end of the week at the latest.

She had lunch with the inhabitants of Vieux-Habitants, pronounced *Zabitan* in Creole, at stopped to see one of her friends on the way back north. She did a bit of shopping before arriving at Bougainvillea Domain, where she was astonished to see the car of one of her friends, a doctor, in the visitors' parking lot.

Without unloading the trunk, she rushed to Eusebius who escorted her to Naima's bungalow, where Dr. Lamblin was.

"What's wrong?" she asked the young lady.

"Nothing serious," the doctor said, a tall man with

graying short hair who looked like a former basketball player. "She was just short of air for a moment, but our dear Jean-Pierre was perfectly able to manage things, apparently. She won't have any aftereffects. All she needs to do is rest today and maybe have a glass of rum to get her colors back."

"You reassure me, Alex," she responded. "I've always appreciated your therapeutic methods. Speaking of which, when you're finished with our sweet Naima, do you have time for a drink at our place?"

"I would have been glad to Sev', but I've got a job to do. I snuck out between two house calls. I'll take a raincheck though."

And he put his equipment back in his bag before leaving Naima to rest peacefully.

CHAPTER 13

Who could have believed that?

Biscarrosse, March 2020

The photo of our group on Jean-Pierre's skiff left us dumbfounded. Naima's smile on the photo, before her dive, before her accident, was full of emotion. Colombe sighed as she put the photo book back down on the coffee table.

"*Leaving Naima to rest peacefully*... Good Lord! Jerome, I can't get those words out of my head and my heart!"

"The same is true for me. Who could have believed that? How could someone imagine that barely two weeks ago, we were having such a good time with that young and friendly lady?"

"While today, when I look at that email we got, it sends shivers down your spine when you know that..."

"Show it to me again."

Colombe picked up her phone.

"You remember that message I'd sent to all of our group, for that shared file that no one got? So, here's the email that I got back, from Naima's inbox."

I read what was on her phone.

"AUTOMATIC ANSWER: JACQUES' email?

FROM: naimabentallah@gmail.com

To: colombe.deschamps@gmail.com

I'M EXTREMELY sorry to inform you by this automatic inbox response, of the death of Naima Bentallah. This email address is thus now null, please don't use it anymore.

May she rest in peace.

Adele."

. . .

"That is just crazy," I whispered. What could have happened to her?"

"Do you think her death could have been linked to her accident in Malendure?" Colombe asked with a broken voice.

"I frankly don't see how. Unless her brain or lungs or something were irremediably impacted, but I'm neither a doctor nor a professional diver."

"But the doctor in Deshaies had said it wasn't serious."

"That would seem to confirm that there's no cause-and-effect relationship," I said, summing it up.

Colombe twisted her mouth, a sign that she was thinking a hundred miles per hour.

"In that case, what did she die from? And like I said earlier, how can we explain those unsettling coincidences, those deaths that took place in such a short time in our group of vacationers. I'm sure there must be a link between all of us. And that common denominator is..."

"Our stay in Guadeloupe?"

"That's all I can see for now."

"But we were there too! I personally didn't see a thing that could explain those tragedies. What about you?"

"Me neither. And that's what's bothering me. I'm sure I missed something."

"But what?"

"I don't know. A detail, a word, an interaction between her and someone else?"

"Are you insinuating that one of the vacationers could be linked to Naima's death? Or know something about it?"

"I'm not insinuating anything, just thinking out loud."

"You know you sometimes scare me with your crazy theories... even though I must say that you often nail it, honey."

"Well aren't you polite," joked Colombe. "So? What about trying to figure this out together?"

"Good investigators always have to try to figure things out. Count me in. But how?"

"We'll keep on going through the album and my notes. Some detail is bound to jump out at us, don't you agree?"

"Like they say, nothing ventured, nothing gained."

COLOMBE LEANED down to the coffee table, put the photo book on her thighs, sending us back to our visual souvenirs of our week in Gwada.

— A —

A HINT OF MUSICALITY

A light drizzle was lazily falling on the cemetery walls, gusts of wind were blowing on them, beating time. The cold weather had invited itself to the party, but that was just an expression. The day drew on sadly, in a grim atmosphere that shocked no one on that day of her burial.

The heavy wrought iron gates opened towards the inside, allowing the hearse to slowly and solemnly make its way into the cemetery.

Behind the undertakers' vehicle, a handful of people, heads bowed, shoulders lowered, were silently and religiously following it.

Only the sound of the hearse's tires on the gravel path brought a hint of musicality to what was going on, covering the discreet purring of the engine in first gear and the smothered sobs of attendees wearing their black clothing for the occasion.

The procession went into the central path.

CHAPTER 14

I call them angelic

NOTHING HAD BEEN PLANNED for the afternoon when Dr. Lamblin was at Naima's place, and everyone could do whatever they wanted. Colombe and I had gone to Anse de la Perle swimming, just because we were intrigued by the name, and we got back right when the doctor was leaving.

We saw Severine who was unloading her trunk, and seeing as it was full, we offered to give her a hand.

"Thanks, but it'll be okay," she replied.

"But we really want to," Colombe insisted.

She hesitated politely, then accepted.

"Okay then, thanks. After all, that way I won't have to do so many round trips."

I took a large PVC crate, filled with isotherm flasks,

that weighed a ton, making sure I didn't fall over from its weight.

"What the heck is in there Severine? Quarts of macerated rum for the whole week or what?"

"Don't be so curious! You need plenty of energy to keep up a steady pace, don't you?" she said with a smile and her arms full of bags. "Looks like you all appreciate it!"

"We never say no to good stuff, especially when we're on vacation," I confirmed, putting the crate down on the table on their patio.

After two other trips to her car, all the groceries were unloaded. Severine thanked us and we left.

I ASKED Colombe if she wanted to eat out tonight in Deshaies. I'd seen a little restaurant there with an outside dining area overlooking the port. A lovely place to dine, plus the daily special was sauté of kid in coconut milk, something that I'd never tried.

Enjoying a bottle of local brew, a Carib for myself and a Gwada for Colombe, we talked about what had taken place.

"Today's outing was quite the event," began Colombe. "Poor Naima, I hope she won't be traumatized by her first dive. I'm sure I would have panicked in her shoes."

"I don't know if she actually realized what was happening. I think she lost consciousness right before coming up. Luckily Jean-Pierre was really reactive. Can you imagine her drowning right in front of our eyes?"

"I prefer not to."

We then remained pensive with that thought, looking out to sea where the masts of the boats docked there were dancing an imaginary aquatic biguine.

The server brought us our meal, and while eating, we talked about our fellow guests that week.

We of course began with Naima and how weak she felt after the incident. Then Severine and Eusebius's warm and friendly welcome. Nathalie's tenacious coldness, she who couldn't raise her nose from her Canson drawing book, her solitary and artistic nature. The only person she seemed to appreciate was Eusebius, and she seemed to discreetly have hooked onto him. Then Gregory's banter and impertinence, someone who never had grown up, a loudmouth who seemed to us to be more uncouth than unpleasant, too close to Naima, at least in her opinion. Then Jacques's discretion and nearly British correction, someone who didn't seem to easily mix with the others. And last but not least, Bruce, who for the moment hadn't sparked any comments from us, but who seemed too smooth, too handsome, too likeable... to be honest?

"You see evil everywhere," remarked Colombe after that reflection.

"Just experience, my dear, and it's taught me to be curious, and above all wary of everything and everyone. I think that there are two ways of seeing others. On one hand, there are those who think others are intrinsically good and who are astonished by deceit and dishonesty. Those are the ones I call angelic. On the other, people like me, who instinctively distrust others and wait for them to prove they are good people. Those people are realists."

"Interesting... But tell me, when we first met in Nice, did you consider me as being potentially dangerous or a bad person?"

"Come on, it's not the same thing with you. As soon as I set eyes on you in that café, Rue de la Préfecture..."

"The Master Home?"

"Exactly! As soon as I set eyes on you, it was love at first sight!"

"Yeah... let's say I believe you."

Right then we saw the silhouette of someone we knew come into the restaurant.

Jean-Pierre also saw us and went to our table.

“Enjoy your meal! So? How is Naima?”

“She’s much better,” said Colombe. “The doctor said it wasn’t serious, just scary. And you must have been scared too this morning. What exactly happened?”

“Of course I was scared. But when things like that happen, the most important thing to remember is not to panic. There’s always a solution.”

“Was there some technical issue?” I insisted.

“I was completely astonished by what happened. When I examined the equipment after coming back, I saw that the collar that linked the bottle to the pressure regulator was cracked. And that’s what caused the leak and lack of oxygen. But I have to tell you, I’m an extremely conscientious person and I’m sure that I checked all the equipment before our outing and didn’t note anything that was abnormal. I don’t understand.”

“Could the pipe have been cracked during the dive?”

“Something that’s extremely rare, but possible, yes. If she rubbed up against a rock or a sharp coral, for example.”

“Could it have been done intentionally?” Colombe asked. “With a knife?”

“You read too many mystery books. I can assure

you that between my checklist in the morning and the time when you put your wetsuits and equipment on, no one walked up with a knife or a cutter!"

"And during our dive, under water?" I insisted.

"I was watching you all. Nearly impossible. But all's well that ends well, right? Well I have to be going now. Have fun here on the island and I think that we'll be seeing each other soon, at least that's what Severine told me."

"Really?"

"An all-day outing in the mangrove, that's something that everyone loves. But don't worry, this time we'll just be diving with snorkeling equipment, so it'll be safe! Can I count you two in?"

"Sure can! Enjoy your meal too and thanks for everything, Jean-Pierre."

"You too!"

He joined his guests at their table letting us finish this nice evening together.

AT TEN, exhausted, we were both sleeping like logs, protected by our mosquito net.

CHAPTER 15

Behind the screen

At the same time in her bed, Severine was also sleeping soundly, tired out from having driven all day and having prepared her outing and surprises at Soufriere Hills volcano.

Right after dinner, she went into her office, as usual, to reread an excerpt from her diary.

Friday, June 18, 2004

I can't wait till school is over. I can't stand my teacher anymore, I can't stand all the kids who keep making fun of me. It's not my fault if I am like this.

Do I make fun of fat Linda? Of that stupid Nicholas who hardly knows how to read? Of Sebastien who's cross eyed? No! I don't make fun of them because I know how much that hurts.

It hurts you inside. In your heart.

I want to move, change schools, and finally go to middle school. I hope that things will be better there. I really hope so, because I can't even imagine how it would be if it was worse. And I don't know if I could bear it.

Come on, just another two weeks and it'll be over.

I hope I can wait.

Luckily my sister is there, she's never too far from me. She's the only one I can talk about that. She's the only one who can understand me. At least she listens to me when things aren't going well. But I made her swear that she'd never tell mom and dad. I'm too ashamed. Adults don't understand things like that.

I really hope I can wait.

Severine turned the page, hoping by that gesture she'd also turn the page of her pain. She had gone through her whole diary to reach a new blank page, and picking up her favorite pen, write a few lines before going to bed. Her eyelids were already as heavy as those of a *chatrou*, that squid that people ate here fried.

Deshaies, February 27, 2020.

I'm exhausted but glad to have prepared my little surprise for my guests.
I hope they'll appreciate it!
Just a few more days. What a farce I've prepared for them!
I'm going to bed, my eyes are closing all by themselves.

When she went to bed, Eusebius was already there, tossing and turning, without being able to fall asleep. She gave him a little kiss and fell asleep immediately.

~

Even the sweet melody of his wife's regular breathing wasn't sufficient to send Eusebius into Morphea's arms. He cursed, sat up and pushed the mosquito net away to get out of bed without waking Severine up. A short walk in the cool night around the deserted domain would undoubtedly do him good.

He could hear the sound of the gravel under his thongs while walking around the paths leading to all the various bungalows. It was completely dark, all his guests must have been sleeping soundly with all the emotions they'd had that afternoon. There was only light on one patio, Nathalie's, who was sitting cross-legged on the bench next to the rattan coffee table, wearing her brightly flowered robe.

"A beautiful night to walk in the moonlight!" murmured the artist.

"Good evening, Nathalie. You're right, the stars and this harvest moon should help me go to sleep. I thought everyone would be in bed by now! You're quite the night owl!"

"Inspiration! That's what's keeping me awake at this time of the night."

Inspiration and a couple of glasses of rum, thought Eusebius by the way she was slurring her words.

"Always drawing, aren't you. You're never without your notebook?"

"That's true, I usually have it with me. Do you want to see the drawings I did of you on the boat?"

"Sure! They'll flatter my narcissistic side!" he joked.

"Come and sit here by me, the light's good. And grab a glass in the kitchen, you know where they are."

Eusebius did just that and discovered his picture that Nathalie had etched. She drew him with his bulging muscles, leaning on the bow of Jean-Pierre's boat as well as in a dozen other postures. While going through her notebook, she looked up at him.

"Did you have time to think about what I asked?"

Eusebius backed up, bit his lower lip, a sign that he was undecided. On the one hand, when he looked at Nathalie's drawings, he was subjugated and curious to find out what different more... liberated poses would look like. But on the other hand, he felt guilty, like he was betraying his wife, who was fast asleep about fifty feet uphill. The advantage was that the whole domain seemed to be fast asleep, except for Nathalie and him. What did he have to lose? He wasn't doing anything forbidden.

"We won't be doing anything wrong," he convinced himself, speaking aloud.

"Nothing at all! Follow me."

She got up, wincing because she had a slight cramp in her leg, and held her hand out to him. Eusebius allowed himself to be led into the bungalow and she closed the door behind them.

“I’ll let you get comfortable,” she continued. “If you’re modest, you can get undressed behind the screen. Or else I can just turn around. I won’t look, promise!”

“You’ll have to look after to draw me.”

“It’s not the same my little chick. An artist’s eye isn’t a woman’s eye. Let’s not mix things up. Plus, I already saw you in your swimsuit.”

Eusebius didn’t really know what the woman was thinking and turned around. He took a deep breath and pulled his T-shirt over his head, took his cut-off jeans off, and then, the most difficult part, his boxer shorts. Nude like the first man on the first day, his voluminous ding-dong swinging between his powerful thighs, he felt intimidated. There was a towel on top of the folding screen, which he grabbed and rolled it around his waist before stepping out.

“I’m ready.”

Nathalie turned around, her eyes twinkling. Was it the alcohol she’d downed? Or perhaps lust? Eusebius preferred not to know.

"I prepared someplace to set your delicate little butt on," she said, pointing at a barstool in the middle of the room. "Just sit down young man. To begin with, you can keep the towel around you, that won't be a problem."

Eusebius was relieved that he'd be putting off the moment where he'd be totally nude in front of her. Nathalie pulled a chair out about six feet from him, sat down and crossed her legs, putting her sketchbook on it. She silently squinted, moving her head from one side to another, drew, raised her head, began drawing again. From time to time she would hold an arm out, advance a hand towards her model, with her thumb and pinkie finger raised and the others closed, then she'd close an eye with that impromptu instrument well known to experienced artists and take measurements. Measurements allowing her to reproduce as closely as possible the model's body in her sketchbook. Eusebius wondered if all the rum she'd downed wouldn't betray his proportions.

She filled three or four pages like that, asking him to change poses, put a hand here, his head like that, raise one of his legs, lower his head, etc. Then the sentence he'd been dreading since the beginning was pronounced.

"Can you take your towel off now?"

He had reached the point of no return. Eusebius, though not shy, still hesitated. He briefly thought of Severine who was sleeping in her bungalow. He was tempted to put a halt to that masquerade, to pick up his clothes and hightail it out of there, far from that poisonous lady. But curiosity and undoubtedly something else he refused to admit made him slide towards temptation.

He untied his towel, unveiling his most intimate anatomy, swallowing the lump he'd had in his throat up till then.

"A true Apollo," Nathalie approved. "You're very well... hung. Mother Nature was generous with you, but I'm sure you know that."

"That's what they say," Eusebius said, trying to laugh, but with the temptation to cup his hands over his sex.

Nathalie brought her pencil up to her lips, nibbling and sucking on the tip, sliding it from side to side of her lips. Eusebius's internal temperature suddenly shot up ten degrees. That lady, whose ethereal robe barely covered her pleasant curves, had a very disturbing aura. Where was that feeling of trouble coming from? Was it from her role as an artist? Was it the ambiguous situation? Was a type of eroticism hanging above their heads?

Nathalie stopped staring at him and concentrated on her drawing. Eusebius was relieved. Then though, when he looked back at the artist, he saw that her robe had risen even higher on her thighs, uncovering untanned skin, then a bit farther on under the frilly lace, a shadow of mysterious depths that titillated the nude male. Strange thoughts ran through his head. He began to confuse the nearly perfect curves of this almost unknown lady with those, more ordinary, of his own wife. He had to force himself not to assimilate his artistic nudity with a rarer, more engaging sexual nudity. It was just art, he tried to convince himself, nothing dirty.

That, however, did soothe him a bit. Right up to the moment when Nathalie put her sketchbook down on the table next to her and got up, slowly walking towards him.

She was looking straight at him, perhaps judging him?

The distance separating them was smaller and smaller. Then she was there, standing right in front of him. He could smell her perfume, the odor of her skin, and more unsettling, her rum-filled breath.

She held a hand out towards him.

"Just let yourself go, I'd like to draw you in a different position."

She brusquely took Eusebius's shoulder, pushing him a few degrees into a different position...

"That way the light will accentuate you better, perfect like that."

... put her hand below his chin to inch his head up...

"Your eyes are more luminous like that."

... put her hand on his brown thigh, her fingers just two inches from the end of his penis...

"You have to dare," she continued. "Dare to break the codes of antique poses, renew angles to make them more modern, seek perfection, open yourself to the unknown..."

What is that lady talking about? wondered Eusebius, who didn't understand a word of her artistic elucubrations. But what he understood however, was that if Nathalie didn't immediately move away from him, he would be having problems controlling his masculine impulses. Because near the lady's hand, Eusebius's sex was trying to live its own life, swelling with impatience, raising the flag, its flesh and blood becoming much too autonomous.

"I'm sorry," he stammered.

"Don't be. It's something normal, you know. You're not the first one. Plus, that's actually quite flattering, to be frank with you."

Eusebius wanted to get up, put a term to his ambiguous moment.

"I think I'd better be going now."

"We haven't finished yet," she said, forcing him to sit down. "I can feel we've nearly reached our goal, touching what is sublime, unprecedented. I can feel the strength in you I want to portray. I have to highlight the substantial backbone of your superb body, put this unique moment on paper."

"Nathalie, I didn't think this would go this far. I don't feel at ease here. It was stupid of me to have accepted your proposal, I shouldn't have."

She put a finger on her lips, telling him to remain silent, to contemplate the complete immersion in the "here and now" that she was seeing with her artist's eyes.

"*Shhh*. The best is yet to come" she whispered. "Relax."

The moon showed its white and pure light through the gaps in the shutters on Eusebius's naked and shining skin.

When she kneeled down at the foot of the stool, he gave in to an irrepressible, cutaneous, sensual and animalistic desire.

HE ONLY WENT BACK to his wife's bed an hour later that night, but with mixed feelings of shame and male contentment.

CHAPTER 16

Pitfalls we couldn't even imagine

THE NEXT MORNING Naima had totally recovered from her fright and fatigue. When she joined us at Eusebius's van in the middle of the morning, her colors were back in her face, that delicious copper-colored one that Moroccans have.

Today's outing would be going to Sofaïa, a magnificent place in Sainte-Rose's uplands, not too far from Bougainvillea Domain. As we'd spent two days on the sea, our hosts had invited us to discover the tropical forest, something omnipresent in Basse-Terre, and that was our hiking goal for the day.

Because it was only a two-and-a-half-mile round trip, the time required for it mentioned on the signs seemed to be vastly exaggerated to us. But we had not factored in how difficult the paths were, pitfalls we couldn't even imagine, especially as the night before, there had been a huge tropical rainstorm here in Guadeloupe. The ground was still damp, causing some of us to comically slip and slide while others swore like sailors.

That dense and damp rainforest was a pure marvel. Our eyes didn't know which way to look, as beauty was omnipresent. Stunning trees, rubber trees, and West Indian chestnut trees were over a hundred feet tall. Farther down, there were pink oleanders and cassava trees and bushes forming a second layer. Then, about six feet tall there were palm trees, Peyi currant bushes, and hordes of deep green ferns. All of that was invaded by entangled vines and suspended plants with sweet names like philodendron giganteum, wild pineapple, and brilliant flamboyant bushes. We slowly walked on a sweet-smelling path that was relatively marked out in the middle of these dense lush gardens, with their huge leaves that could have elegantly wrapped around a woman. Our progression was slowed by countless roots that were above ground, forcing us to do perilous contortions because of the slippery texture that those wooden veins on the surface had.

To continue, we sometimes had to take each other by the hand, something some of the group loved, while it annoyed others. Nathalie was wearing shoes that weren't really suited for this type of hike and was constantly complaining that it was much too slippery, gripping Eusebius's powerful and experienced hand as his native feet advanced slowly but surely. Severine was at the end of our group and didn't seem to appreciate unfair competition like that.

Gregory and Bruce were both vying to assist Naima, but she refused any help, too agile and proud to want to depend on any given male.

Jacques, bucolic, advanced carefully, his eyes attracted by a particular tree, a delicate fern, a rugged and crooked root. His eyes never looked at the path and he often nearly fell into puddles of muddy water. Such a slippery and muddy path though was a tricky one, I had to admit. Often our shoes sunk in the mud up to our ankles, and needless to say, we would be bidding adieu to our socks upon arrival.

Colombe and I were having fun just like little kids, jumping, running, and sliding in the midst of those vegetal interlaces.

"Keep up the good work!" Eusebius hollered out. "Your efforts will soon be rewarded."

"There's a surprise when we get there?" asked Gregory.

"There is, but before that there's something else,

you'll see. You hear the running water? We're nearing the *Saut des Trois-Cornes* waterfall."

"Love the name," Jacques approved.

"You'll love the site even more."

And about ten minutes later, we reached the banks of a mountain stream winding around polished rocks.

"Who wants to continue to the waterfall?"

"We have to cross the stream on foot?" asked Nathalie.

"Yup, you just jump from rock to rock, it's loads of fun, you'll see. Give me your hand."

In single file, after slipping a few times, we did reach the opposite bank. About five or six hundred feet further, the waterfall streaming down the rocks with trees and shrubs surrounding it left us flabbergasted.

"Anyone want to cool off under a good natural shower?"

I dipped my toes into the water at the foot of the falls.

"It's freezing!" I shouted.

"Jerome, it's good for your blood flow," Severine taunted me, running below its powerful water jet, without even taking her sarouel off.

As I didn't want the others to think I was a chicken, I immediately followed her, and then Gregory and Bruce also ran in.

Nearing the waterfall, there was a type of mist made from droplets that gave us an idea of the water temperature. That though was nothing at all compared to the shock I had when I went under the falls. I crossed the energizing curtain of water to shelter myself behind it, my back up against the rocks.

"Holy cow!" I hollered out, contracting my skin in an illusory effort to warm it up.

Colombe immortalized that moment with my mouth wide open while I was shouting, a burlesque reproduction of Munch's famous painting.

Gregory, behind me, also shuttered his male pride shouting out high pitched squawks. Bruce, stoic, an experienced surfer, was completely serene.

Once you got used to the cold water however, it wasn't unpleasant to massage your back and shoulders with the powerful waterfall streaming down on them. That was one of the highlights of our stay here.

We turned around to return taking a steep trail, almost like we were rock climbing, nearly crawling between the roots that we had to hold on to so we wouldn't slide down in that natural muddy slope. Our dear Gregory drew attention to himself when he slipped and slid down about ten feet in the mud, leaving him filthy from head to toe with a thick brown coating. He didn't seem to appreciate our friendly sarcasm and muttered to himself until the end of the walk.

"What's the surprise?" asked Naima impatiently.

"Here it is!" replied Eusebius, holding out his hand. "This time it's a real shower. Some of you seem to need one, right Greg?"

"Ha ha."

"So my friends, these are the natural showers of Sofaïa!" said our host proudly, pointing at an artificial space with four showerheads that seemed to be spouting out hot water.

We all approached them.

"Smells like someone's been farting around here!" yelled out Gregory with his legendary discretion.

"My dear Greg," Eusebius interrupted him. "Maybe you don't smell your own farts, but let me reassure you, that's not what you're smelling here, nor is it rotten eggs. It's merely the sulfur that this water coming out of the showers contains. Water that comes from the entrails of the mountains, full of sulfur and that is naturally heated to over a hundred degrees! People often say it has therapeutic virtues. So a free spa in the middle of nature, go for it!"

Gregory, convinced, immediately got undressed and rushed in. We all followed him.

A PURE MOMENT OF BLISS, in communion with Mother Nature! Despite that characteristic and a bit unpleasant smell, it was like divine nectar was falling upon us. The water, that was nearly oily when touching it, wrapped us in a veil of well-being that no one wanted to leave. But as there were only four showerheads, we had to let the others enjoy that too.

Eusebius, with his muscular ebony body was shining under the water, attracting feminine looks, and I'm sure you know who I'm talking about here. I even surprised my sweet Colombe giving him a few gourmet looks and couldn't help but roll my eyes at her. After all though, I knew that I couldn't physically compete with his body, not being athletic for two cents!

WHIFFS of rotten eggs accompanied us back to the van for our return to Deshaies. Eusebius dropped us all off there and we all had lunch privately, or at least with those we wanted to. Nothing else was planned for that afternoon, but Severine warned us.

"Don't go to be too late! Remember, tomorrow is

our big outing: we're going to climb the Soufriere Hills volcano. It's about a two-hour drive from here, so we'll be leaving at five a.m."

"Five?" Gregory choked. "But that's when I get my best beauty sleep!"

"Tough luck, you'll have to hit the sack at the same time as the wild chickens tonight. You weren't planning on dancing the biguine at Pointe à Pitre, were you? Plus it's a weekday, the discotheques are all closed."

"Not in a discotheque. But how do you know I wasn't planning on spending the night with a charming little lady?"

Then he winked salaciously towards Naima.

"Not even in your dreams," she replied, cooling him off immediately.

"Maybe Nathalie then?" he tried.

"You're just a kid. Stop dreaming and make sure you're on time tomorrow."

So everyone had free time that afternoon. Colombe and I just took advantage once again of the pool at the resort. Jacques was with us most of the time. When speaking about how beautiful the scenery was here, how friendly our hosts were and how little this vacation was costing us, we got to know him a bit better, discovering a charming and well-educated man, though a bit too proud of his professional success, something that did impact our good impression of him. He boasted about all the money he'd made last year thanks to his job as a trader, something allowing him to satisfy each and every fantasy he had. Buying sports cars and filling them with beautiful dolls – and he showed us pictures of them on his phone, or playing golf whenever he wanted to with all the movers and shakers of his region, and there he showed us a video of one of his most successful swings. In a nutshell, a nice guy though he spent much too much time listening to himself speak and admiring what he had just said.

CHAPTER 17
Downplaying

Biscarrosse, March 2020

Once again Colombe pushed the photobook on her thighs away, delicately opening it to the double-page about our trip to Sofaïa. That was when we got to know Jacques a bit better, during our free afternoon.

"One more!" she exclaimed. "That's starting to add up..."

I needed some time to digest what Colombe had just said. That lady, who began as my intern, then my girlfriend and now my partner, was often carried away by wacky ideas, outlandish theories. I did however have to admit that she had a knack for unearthing good tips, clues, and solving improbable mysteries, logical puzzles. I went into the kitchen to prepare us some tea and brought the mugs back with a box of cookies.

"Show me that answer you got again," I asked, sitting down.

Colombe handed me her phone and I reread the automatic message from the host.

"Mail delivery sub system.

Your message did not reach jacques.damiens666@sfr.fr. Either the address cannot be found or can no longer receive any messages.

Distant server's response: 552 5.2.2 <jacques.damiens666@sfr.fr>: Recipient address rejected: Over quota."

"What did you ask Jacques?"

"Remember, he assured us all that he was going to create a shared file on the cloud so that we all could post our vacation photos and exchange them."

"Right, I remember, he told us he'd do that the last evening, at the poolside. He promised he'd upload his underwater videos."

"And as he never did, I sent him a little mail as a reminder. And got that automatic message back. When it happened I really didn't think it was a big deal."

"Of course, most people don't clean their inboxes up that often and sometimes they're over quota."

"That sort of surprises me coming from a guy like Jacques who seems pretty savvy tech wise, don't you agree?"

"True, but still, sometimes people don't regularly clean up their inboxes."

"I know. That's what I said to myself. But I couldn't help but googling around to try to find another method of contacting him. And that's when I found that article about his death..."

Mr. Jacques Damiens passed away in Dijon on March 7, 2020, at the age of 55. He was single and had no children.

The police, alerted by the mailman who had a registered letter for him, found Mr. Damiens dead at his home. The mailman, in his declaration to the police, said he had been intrigued by music - guitar music -

that was playing very loudly in his house, though he rang the doorbell three times. Convinced that Mr. Damiens must be inside, he looked in the window and saw him sitting in an armchair in the living room, unconscious.

An investigation is ongoing to determine Jacques Damien's cause of death.

"TRUE, it's not as easy to clean your inbox in those conditions," I said with my habitual dark humor.

"Stop fucking with me. Two deaths in our little group of vacationers that week is something I don't find funny at all."

"You're right, I'm just trying to downplay this a bit."

"Downplay?" asked Colombe, irritated. "It's dramatic, on the contrary! An improbable curse... How many other deaths will there be Jerome? One, two, everyone who was there? Including us? I'm really starting to get scared here. And the worst thing in all of this is that I don't understand a thing. Why did these people die after they got back from Guadeloupe? Are we the next ones on the list? Who's the guilty person causing all this? Where is the threat?"

I grabbed her hand to try to reassure her.

"Calm down, honey. We don't have anything to fear. We'll try to understand what is going on here... or what went on. I'm sure we'll get to the bottom of all this, okay?"

Colombe took a deep breath.

"But how?"

"Let's continue to go through our photos, trying to remember each day in Guadeloupe, each and every tiny detail. I'm sure something will stand out."

I PUT my half empty mug down next to our photobook and picked it up.

Back to Gwada.

— *B* —

A MOROSE DRIZZLE

The wide gravel covered straight path, through two rows of trees, guided the procession that accompanied the deceased towards their permanent destination. A destination everyone would eventually have, whatever color their skin was, whatever social category they were in, whatever age, sex, history or family connections they had had. Ever since the dawn of time, and as long as Mother Earth would exist, men and women would be born, grow up, fall in love, reproduce, give birth to other beings who would then reproduce the same cycle, would grow old and would finally return to the earth, as that was what happened ever since mankind had appeared.

That day, there was a morose drizzle surrounding the cemetery, one more life amongst so many others that was slowly making its way towards its final resting place.

A life like so many other, a death just like another. Here, as elsewhere, their friends and family were mourning, sad, their eyes damp like the mist, arms dangling along their bodies, the soles of their shoes dragging on the gravel – the same heartache that billions of others before them had experienced.

There weren't many gawkers that day following the hearse as it stopped, silently so as not to disturb anyone in the neighborhood, about six hundred feet down the central path. Where another smaller path branched off with dozens of marble, granite, or stone tombstones were. A narrow path with a handful of sad people walking down it...

CHAPTER 18

Need to decompress

WHILE EVERYONE in Bougainvillea Domain was relaxing on that afternoon before the outing to Soufriere Hills volcano, Eusebius felt exhausted and told Severine that he was going to nap for an hour or two in their bedroom. After his short night and the hike to Sofaïa, he needed a rest. Though he did invite his wife to join him should she feel a bit mischievous, he was hoping deep down inside that she'd let him sleep in peace.

Luckily for him, Severine declined his offer and while he was snoring away in the adjacent room, she was lying in the hammock on the veranda with her black diary.

Currently in a profoundly nostalgic mood, once

again Severine browsed through the pages of her past. What she read that day brought bitter tears to her eyes.

Thursday, December 16, 2004

My Dear Diary,

That didn't last long.

We moved again because of Dad's job. We always have to follow him to a new city. At first, I was glad when he told me we'd be leaving Auxerre. I was sick and tired of Auxerre and my school.

I couldn't stand the Bitch anymore. I couldn't stand it, she was always harassing me. And I could tell she liked to. And that made all the other kids laugh. It's easy to make fun of weaker people, those who can't fight back, who are afraid to.

I was used to it, that's all.

Plus, Auxerre wasn't a very nice place to live. That's what I thought before knowing where we'd be going this time.

But when I discovered Guéret, what could I say?

Of course, it's beautiful around Guéret.

But it's even smaller and more boring than Auxerre. Smack in the middle of France, next to nothing!

At the same time, I don't care where we live. Though each time I must say they have a nice house for us. That isn't the problem though.

The problem is what goes on at school.

I thought they'd leave me alone in middle school. I didn't know a soul, and no one knew me either. Like when you start over again. But still, it's not easy because I have to make new friends.

Well, friends... that's saying a lot: Did I ever have any real friends?

And what is friendship? I thought that a friend was someone who liked you, even with your imperfections, someone who never made fun of you, someone who had your back. That's what I believed.

So I thought middle school would be better than primary school, but I was wrong.

There are the same nasty ones, they're just a bit bigger, a bit older, a lot more stupid than before. And me, I'm the same, meaning I'm not better.

I've already seen people staring at me, smiling strangely, making fun of me, whispering behind my back. But that's nothing.

The worst is when you become someone's scapegoat. Scapegoat, what a weird word! I had no idea that I looked like a scapegoat, people always told me I looked like an asshole.

Pretty soon I'd become the Sucker's scapegoat.

The Sucker, that's what I nicknamed that big stupid guy in my sixth-grade class, who thought it was funny to mock me all the time. As soon as school started in September, he started to call me names. Not nice ones, I'm sure you know that. Not sweet ones! And I never had a sweetie, I'll never have one either with the way I look… anyway I don't want one.

Anyway, I've been his target for the past three months and I want to change schools. But of course that's not easy.

The Sucker is the butcher's son, the butcher from downtown Guéret. He outdid himself today. I don't have any proof but I'm sure that he was the one who did it, like he'd signed it!

I don't know how he did it, but when the bell rang saying school was over and I picked up my schoolbag, I had never been so scared in my whole life.

There was like a stain on the floor. Like something had run from my bag that was damp.

It was blood!

I nearly screamed! When everyone had left, including the math teacher, I carefully opened my schoolbag, I was afraid of what I'd find inside it.

My hand touched something that was hard but soft and sticky at the same time. I quickly took my hand out and it was covered with blood.

I thought I was going to faint, and I was all alone.

I put my hand back in and I picked up the thing.

I almost threw up my lunch - chicken wings and Brussel sprouts - when I saw a rabbit's head full of blood with its huge white eyes full of veins.

A rabbit's head like old-fashioned butchers sometimes have in their windows, without the skin on it, without the pretty white fur of soft little bunnies, and I was sure that it was the Sucker who'd put it there.

I stayed a long time in the math room. I cried until I had no more tears left. When the cleaning lady came in, I was still there.

I didn't say anything to her except "Goodbye, ma'am."

Then I walked home, alone, like I always did.

When I saw the dumpster in front of the building, I threw that bloody rabbit's head in it.

CHAPTER 19

A true treasure hunt

FIVE IN THE morning in Deshaies. The sun was still sleeping on the other side of the horizon, but everyone in Bougainvillea Domain was up and about, rushing to the van.

Today was the big day, the highlight of our stay here, the one that would take us to the foot, and then to the top of Soufriere Hills volcano. That dormant volcano sneezed a bit every once in a while, just so no one would think it was extinct and that it remained the King of Gwada!

Us sleepyheads climbed into the van, muttering vague greetings between two yawns. I was used to seeing Colombe when she woke up and I knew that this early in the morning she was having trouble opening her eyelids completely. As for me, I was a morning person.

Eusebius was in the front seat, stuck between Severine, our driver, and Nathalie who was looking out the window watching the sun rise over the sea as we drove.

Colombe, Jacques and I were in the middle seat. The kids, as we now called Bruce and Gregory, were on each side of Naima, who took advantage of the drive to finish up her beauty sleep. That was both a funny and quirky scene, – we'd then reached Bouillante – that I saw in the rear-view mirror. I saw Gregory's head, frowning with vexation, unless it was actually jealousy. Next to him, Naima, sound asleep, had her head on her other neighbor's large shoulder.

I whispered that to Colombe, who smiled. We'd learned last night that during his free afternoon, Bruce had gone to one of the surfing sports that Eusebius had told him about. And when he'd come back to the resort, we saw Naima getting out of the blond surfer's rental car. And Gregory had probably discovered the same thing.

The sun was already up when Severine turned around.

"Here we are at Saint-Claude! Get prepared for out big ascension and the big... surprise!"

"A surprise? What surprise?" asked Gregory, excited like a little kid.

"A treasure hunt!"

"You're joking!"

"Not at all! I prepared a real treasure hunt for you, with riddles to solve, to help you in your long climb up to the top!"

"Sort of like things you do for birthday parties for children?" asked Naima, who sometimes organized things like that in her job.

"Exactly! You wanna go?"

Like a tsunami, there was an enthusiastic *yes* that rolled out in the van.

As we'd made the effort to get up before sunrise, our reward was that we were amongst the first hikers of the day. We were able to park right next to the trail, next to the Bains Jaunes. Severine gave us our bags, full of water bottles, as well as the first little piece of paper for our treasure hunt.

"Who wants to be the team leader?" she asked.

Not surprisingly, Gregory was the only one raising his hand there and we all accepted his invading leadership. He read the clue that she had written:

In order to begin, you must go to the natural border…

"What the heck is going on here? A border?" muttered our dear leader. "There aren't any borders in Guadeloupe, it's an island!"

"Each word is important…" Severine pointed out.

"Maybe we have to find synonyms with the word border?" suggested Colombe, who loved word games. "For example: limit, separation, fence, passage, etc. See if that rings a bell someplace."

"Natural…" Jacques thought out loud. "That seems important too. Maybe it's an allusion to that lush scenery surrounding us?"

Severine, with her backpack, cut us all off.

"Why don't you think while we're hiking? I just want to tell you that there's a bit of a climb and that you'll have plenty of time to think about that riddle while you're climbing."

He took the lead and we followed him, in Indian file. At first the path was cleared out, presenting steps that men had made, but little by little they narrowed out and suddenly it became more rugged. We could feel that climbing up to the top wasn't going to be an easy ride. Nonetheless, the luxuriance of the tropical forest filled our eyes and souls with contagious well-being.

Of course, it was easy to imagine in what order we were progressing, each person joining the other according to the affinities they'd felt during the previous days. As for me, I was following Colombe, who was walking dangerously, her nose in our guide-book. She suddenly ground to a halt.

"I got it!"

"Halleluia!" shouted out Gregory, bantering but glad as he'd given up trying to find the answer. "Tell us!"

"I just read something interesting. It says here we're going to have a fantastic natural show at an altitude of about 3,300 feet. There, we should see the vegetation suddenly changing, transforming from a tropical forest to a dense humid scrubland. In the guidebook, they say that the border is well defined."

"A natural border!" said Naima. "That's it! Let's go!"

Stimulated by that discovery, we advanced with enthusiasm, without however depriving us of appreciating the scenery and the sweet smells of humus, dew, unknown species of trees, at least ones that were unknown to our French metropolitan noses.

The border appeared evident to us, sides of the path were clearing out, the types of species were changing, it was beautifully light, we'd arrived.

"What now?" asked Gregory impatiently. "Where is that clue? Do we have to dig it up? Climb a tree? Lift the rocks up?"

"All you gotta do is close your mouth and open your eyes," joked our hostess.

"We don't even know what we're supposed to be looking for!"

"For a new clue on a new piece of paper. Sometimes you have to go off the beaten path..."

"Ah! Okay! Got it! It's not on the path, it's next to it!"

"You're really impressing me, Greg!" Bruce said. "You really got an exceptional IQ!"

"Ha ha you should do stand-up! Normal, I'm not a blond!"

"That was under the belt!"

"Children," Nathalie said. "Instead of squabbling, what about looking for that piece of paper?"

Methodically, looking through that vegetal border, we found a piece of paper, well wrapped in a layer of cellophane to protect it from the humidity. Gregory, as our self-proclaimed leader, grabbed it.

In the savanna, you will run across mules...

"Curiouser and curiouser! Now the savanna. I thought the savanna was in Africa!"

I saw Colombe tapping her phone, before beginning to read.

"A savanna or savannah is a mixed woodland-grassland (i.e. grassy woodland) ecosystem characterized by the trees being sufficiently widely spaced so that the canopy does not close. The open canopy allows sufficient light to reach the ground to support an unbroken herbaceous layer consisting primarily of grasses. According to Britannica, there exists four savanna forms..."

"Thank you, Wikipedia!" I said cutting her off gently.

"They predominate in zones subject to a tropical savanna climate, principally in Eastern Africa, South America, and in the Caribbean Area," she continued, unflappable.

"The Caribbean! We're on the right track."

While continuing, we suddenly noticed that we could now see the horizon. The shrubs disappeared little by little, the silhouette of the top of Soufriere could be seen, immense, majestic, authentic, at the end of the trail.

We then came to a plateau that had all the characteristics of what Colombe had just read us.

“The Mule Savanna!” read Bruce on the sign.

Except that we only saw a huge brown rock on the cemented square, not a single mule.

“I bet we’re going to find our next clue near that rock, the one all alone in the middle of nowhere...” I proposed.

“It’s an enormous block of volcanic rock that came from up there,” said Eusebius, who had remained silent up until now.

As it was evident that no paper was hidden elsewhere than towards this rock that was about twelve feet high, one that each and every visitor climbed to get their pictures taken with the still smoking crater in the background, we sacrificed ourselves to obey that tradition.

While one person was taking the photos, the others were rummaging around each nook and cranny of the rock looking for the clue. Suddenly Nathalie shouted.

“Got it!”

. . .

FAUJAS THOUGHT HE WOULD DIE WHEN HE HEARD THE EXPLOSION IN 1798...

"WHO THE HECK IS FAUJAS?"

"A famous unknown person," tried Greg, trying to be witty.

"In 1798..."

"Must be talking about the French Revolution."

"More precisely the Directory," added Bruce, who astounded us by his historical erudition.

"So how's that helping us?"

"We gotta find out who Faujas was."

"A scientific," shouted Colombe, on her phone again.

"You're cheating," confirmed Severine. "But it's not gonna be Faujas who'll be finding the next clue."

"My guidebook says that this Faujas guy gave his name to a rockslide that occurred after the Soufriere volcano exploded that year. Meaning that we'll see a place named Faujas Rockslide. Let's go!"

WE WERE all playing amateur detectives with this treasure hunt and its clues, making us forget how difficult the ascension was, encouraging us to continue higher and higher. No one though forgot to drink, because ever since we'd reached the "savanna," the sun was pounding down on us.

We also immortalized our hike when we asked another tourist to take a picture of us, all together on the dome of the brownish red rock. A picture that would become a collector's item!

"And this is where things get serious!" said Severine, now taking the lead. "Up till now, it was for sissies!"

In Indian file, we followed her footsteps on the side of the dome to the top, where the fumaroles looked like a cloudy cap.

The landscape was more arid, the slope much steeper. We had to make several regular stops to drink as the sun was burning us up.

We finally reached the so-called Faujas Rockslide, that had a sign on it for tourists. It was easy to see the fault that the rockslide had caused when Faujas was there, that scientist who had named the place. It was a like a type of downspout with low-growing vegetation on its sides, a mixture of red, yellow, orange and green humps, composed of lichens and ferns growing on the iron-filled rocks, something so beautiful and unusual and that our cameras and phones largely immortalized.

Jacques was the first one who had the reflex to look behind the sign and he discovered the next clue there.

There are no flaws for the next clue...

"That's an easy one, Severine," said Gregory, looking like the cat who had finished the cream.

"What's your theory then?"

"Being flawed! A flaw, get it?"

"Sort of. Continue."

"I saw a sign a while ago pointing at "The Great Flaw. So we'll find our next clue up there. Elementary, my dear Watson!"

"Wow, to boot he knows his classics! I am *imprepreprессed*," said Naima ironically.

"Oh come on... You don't have a monopoly on IQ, Miss!"

"And political classics! Congrats!"

As the cat and dog duo were fighting, we were making progress towards the top of the volcano, a bit less talkative than we were five hundred feet below, because we now had to concentrate on our ascension. The rocky path, filled with dry earth, was now abrupt. Sometimes you even had to climb on top of a rock to gain headway.

The Great Flaw, indicated by a yellow sign, looked more or less like the Faujas Rockslide, though it was much more imposing.

Our team of amateur sleuths needed a bit more time to unearth Severine's clue and we all thought how well she'd done, preparing everything in advance. The plastic covered clue was discovered on the back of a brown rock surrounded by ferns. It said:

LOOK BELOW THE LARGE VIOLET ROCK TO FIND GWADA'S YELLOW TREASURE...

"AHHA! METHINKS WE'RE ALMOST THERE," exclaimed Bruce. "In my humble opinion, this is our last clue. The treasure is up there, at the crater, within reach guys!"

He accelerated with enthusiasm, forcing the group to try to keep up with him.

"Hey, you young'uns, slowly but surely," complained Nathalie. "My legs aren't twenty years old anymore! Take it easy!"

"Totally agree with that!" added Jacques, the oldest member of our group.

"One for all, all for one, okay," said Naima. "We'll reach the treasure together or not at all."

Anyway, because of the topography, our ascension was slow. The last five hundred feet were the hardest. There was one passage, where a rockslide had gone through, that was very difficult. We had to use rock climbing techniques for about sixty feet, and Nathalie was ready to give up.

"I'll never be able to climb that!" she lamented.

"Sure you can," Eusebius encouraged her.

She allowed herself to be convinced, carefully placing her feet between two rocks, but slipped and scratched her tibia. Luckily our hosts were equipped to take care of any eventual scratches and scrapes and Eusebius disinfected the wound. While he was playing nurse, closely and suspiciously watched by his wife, we took advantage of the halt to rest a bit and take photos of the coastline below, from Saint-Claude and Basse-Terre. We could see the nine Iles des Saintes, or Saint's Islands, peaking through the mist.

Spurred by the desire to discover a sensational site, we all climbed the last few feet. I personally couldn't wait to touch the grail and was totally amazed to be climbing up an extinct volcano. I kept on repeating to myself that I wasn't at risk, that it wouldn't suddenly be waking up, that the seismologists would have been alerted by signs of an impending eruption. Still, images of that huge crater, reddish, boiling over, were dancing in my mind.

Just like my fellow vacationers, I was aware that I was living a unique moment, one that was exceptional, the highlight of our vacation.

We finally were rewarded. We had climbed the 4,913 feet of what was called *Découverte*, the peak of Soufriere Hills volcano.

Some of our group shouted out loud whereas others were silent and flabbergasted, as the bird's eye views we had over the craters were striking.

We saw a lunar landscape, sometimes broad and open, sometimes filled with clouds that the wind quickly pushed away. Contrary to our preconceived notions, probably stemming from documentaries produced by vulcanologists such as Stanley Williams or Harry Glicken, the crater below wasn't boiling over with molten lava. There were just some crannies where sulfurous vapors escaped from. At the same time though, we could hear a slight rumbling but above all, see that phenomenon of fumaroles, those emanations of gas and vapor that shot up from the earth with a sound like a jet plane's engine.

We were so attentive to that natural show, taking photos, videos, selfies, that we forgot about the treasure hunt.

"I'm so happy you found the treasure," Severine suddenly declared.

"What do you mean? I feel like I've been ripped off!" Greg replied.

"What? Wasn't that marvelous? A treasure that Mother Nature gave you for the delight of your eyes?"

"And our noses!" I joked, referring to the sulfur.

"You'll never forget this moment!" added Eusebius proudly. "One of Gwada's jewels. Take it all in!"

"What about that violet rock?" asked Colombe, who hadn't forgotten the treasure hunt. "We've still got that clue."

Turning talk into action, she urged us to find the last piece of paper, one we did find under a shallow volcanic rock.

The treasure is here, right below your eyes. You'll soon discover the surprise...

"A surprise? What, where, when?" our leader asked.

"Everything in its own good time! For right now, just take advantage of this while you've got time."

"That's disgusting, it's not a game!"

"Life is a game, Greg! And this week, I'm the one making the rules. And there's no jokers! Let's go back down now and have our picnic."

The strong wind at the top of the volcano was freezing. Luckily we'd taken windbreakers, and we appreciated them when the sun was hidden by the clouds. We all enjoyed our picnic next to the Mule Savanna parking lot.

THAT EVENING, when we returned to our resort, everyone was exhausted.

CHAPTER 20

The patina of time

IT WASN'T EVEN ten and everyone was already sound asleep.

Everyone except Severine, going through her diary which was like her bedside book. It was impossible for her, at least during that week, to go to bed without having reread a passage, going back into the past that was engraved on those white pages, touched by the patina of time.

Thursday, January 31, 2008

If there really is a god up there, he must have heard my prayers.

We finally moved. We left Guéret. This

must be the first time that I'm so overjoyed be following my dad to a new city.

A new life?

Each time I've got the impression that it'll be a good one. That those Suckers or Assholes won't bother me anymore.

Because that Sucker from Guéret, he went pretty far. But I didn't give in, I never did.

Maybe as I've gotten older, I've developed a thicker and stronger shell. Like it's a hide now!

All those people making fun of me, their sarcasm, their cheap shots that broke my heart, now I can take all that a bit better.

Plus, I really can't complain. Going from Guéret to Strasbourg is much better than when we moved from Auxerre to Guéret. At least this is a city, a real one. One where you can find anything you want.

And even what you don't.

Plus, and as crazy as it may seem to you, though I was sure that it would never happen, I finally found a friend, a true friend. We're in the same 8th grade class together.

I almost want to write that word with a capital letter: Friend. A capital letter for a capital Friend.

A Friend who doesn't judge me because of the way I look.

A Friend who sees my inner beauty.

A Friend I can tell secrets to. My doubts, my pain, my desires, my dreams. Everything.

I'm calling this Friend Scheherazade, because she's beautiful like the character in One Thousand and One Nights, that story I've read and reread over and over. Like her, my Friend has long dark hair that falls to the bottom of her back. I know, next to her I look like a toad with warts.

Her and me, we're an odd couple: Beauty and the Beast, another story I read when I was a kid.

Here at school, it nearly started again, like in all the schools I attended. There were mocking Suckers, but my Scheherazade pushed them away. She's my shield, my guardian angel.

I love her.

. . .

THOSE OPTIMISTIC WORDS, one of the rare passages with them, always made Severine smile. Nonetheless, a wry smile, one that quickly disappeared when she read what followed, where she felt she'd been stabbed in the back, her soul sliced open.

Saturday March 21, 2009

My Dear Diary,

Have you ever noticed that fairy tales usually don't end well? Or that when they do, they're often cruel? Just look, what about Tom Thumb and his brothers, abandoned by their parents in the forest... Same thing for poor Hansel and Gretel. Little Red Riding Hood who gets eaten alive by a wolf... Snow White who is imprisoned by her mother-in-law disguised as a witch... Cinderella, who was treated like a worthless maid by her wicked step-mother and step-sisters. And what about the Ugly Duckling who everyone rejected because he wasn't like the others... The other day on the radio I heard them speaking about "racial profiling" and we talked about that in our civil education class. That was exactly what that poor duckling had, that poor duckling who wasn't a duckling at all, but in reality, would become a beautiful swan.

So me, I feel like that Ugly Duckling. I know I'm ugly outside but inside, I'm a swan.

I have to convince myself of that.

Alone. Or almost, because my sister is there to listen to me. I'm lucky I have a sister! What would I become without her? Would I still be alive to talk about my little misfortunes? Thank you my sister, my double, my confidant, for being there. When I say my double, we're neither twins nor joined at the hip. My sister was much luckier than me when God dealt out his cards. No one makes fun of her. My sister is beautiful.

Anyway, my own fairy tale is over. Scheherazade no longer tells me beautiful stories. Stories in which I was her princess, I had a type of beauty others didn't see.

All that was just smoke and mirrors! Words! She was pretending.

She abandoned me like a coward. She chose the others and this time the scales *weren't on my side. I lost my shell, now I have to resist all alone, like a big girl.*

I thought she was my Friend. I must have dreamed it. Back to harsh reality, the fairy tale is over!

I hate her.

Smothering a yawn, after having dried her eyes, Severine scribbled a few short and dry lines on the last page of her diary. There were no blank pages left. But that wasn't important, as soon it all would be over.

CHAPTER 21

Libido, a vast subject!

A GOOD NIGHT's sleep after having spent the day climbing up the volcano, had finally rested Naima. The young lady woke up early, right as the sun was beginning to rise behind the hill.

While having a cup of coffee on the patio of her bungalow, she relaxed and decided to write a couple of postcards that she'd promised to send to her friends and family in France.

She'd always liked getting up before everyone else. Still rubbing her eyes and drinking her first cup of joe of the morning, she took time to think about herself and her vacation.

She chose the prettiest postcard, one that represented a magnificent landscape of mangroves, and began to write, innocently.

. . .

Darling,

I know I heard the sound of your voice last night again before falling asleep, yet, when I woke up this morning, you were still on my mind. And you're the first person I'm writing to.

I'm sure though that I'll already be back with you before it reaches you. But that's not a big deal, what postcards are all about is writing them and then reading them. What happens in between is unimportant. Some take only two days to cross the ocean, others sometimes seem to be globetrotters, taking months to reach their destination. What will be the fate of this one? Time will tell.

My Darling,

I miss you terribly, though I must admit that this week, a junket you could say, is just perfect. I'm staying with adorable hosts, and the other members of our group are friendly too. Though some *of them are a bit... invading!*

Let me tell you about, and don't get mad here, Gregory. Quite the character! I think he thinks he'll "conclude" with me by the end of the week... But don't worry my dear, you know I'd never cheat on you and there's no way I would give in to his advances.

But he makes me laugh with his loudmouth and his "bad boy" manners. I'm sure that he must have lacked love when he was a little kid.

Despite her tiny handwriting, Naima had already filled the postcard. As she was a chatterbox, she continued on a second one.

So I'm just having fun, that doesn't hurt anyone. I'm trying to make him jealous. There's another young, handsome, blond guy with us, surfer style, see? Yesterday, to make Greg jealous in the van that was taking us to Soufriere Hills volcano, I pretended to sleep, and I put my head on Bruce the surfer's big shoulder. You should have seen how Gregory glared at him.

There's nothing to fear concerning Bruce and me though. He doesn't stand a chance, though he is quite the hunk. But you know me. There's no ambiguity between us. We're like two good friends. And we laugh behind Greg's back.

Otherwise, there's one person I find sort of strange, she's not very talkative or outgoing, her name is Nathalie. She spends her days drawing in a sketchbook, I wonder even if she's drawing all of us. I also noticed that she couldn't help discreetly - at least that's what she thinks - trying to get closer to Eusebius, a super cool tall black rasta, Severine's husband.

Ah! Vacations and libido, a vast subject!

I'm out of room, hugs and kisses, darling.

I love you.

AT THE SAME time in her nearby bungalow, Nathalie was also having breakfast. For her, it was tea and oatmeal mixed with chia seeds, totally healthy to the last bite. Generally, her health and physical appearance guided her choice of meals. She wouldn't have turned down a good continental breakfast with bacon, scrambled eggs, sausages, and buttered toast, but her scale would have reproached it. She never liked her scale to be angry with her.

While sipping her green tea, lulled by the sweet chirps of hummingbirds, she multitasked, performing something she did with passion.

On the table, she'd spread nine or ten sheets of paper that she'd taken from her omnipresent sketchbook. She looked at them one after the other, with a critical and expert eye. She knew how to judge the quality of drawings, especially her own. That morning though she wasn't judging their quality, but rather their content.

She picked up one of the sheets, raised it to eye level in the budding light of the day, squinted to better concentrate, and then put it down again. And repeated that for each drawing.

Then she put them in a certain order, that she was the only one to understand. She sometimes hesitated, sorted them again, changed places, put one on the right, another one on the left.

When she was finally satisfied, she looked at them all with a satisfied rictus on her lips. She had portraits of Eusebius, Naima, Colombe, Vanessa, Toussaint, Bruce, Jerome, Gregory, Jacques and Jean-Pierre, and to finish, that of Severine.

That was her classification of the anthropomorphic way beauty was ranked, in her opinion, which was close to how Italian painters in the Renaissance era considered beauty. As an artist, she'd always loved the perfection of models that Raphael, Botticelli, Michelangelo and Da Vinci portrayed. In her collection of portraits, she put the first six in that category, the following four in the category of commonplace, and she associated the last one, Severine's portrait, with the category of Jerome Bosch's monsters! Nathalie hated imperfections! Especially at breakfast where that gave her heartburn.

A BIT FARTHER DOWN, in Jacques's bungalow, the atmosphere was totally different. He was lying in his hammock, smoking a cigarette. Not that he smoked much, but he did appreciate a cigarette when he was relaxing. He was wearing headphones, listening to the compelling, irregular and lively notes of Rodrigo y Gabriela playing his guitar.

Jacques had started to play the guitar when he was younger, learning quickly, progressing regularly. First as a simple hobby, he'd then thought of passing his knowledge on, especially to the younger generations. Isn't music, like all arts, something that you transmit from generation to generation? Men are born and die on Earth, but Art, as it is shared, is eternal.

His eyes closed, ears filled with sounds that made him shiver with contentment, he began to daydream, his thoughts bringing him back to a few years ago. At a time of his life when he had begun to lose control...

He dreamt of a young lady, a student who was quite talented, something innate that made her attractive, despite... As they say, physical beauty isn't always the main criterion when two people are attracted to one another. Beauty is in the eye of the beholder, according to the old saying. Some people are attracted by midgets, obese people, hunchbacks, those with lots of hair, anorexic people, legless cripples, animals, costumes: the list of paraphilias, – or in other words sexual deviances – was as long as human imagination.

And Jacques, you could say, never lacked imagination.

HE WAS FINDING it hard to open his eyes that morning. Climbing up to the top of the volcano had worn him out. Plus the image that was looping through his mind and haunting him was Naima's head dozing on Bruce's shoulder. Gregory had to admit to himself that he had a crush on her, he knew it the first time he'd set eyes on her. What attracted him was that she knew how to respond, to assert herself when he was messing with her, he liked gals who knew how to resist a bit. That was his way of getting close to others, by horsing around, by trying to show he wasn't interested in the person he was targeting. He always criticized rather than giving compliments, provoked rather than being friendly. Sometimes it worked, other times it didn't. This week it looked to him like that cute Moroccan babe would be resisting him.

But what a body she had, he thought, as his hand

slipped beneath the sheets. That nervous yet supple body, that long mesmerizing wavy black hair, those eyes like those of a deer in headlights, and that mouth! That mouth he mentally visualized, his eyes closed, his hand moving up and down in rhythm with his solitary dreams. Gregory wasn't dreaming, he was slowly waking up. He pleasured himself, alone in his bungalow, imagining that she'd joined him under the shelter of his mosquito net, that she was lying next to him, languidly taking off her clothes, that she wanted him. Suddenly it was no longer his own hand giving him pleasure, but that fanaticizing mouth.

Gregory was breathing harder and harder, his erotic dream gaining consistency to the point that he did believe that Naima was leaning down over his virility. He could nearly smell her perfume, the weight of her body against him and the moist heat of her mouth on his sex that was ready to explode. He finally had an irrepressible wave, beginning at this nape, descending down his backbone, warming his hips then... flooding his sheets.

Naima's face faded away when Gregory reared, empty.

In the bungalow above him, Bruce had been up for quite a while already. He'd had his bowl of muesli, a banana and a glass of guava juice and was now doing his morning drill.

A series of pullups, squats, steps, and stretching. His morning ritual included a mixture of stretching and musculation, his own personal recipe for a fit body, with firm and well-shaped muscles, something he was proud of when wearing T-shirts that were a size or two too small for him.

Ever since he was a kid, he had known he was good-looking. He'd always taken care of himself. A good tan, white teeth, a hairdo that he put gel in to keep it in place. Bruce knew that the girls liked him, even in middle school they'd proved it. He was the best-looking guy in his class, and as he was also tall, he could boast that he'd seduced girls that were even older than he was. Something others respected.

Though he did cultivate his body, he was a serious student, one who got good grades. Both muscles and brains!

Plus he had a good sense of humor and was a good listener, something the girls always appreciated. That week in Guadeloupe proved it: Naima instinctively got closer to him, without any ulterior motives. They'd spent moments alone as friends, telling each other about their lives, their joys, their heartaches. And because of him, she'd felt less harassed by that little shithole, Gregory. Not that he was dangerous, just a bit slow in the head.

After his fifty pushups, Bruce got back up, took a couple of deep breaths, let his cardiac rhythm slow down, and took a shower.

CHAPTER 22

Strangely excited

I'll never forget the day after our hike to Soufriere Hills volcano.

Everything had begun early in the morning, in the van driving us to Grand-Terre, which was the eastern part of the island, one we hadn't yet visited. We'd be seeing magnificent sites, ones that were totally different from the mountainous and volcanic landscapes in Basse-Terre. Here the topography was nearly flat, there were many more towns, with fields here and there. The more touristic beaches didn't have the natural appearance that the cricks and cliffs in Basse-Terre had.

Everyone had their eyes peeled on the countryside

while Eusebius drove us to the most eastern part of the island: Pointe des Châteaux Peninsula. Jacques suddenly asked a question.

"Is what I saw last night on the news true? They were talking about witchcraft. Undertakers at Saint-François Cemetery discovered a black chicken that had been sacrificed."

"Ah! Here, that's what we call *quimbois*! That's true, stuff like that still does go on, of course secretly now, in some villages or some very precise sites."

"All that's just made-up stuff," Nathalie added. "I don't believe in foolishness like that at all."

"Nathalie, you know black magic is something that's very powerful," Eusebius insinuated.

"Maybe, but I'm like Saint Thomas, I only believe what I see."

"Would you like to see it then?"

"What? Witchcraft rites?"

"Yup. I know people. And maybe you'd also like to attend a black magic session?"

No one said a word, taking the time required to assimilate what we'd just heard.

"I'm quite curious by nature," I finally admitted.

"So am I," agreed Colombe.

"I wouldn't chicken out," boasted Greg.

“If Greg’s going, I am too,” Bruce joined in. “What about you, Naima?”

“Let’s just say that because of my origins, I sort of believe that some people have powers like those. But I’m still sort of scared.”

“Oh, come on,” Greg continued. “Eusebius, when you said that you know people, does that mean that you could organize that for us?”

“A session with a *quimboiseur*? That’s what we call the people who practice black magic here. Can do. If everyone agrees, I can set that up for tonight...”

As the majority had agreed, it became a unanimous decision, though some members of the group were still a bit half-hearted. Most of the group though were strangely excited.

We reached Pointe des Châteaux Peninsula, end of the line for waves from the Atlantic, and Eusebius invited us to climb up to the cross on top of Morne Pavillion. There was a belvedere there where we could enjoy a breathtaking view of the ocean as well as the neighboring Desirade Island.

He left us and walked down to the beach to make a few calls. When he came back an hour later, he was overjoyed.

“It’s a done deal! Tonight you’re going to have a real *quimbois* experience!”

"Where's it gonna take place?"

"Not far from Hell's Gate."

Talk about a predestined name, I thought to myself.

While shivering with expectation though.

THE IMMINENCE of a black magic experience, spiritualism, witchcraft, of whatever it was called, had put us in a strange state. As for me, this would be my very first incursion in the realm of "paranormal," in the literal sense of that word, meaning what was outside of normality. I enjoyed today's visit very much, from the two ends of Grand-Terre, including Vigie Point, the most northern part of the island, with its breathtaking views.

Just like my fellow vacationers, I was bowled over by the diversity of landscapes in Guadeloupe. We'd left the tropical rainforest in the morning and were now in a mineral landscape, almost like the ones back home in Brittany. Here all we could see was the unbridled ocean, foamy sprays of water, rugged rocks, low-lying shrubs and heather, and dry lichen resisting the strong winds. Our hosts had told us last night to take hiking shoes and to leave our sandals or thongs back home today. And on this limestone, arid and harsh ground, full of edges of rocks that were sharp, our hiking gear was really appreciated.

We stayed there a long while, contemplating the waves pounding against the cliffs, subjugated.

AT THE END of the afternoon, Eusebius drove us to Hell's Gate. Severine had joined us as she also wanted to attend that *quimbois* session.

"So, you'll be meeting Jean-Felix. He's one of the best *quimboiseurs* on the island. If you've got any wishes you want to make, any spells or enchantments to cast, someone you want to bewitch, any desires of power, success, love, all that, tonight's the time to ask him. He's really powerful, Jean-Felix!"

"You believe that stuff?" Nathalie asked. "Because I'm personally convinced that it's just a show, they're all quacks. Sort of like those pseudo-psychics who put their business cards under your windshield wipers at the store. The ones where they say that in twenty-four hours, your husband or lover will come back, or in a week you'll become rich, and all of that a hundred percent guaranteed in just one phone call!"

"I can see that you've got a lot of preconceived ideas. But I can assure you that Jean-Felix isn't like that. He's from Haiti, a descendent of witches from generation to generation. All his ancestors did voodoo, and had extra lucid gifts that were known throughout the island."

"Okay. Can't wait then to see this."

"So you can all start thinking about what you want to ask him. Tonight will be an unforgettable experience!"

"Plus," Eusebius added, looking at the calendar on a phone app, "it's almost the full moon."

"We also call that the black moon..." his wife completed.

"Black moon, a conducive moment for black magic!"

BLACK MAGIC, spells, bewitching, *quimbois*, and Hell's Gate! Today's theme was light years away from yesterday's, which targeted nature.

But when we reached Hell's Gate, it wasn't really that infernal at all. On the contrary, it was a magnificent and peaceful site, one where the sea advanced into the land, forming a narrow fault where walking anglers could fish up to their hips. This tongue of the sea originally was closed halfway by a natural arch above it, which is where its name originated, but it collapsed in an earthquake in 1843, Eusebius explained. There was a hiking path there leading us to a site named the *Trou de Man Coco*, or Man Coco's Hole.

Here, Eusebius donned his guide hat again.

"One of the legends – and there are a couple of versions of it – says that a certain Madame Coco, in Creole, *Man Coco*, a rival of Man Grand-Fonds, had sold her soul to the devil to become stronger than her. But as she didn't fulfill the promises she'd made to Satan, he threw her into this here chasm, where she perished."

"That's awful," said Colombe, shivering, leaning over the hole where the waves were rushing into the cave.

"And some sailors even say they've seen a feminine silhouette carrying a parasol, walking on the sea, accompanied by a cavalier, before disappearing into the Hole."

"Wow! Now we've got ghost stories too? I'm out of here!"

That was our brave Gregory's voice.

"Oh no, you're not going to leave," Eusebius cut him off, "because tonight there will be a *quimbois* session here, right in this very cave."

"You're shitting me! You are crazy! I don't even see how we can descend into that devil's hole! Did you see the waves? I don't wanna die like Old Lady Coco!"

Eusebius burst out laughing, a diabolical laugh, bent over, before calming down.

"Just joking man! But sometimes we've got *quimboiseurs* who come here at low tide, for their black magic. We often find candles and dead animals down there. But usually sessions like that don't have a public. We'll be meeting Jean-Felix above here, in a dry cave that's on the hiking trail to Souffleur Point."

"Sue Flare Point?" asked Jacques, who must not have heard correctly because of the noise of the wind and the waves.

That relaxed us all a bit as we were all starting to get tense and slightly nervous.

"So, while we wait for the *quimboiseur*, how about a cocktail before we eat?"

No one refused. Our hosts took us to a nearby restaurant, Chez Coco, at the entrance to Hell's Gate.

The food, like everywhere on the island, was excellent and fresh. Cocktails flowed like water as we all seemed to have a need to intoxicate ourselves slightly before the black magic session. This was something that hadn't been planned, a challenge, a curiosity. But as time went by, we were no longer so sure of ourselves.

After one last drink of macerated rum, Eusebius got up.

"Time to go my friends. Jean-Felix is expecting us."

CHAPTER 23

Feeling nauseous

THE WIND WAS HOWLING GRIMLY, licking the rocks of the hiking trail to the Big Cliff. Using the built-in flashlights in our phones, we were heading towards the *quimboiseur*. The noise of the waves embracing the rocks down below seemed to me to be Man Coco's relentlessly repeated lament. Eusebius and Severine had filled our heads with their stories of witchcraft, beliefs, ghosts and West Indian legends. They'd intelligently conditioned and prepared us for our meeting with Jean-Felix.

Someone spoke up.

"By the way, what does '*quimbois*' actually mean?"

Eusebius answered, explaining things he hadn't yet told us.

"A pertinent question! *Quimbois*, or *kembwa*, is a Creole word stemming from *kimbw*, which means 'knowledge' in the Kikongo language. That's a Bantu dialect. Sec, that comes from far away, an ancestral belief in the African culture, and consequently, in the West Indian culture. You could also say that it's the Creole form of '*Tiens, bois*,' meaning 'Come and drink,' as sometimes witches use potions that they give to those who come to consult them."

"There's no way I'm going to be drinking anything there!" Nathalie burst out.

"We'll see," Eusebius replied to her calmly. "Everything depends on what you're asking."

WE'D AGREED to meet in a cave that was accessible by foot on the bottom of the cliffs, not too far from the *Trou du Souffleur*, a blow hole and natural curiosity of the site. It was a hole that communicated with the sea, and geysers of saltwater and foam ten to twelve feet high blew out of it, like the violent and noisy ejections of a monster hidden below the rocks.

No one dared to speak during that dark night, not even Gregory who always had something to add or say. We walked along in a single file, all lost in our own thoughts. Thoughts that, and I was sure of this, targeted the experience that we were getting ready to live together.

"Here we are!"

For a second, I was regretting having been dragged into this. But, just like my fellow vacationers, including of course Colombe, I walked down to that rocky cavity that was sheltered from the gusts of wind, towards a weak light that was now guiding us, one that the many candles with their flickering lights emitted.

The decor, atmosphere, and site, all that made me feel like I was a character in a poorly made horror film. When I was younger, I'd watched a slew of B or Z series movies, full of witches, monsters, ghosts and paranormal phenomena. But it sure was different than just watching those movies and starring in one.

"Welcome," a deep voice said, a cavernous one actually, matching the venue.

"This is Jean-Felix," said Eusebius.

When we'd all introduced ourselves, he had us sit down in a circle, facing him. He was wearing a type of multicolored boubou, and his face was covered with cabalistic signs, probably made with coal, unless it was chicken blood or something like that, making me think of some Haitian voodoo witch, something he more or less actually was, I guess. He was wearing a heavy wooden crucifix around his neck.

There was a strong smell of melted wax and acrid smoke in the cave giving it a dizzying atmosphere. The candles were in a circle in the center of the cave, making our shadows waltz on the rocky sides of the limestone cave, just like will-o'-the-wisps that had escaped from abandoned cemeteries.

We were all duly impressed by his staging. Around the circle of candles there was another circle, about six feet in diameter, that was probably drawn by using salt, as it was white. There were four elements lying on the circumference of the circle, sort of like the four cardinal points: a bowl filled with water, a feather, a little heap of earth, and another candle.

Jean-Felix was smack in the middle of this circle.

"My dear *quémandeurs*," he murmured to us, "you are now protected by this cabalistic circle, one that will not allow any evil spirits to enter here. It uses the four elements that compose our universe: water, air, earth, and fire. I'm going to begin by consecrating this protective figure, then you can formulate your wishes, hopes, desires and I'll try to fulfill them, using friendly or... evil spirits depending on what you've asked me."

He stood up but gestured to us to remain seated.

Some people were kneeling, others were crouched, whereas others were sitting Indian style. The rocky ground, damp with sea spray, was nice and cool.

The witchdoctor suddenly put a hand under his boubou and took a knife out.

"Don't fear, this is the consecrated athame. If needed, it will push evil spirits from you and cut the ties with harmful energies."

With the tip of his knife, he pointed at the candle, on the eastern side of the circle, and made a big circle clockwise. After that he began to chant, pointing his athame towards the feather.

"By this feather, I consecrate this circle and invoke the presence of the Guard of the Eastern Tower, he who guards the heavens and guards the air, let him come to me, let him hear me, let him protect me. May my will be done."

Then he pointed at the candle.

"By the Fire, I consecrate this circle and invoke the presence of the Guard of the Southern Tower, he who guards the sacred fire and he who protects this element, let him come to me, let him hear my prayers, protect me and guide my steps by giving me his light. May my will be done."

Same principle for the bowl.

"By this Water, I call the Guard of the Western

Tower, he who guards the sacred waters and governs this element, may he come to me, may he guide and protect me. May my will be done."

THEN HE CONCLUDED with the handful of dirt.

"By the Earth, I call for the power of the Guard of the Northern Tower, may he who guards the earth and governs this element come to me, may he protect me and guide my steps on the path of life. May my will be done."

A deathly silence followed each of his phrases. He went back into the center of the circle.

"O spirits, I thank you for your presence now, may magic begin, may it be inside me and around me and guide my steps."

A breeze came into the cave, stroking my nape, I nearly screamed. Though I knew logically that everything was just staging, and the text was to create an atmosphere, the result was totally successful.

The *quimboiseur* closed his eyes for a few seconds that seemed to me to be an eternity, while continuing to move his lips. None of us though could make out what he was saying.

"It's finished!" he said gravely. "Now, we'll take turns and I'm going to ask you to raise your hand when you're ready to formulate your request to the spirits who have entered into the circle with me. With my intermediary, you will be able, or maybe not, to have your wish granted. You can ask them for anything: love, protection, money, success, healing, revenge... It doesn't hurt to ask. Of course, it will be done discretely, I'll come to you, and you'll whisper your request into my ear. So? Who wants to start?"

There was a moment of collective silence. No one wanted to be the first one to adventure into the troubled waters of voodoo cults. While we were all hesitating, the *quimboiseur* walked to a trunk in a dark corner of the cave. He took a bunch of eclectic objects out of it and placed them inside the cabalistic circle.

"Me! I'll start."

It was Jacques and he spoke calmly.

Jean-Felix slowly walked up to him, leaned towards his face and then put his ear against Jacques's mouth. He began to speak. We could only hear an unintelligible murmur of what he was saying, especially as the wind had picked up and was blasting through the cave we were using as a magical den.

Jean-Felix, his eyes closed, regularly nodded, while Jacques must have been formulating his secret request. He must have listened to him for a good minute before saying anything. Then he opened his eyes and looked intensely and silently into Jacques's eyes.

"I understood you," he said, going back to the objects he'd put into the dark part of the circle.

We saw him pick one of them up and heard him chanting incantations, in a language that was impossible to identify, probably a mixture of divers dialects, sprinkled with an unknown magical lexica that was not for profane people like us.

He turned towards Jacques, walked up to him and held his hand out.

"You'll wear this cinnamon stick around your neck for twenty-eight days, not one more, not one less. And never take it off, is that clear?"

He opened his hand and gave him the cinnamon stick, with a string around it and put it over Jacques's head, like a necklace.

"The spirits are watching over you and your wish shall be granted, please be assured of that."

"Thank you," was all Jacques had to say.

"I don't need any thank yous," grumbled Jean-Felix, going back to the center of the circle. "Spirits know how to read into the heart and soul of sincere *quemandeurs*. Next!"

I raised my hand.

"Okay, young man," whispered the witchdoctor bending towards me.

His long thick dreads fell onto my head, giving me the feeling that a hoard of spiders were crawling around in my hair.

The quimboiseur's breath smelled of old rum mixed in with a bitter stench that I mentally associated with what Howard Carter and Lord Carnavon must have smelled when they first went into Tutankhamun's tomb. The odor of death? The fragrance of spirits?

"Speak. What is your wish?"

With a few carefully constructed sentences, I formulated the wish that I'd thought of. I had no idea how that so-called witchdoctor could grant it, but nothing ventured nothing gained.

He did about the same thing he'd done for Jacques, coming back to me with a flask containing a liquid whose characteristic odor reminded me of when I'd had PT and that I identified as camphor. I was aware of its tonic and stimulating properties for the body but was far from imagining that it could also be magic. I put the flask in my pocket.

"Twenty-eight days also," the witchdoctor prescribed. "A complete lunar cycle."

For a moment I thought he was going to continue

with the price of the visit and ask for my insurance, but of course he didn't.

The session continued in the same way for the other participants. Colombe left with a dried hibiscus flower, Naima with some vinegar, Eusebius with dried red peppers and Nathalie with a branch of dill, overjoyed that she didn't have to swallow anything.

Gregory got a good-sized sweet potato, in which the *quimboiseur* had patiently stuck six needles into while chanting some vague incantations.

Up till then, everything seemed under control and not that extraordinary after all. But suddenly things took a turn for the worse and we began to slip down a slippery and frightening for some slope.

Severine was the first surprised by what Jean-Felix brought her from the back of the cave. She made a face, repulsed, when she saw that dried toad, with its mouth curiously closed by a padlock, going through its body.

We all began to feel quite nauseous.

But more was yet to come.

Bruce's turn, the last person to volunteer, was tough.

The temperature seemed to have ratcheted up a notch in the cave. Was it the heat given off by the candles or fear that was making us sweat?

And had Bruce known what was to come, would he have formulated a different request?

After the *quimboiseur* had religiously listened to the young blond man, he went back for the last time to his trunk filled with a thousand surprises.

He brought with him – and here we didn't believe our eyes – a white hen who was still alive, though up till now it hadn't clucked or anything. He put it down in the center of the circle, forcing it to lay its head below a wing, to artificially put it to sleep, after which he took his athame, that knife with the artistically carved handle that he'd used at the beginning of the session to bless the circle.

I was fearing the worst, yet what was to come would be even worse than what I had feared.

Jean-Felix chanted a few incantations before cutting through the throat of that poor hen in one fell swoop. A powerful jet of slimy red blood escaped, that he collected in a bowl.

We were all stupefied, both the men and women emitting gasps of surprise or horror. I saw Colombe turn her head while she grabbed my hand tightly.

I mechanically looked at Bruce, the person who

was the most concerned by that barbaric act taking place right in front of our flabbergasted eyes.

The witchdoctor let the hen's blood fill the bowl, chanting who knew what but which seemed satanic to me. When the bowl was full, he turned to Bruce.

"Here, drink this!"

Bruce backed up, his eyes wide with fear.

Nathalie put her hand in front of her mouth, as if trying to prevent herself from vomiting.

Colombe closed her eyes.

"Do you want your wish to come true or not? Do you want the spirits to help you in your quest?"

"I didn't think it would go this far," the young man whined.

Jean-Felix put the bowl in front of him.

"*Quimbois*, that's serious stuff, young man."

"Jean-Felix!" Eusebius said. "Never mind, it's not a big deal."

Bruce took a deep breath and abdicated after thinking it over.

"Okay. I'll do it. When I was a kid, my parents gave me fish liver oil, it can't be any worse."

With a trembling hand, he grabbed the bowl and brought it to his lips. At first there was a nauseous and nearly sadistic grin on his face, then he closed his eyes and let the chicken blood run down his throat.

That atmosphere in the cave had now changed. It seemed like an eternity between the moment where we'd accepted, by curiosity, Eusebius's proposal to come there and the present instant, a traumatic one which each of us had successively solicited otherworld spirits through the quimboiseur's gifts.

"It's over now," declared the witchdoctor.

We were about to get up, but he stopped us with an authoritarian gesture.

"Wait! We have to reopen the circle in compliance with the rules."

He began the same ritual as when we arrived, thanking the four cardinal points, beginning with the heap of dirt and turning counterclockwise.

"I thank thee, Guard of the Northen Tower. I thank thee for thy presence and protection, for what thee did, for what is taking place now and for what thee will do in the future. Go back to where thee came from and now, everything will be as it was before. May my will be done."

What followed was strictly similar. We couldn't wait to leave and get back to normality.

He freed us from this difficult yet very interesting moment we spent as a group.

. . .

On the road back to Deshaies, as Severine had joined us with her pickup truck, we split into two groups. Colombe and I went with her.

We spoke about what we had just experienced on the way back. I was able to see that she was also, as we all were, overwhelmed and distraught by the witchdoctor's session.

Yet, that was not what surprised me the most in everything she told us that night while she was driving us back home.

CHAPTER 24

Erasing the Blackboard

All the emotions we had during that evening in addition to our fatigue plus the rum we'd downed at dinner transformed the interior of the pickup into a boudoir that sparked secrets.

"What an incredible experience, don't you agree?" began Severine.

"I must say that I never thought I'd experience something like that one day. I certainly wasn't expecting to discover that facet of Guadeloupe when I reserved our vacation."

"Much more authentic than those so-called haunted manors in Scotland."

The road was nearly deserted at that hour of the night, except when we reached the road leading to

Pointe à Pitre. Not much to see or to comment on. All that was left to do was to talk.

"I wonder what everyone asked the *quimboiseur*," I thought aloud.

"Me too! I'd sell my mother and father to find out!" exclaimed Severine.

Colombe had dozed off in the back seat. Our hostess and I were now united in a nocturnal face to face.

"But, just like wishes you make when you see a shooting star or something, if you tell someone else about what you wished for, that wish won't come true."

"We can't even know the subject or theme of it?"

"Um. It all depends on whether or not you believe those phenomena?"

"Do you?"

"I want to, in the same way that I've always dreamed of going back in time, like they did in *Back to the Future*."

"I certainly do, McFly! That's what lots of us dream of, including all sorts of scientists. Just imagine that technically that would be possible - what would you do with a power like that? Most people answer that question saying something like 'Go back before 1933 and try to eliminate Hitler before he became the

Chancellor of the Reich!' or 'Go back before my grandpa who I never knew, died.'"

Severine thought for a moment.

"Without trying to rewrite History, I'd like to go back twenty years, but in my own family. I'd imagine we all have things to forget, things we would have done differently… Most people have at least one or two major things they regret. Don't you agree?"

Quickly rewinding my own existence, I realized that she was right here.

"I do. Something we didn't do, something we said, a decision taken too quickly, a thoughtless act. We'd like to erase our living blackboard and restart what was just a draft of our lives."

"Do you believe in reincarnation or life after death? Do you think we get several tries before living the life we were meant to?"

"No idea. I sometimes wonder about the déjà-vu impressions I have, you understand? What if they were unconscious reminiscences of experiences in former lives? What do you think?"

"I've already asked myself the same question. In real life though, you quickly realize you can't change the past. All we can do is survive our present and try to influence, each second of our lives, our own future and by extension, the future of our friends and family. That reminds me of a book I loved that took place in New York, *Ten Seconds Before Dying*, something like that."

"*Thirty seconds...*"

"You're right, a thriller where the destinies of several people are intertwined and influenced, sometimes with just a couple of seconds."*

"So if you could change one thing about your past?"

"Just one?"

"Just one. And no joker here."

"In that case, I wouldn't change a thing, I'd change a person!"

"Even more complicated, I bet. What person?"

"Me!"

"I think most people have a poor self-image of themselves."

"Jerome, have you ever taken a good look at me?"

I looked at her, but she didn't answer. I felt that at that precise moment, she needed some introspection. She continued.

"Each evening, after my shower, when I'm untangling my hair and looking in the mirror, all I can think about is one thing: breaking it so I won't have to see myself!"

---

* *Thirty Seconds Before Dying*, Nino S. Theveny, 2018.

I didn't know how to answer that. Only Colombe's regular breathing, as she was still asleep, was mixed in with the noise of the car engine.

"Jerome, do you think I'm beautiful?"

Didn't know how to answer that one either.

"Well... beauty is something that's subjective, I think."

"There's beauty and then there's beauty. I'm not talking about those stereotyped beauties on magazine covers."

I knew what she was talking about now.

"That scar... What happened?"

She sighed noisily.

"An accident... in my life. Can you imagine what I feel when I'm looking at myself? That image sends me back to my daily life. But can you imagine what it was like to have been mocked and insulted all the time when I was a child?"

"I do know Mankind well enough to imagine it. You must have suffered a lot when you were young. Kids are so cruel to one another."

"Not just kids..."

We had nearly reached Route de la Traversée, just a couple of miles from our destination, Deshaies. I could hear in Severine's voice the wounds of her past, the bitterness of her present.

Colombe, in the back seat, stretched and yawned. "Did I miss anything?"

CHAPTER 25
All the anger

Biscarrosse, March 2020

"Did we miss anything?" asked Colombe, like an echo to the question she'd asked a couple of days ago.

We were no longer in Guadeloupe, we were at home, sitting on our couch, in our house on the Atlantic coast.

In no danger… But could we be sure of that?

We needed a new pause in the souvenirs of our vacation. Colombe pushed the photobook aside.

"Three now!" I exclaimed. "You're right, that's starting to be a lot."

Colombe took another sip of her tea.

"If it would just stop there! But it's not going to, and you know it too."

"Did you get any answers to your group email from the others?"

"Not a one. And that's what's worrying me too. Like they'd all disappeared!"

"You know everyone doesn't have their nose in their inbox all the time."

"But still... young people all synchronize their inboxes with their phone, something that's always within reach."

"And that doesn't mean that they don't have the intention of answering you immediately!"

"I know. I'd better wait before brooding in my dark thoughts. But look at this."

She opened Facebook on her phone and started looking. In just a second, Mark Zuckerberg's social networking service gave her a non-ambiguous response on Bruce Boutefeux's profile. And it was the right profile: his blond hair, his surfboard next to him, his *Crest* toothpaste smile, it was the same Bruce who was on vacation with us. We scrolled down his public profile.

As we weren't part of his contact list, most of the posts we could access were just Happy Birthday publications year after year. Plus a couple of typical things between colleagues in which he was identified or tagged. But all that was nothing in comparison with the post on top of his profile, leaving us speechless:

RIP Bruce.

That last wave was the very last one for you, my brother. You skimmed above the froth, you dove right into the ocean of life, you mastered all those rolling waves like a pro, the last wave, the most powerful one, took you away.

So quickly!

You were dead in only four days.

The doctors, incapable of saving you, had to resign themselves to allowing you to escape to the seas, to the unknown depths of death.

What happened to you?

That was how the post of a guy named Medhi Chafik ended, on that unanswered question.

"What did happen?" added Colombe. "What did

you die from Bruce? Why? And what about Naima and Jacques? Why? And how? I've got a thousand questions and no true clues."

By the inflections in her voice, I knew that my girlfriend was angry at her own incomprehension.

"I must admit I'm like you, no idea. Three deaths in such a short time, with the only thing in common was that they spent a week of vacation together and died upon returning, something's rotten in Denmark there."

"Not just in Denmark, in France and Gwada too. Maybe you're going to say that I'm being ridiculous here, but do you think we could find some explanation in the ... voodoo witchcraft session?"

"The *quimbois*? Come on!"

I chuckled, now incredulous.

"Bruce did drink that chicken blood..." Colombe hesitated, not really convinced herself.

"So what? I drink weird stuff too and I'm still alive and kicking! That's nonsense!"

"It's not chicken blood that casts spells but the witchdoctor's magic, his gift of witchcraft, his capacity to contact evil spirits..."

"I don't think that's where we'll find the solution, frankly. Colombe, we're in the twenty-first century, not in the Middle Ages! I refuse to believe that in 2020 people can die because they are victims of some dumb spell cast by a witchdoctor in a cave in Guadeloupe, even though that cave was near Hell's Gate."

Colombe picked the photo album up, though she didn't buy into what I'd said.

"Okay. Forget that then. But we need to find something else to explain it. And it must be right in front of us."

"Or else, just have those brain cells work like Hercule Poirot!" I joked, trying to relax her.

A NEW IMMERSION next to the Antilles, with photos from the last days of our vacation.

A TON OF EARTH

For a fleeting second, the overcast sky opened up to let a timid ray of sun pass, which lit up the round, polished and discreet fluviatile gravel on the cemetery path and carefully aligned tombstones. Funeral arts were charming only to a chosen few. Generally speaking, those who came here never appreciated that harmony which nonetheless was born from human minds, inherited from centuries of trial and error in funeral experiences. Since the beginning of Time, Mankind has always valued the memory of those who have passed, whatever religion, civilization, or continent on which those funeral rites were taking place. Universal funeral arts weren't born yesterday!

One of the undertakers opened the back door of the hearse and delicately pulled out the coffin, so as not to disturb the eternal rest of its dear occupant. The slight drizzle placed brilliant tears on the enameled wood, adding to the solemnity of the moment.

They carried the coffin to where the small group had stopped in front of a hole they'd dug out a few hours earlier. The body would soon be resting forever in that hole, covered with a ton of earth, gravel, stones, and heartache.

The heartache that those rare friends and family members had on their faces around that freshly dug tomb.

CHAPTER 26

Under the spell

In her bathroom, Severine looked at herself in the mirror sternly.

"What got into you to blab away like that?" she winced as she saw her image that was blurred by the steam. "Complaining like a little kid to near strangers... You are crazy, sister!"

Oh, come on, no one died, did they?

Was she dreaming or had her lips moved by themselves? Or had she had too much rum? Was she still under the *quimboiseur's* spell? Had one of the participants cast a spell on her through the witchdoctor, provoking hallucinations and delusions?

Was that what weakened her so much that she'd complained to Jerome?

She tried to be logical.

"No, no one died, but danger is near. I have to get myself under control, I can't fail now. If so, that would result in so many lost years. For nothing."

Everything's gonna be alright, don't worry.

Severine grinned mockingly, making fun of that reflection that was hers without being able to affirm that it actually was her. The ambiguity of her existence was summed up there, between herself and her reflection in the mirror.

"Who are you really? Who am I actually?"

You're me, I'm you. We're the addition of both of us.

"Shut up, you're me!" said the woman to the other woman.

My poor Severine, you really had too much to drink tonight.

She put a baby-doll nightie on and went into her office before going to bed.

Thursday, April 1st, 2010

For a moment I thought it was a joke, one more. An April Fool's Day joke!

That really wouldn't have astonished me 'cuz I'm used to jokes, used to being the target of cheap shots.

Frankly, when Adonis – he's so handsome

that's what I'm naming him – asked me if I'd be interested in going to the movies with him last night, I didn't believe my ears. I was already imagining what would come next! I was going to say yes, that I'd be delighted, ask him what time it was playing, what he wanted to see, if he was coming to pick me up or if we'd be meeting in front of the cinema, Place Darcy – or maybe if he preferred going to the Quetigny Complex. After my tirade, I could well see him laughing his guts out and saying: April Fools! Really, just look at yourself! You really thought I wanted to go out with you? Seriously, I don't feel like starring in Beauty and the Beast. Between us two there's a chasm that can't be crossed. Can you imagine my reputation if people saw us together? Stop trying to turn your dreams into reality and get back to Earth! I was joking!

That's what I would have found logical.

But no, he wasn't joking. He really wanted to take me to the movies. He even let me pick the movie. They were playing All That Glitters, with Geraldine Nakache and Leila Bekhti. I know, a chick film. I thought that if he agreed to watch that one with me he was really sincere. Oh! Plus I loved Veronique Samson's song that they played in the preview: Chanson sur ma drôle de vie, you can sort of say it's "A Song about my Crazy Life," something like that. Great rhythm and one that fits me to a T!

"If I know that deep down inside you love the life you're living,

That's something that touches me right to the tips of my fingers,

Though you've got problems, you know I love you, that'll help,

Just leave everything else, your strange poems, and come with me."

Come with me, that's what I wanted to sing to Adonis!

And he really did come with me to the movies.

When they turned off the lights, I was amazed that he was sitting there, right next to me. I could feel his presence and sniff the way he smelled... so deliciously intoxicating. I couldn't stop repeating to myself that I was just dreaming, that I'd soon wake up in my bed and see that this was just the fruit of my too fertile imagination.

I pinched myself, and all I did was hurt myself. My skin got all red and Adonis was still there, next to me, watching the movie.

How could the most popular guy in high school want to go out with me? Someone who up to now had always had the prettiest girls with him, hanging on to his arm, listening to his every word, snuggled in his so muscular arms.

The only answer to that question was his presence in flesh and blood, in the seat next to mine. My eyes relentlessly were drawn to his hand that was on the armrest between our two seats, so close to mine, so accessible, so tempting. I wanted to mix his fingers with mine, to squeeze them, to hold onto them for the whole film, still looking at the screen, just knowing that he was there, that he was linked to me.

But I was afraid to.

Luckily, he wasn't.

His fingers were the ones that made their way to mine. What a feeling! I can't even describe it! That heat that went right *through me, from his hand up to my heart without forgetting my tortured, distraught and lost soul. But that was nothing compared to the tsunami that furled over me when he kissed me…*

How could he have done that without having been disgusted? How can anyone kiss a mouth like mine? A mystery that can't be explained.

It wasn't the first time that I was in love.

This time though, I think it was the first time… that someone loved me!

It wasn't a bad idea to have read this part of her diary for Severine. After an exhausting and tough day, she was really lucky to have happened upon a happy souvenir.

One of the few.

CHAPTER 27

A whole chain of consequences

As all good things come to an end, it was now our last outing.

We all couldn't wait to go on the boat trip that was planned, as we knew we'd be seeing Jean-Pierre again, our diving instructor. He'd asked us if we'd like to spend the whole day on his electric flat-bottomed catamaran, discovering the treasures of the mangrove and the coral reef in a site called *Grand Cul-de-Sac Marin*. We'd go snorkeling, to Caret Islet, have lunch on the boat, then go birdwatching at l'Ile aux Oiseaux, Bird Island, an interesting program that would whet our chops once again, but nice and relaxed. No way could we refuse that.

Eusebius and Severine wouldn't be going with us,

but lent us their van, and Jacques, the oldest one in our group, was the designated driver.

We met Jean-Pierre at Sainte-Rose Port.

"Hello my friends," he greeted us warmly. "Ah! Naima my dear, how are you doing? I hope you're not mad at me!"

"It wasn't your fault," she said, kissing him on a cheek. "Quite the opposite, I'm probably alive because of you."

"Come on, that's nonsense. And don't worry, today it's cool. Slow and easy, like they say here. We missing anyone? No, well, let's go sailors!"

While going there, Jean-Pierre gave us a fascinating lecture about the fauna and flora in a mangrove, something typical of the Caribbean Area.

"Do you know exactly what a mangrove is?"

"Not really," admitted Colombe, the spokesperson of our collective ignorance.

"I thought so. A word you've often heard without really knowing what it meant. I'll give you the simple version. A mangrove is an ecosystem of maritime swamps. In other words, things you only find on the littoral in countries that are in an intertropical zone. And Guadeloupe is one of those countries! So, what grows in a mangrove? Mostly shrubs, vines and some types of palm trees. Amongst the most well-known trees, you have those famous purple rooted mangroves that emerge from the water like tentacles. You see what I'm talking about? Landscapes like those are unique but above all, fragile! The mangrove is fragile, the coral reef is fragile, the coast is threatened!"

"Threatened by what?"

"By submersion, for example, but also by the disappearance of many animal and vegetal species. A catastrophe, one that's imminent, I can guarantee that."

"What is causing it? Whose fault is it?"

"Men caused it, as usual... Pollution, climate change, rising water levels. You'll see that later when we disembark at Caret Islet, it'll be evident to you. Same thing with the coral reef we'll be swimming above, you'll see. It's slowly dying! One of the roles it has, as it says in its name, is to block the ecosystem of the littoral. But when there are storms, you've got tidal waves and land on the coast, and of course on the mangrove. From there, there's a whole chain of consequences for the fauna, because the mangrove is home for many species."

"Not a very optimistic picture," Jacques agreed.

"You're right, Mother Nature's future looks bleak. But I'm not here to sap your morale, right? Let's head to Caret Islet."

Turquois colored waters less than three feet deep

with a sand bottom, an island that's so tiny that you'd think it was maybe Robinson Crusoe's island, with four little shacks made from this and that, sand from the coral bank, that's what Caret Islet was... or at least what's left of it today.

"What if I told you that the island has already lost eighty percent of its area in less than twenty years?"

"We'd need proof of that!"

Jean-Pierre took out an enlarged photo.

"Here's Caret Islet twenty years ago! See what I mean when I'm talking about rising water levels? It's inevitable, in a couple of years, this little island will be underwater, like many others before it. So, put your fins on, your snorkeling equipment, and you'll see it up close and personal."

Indeed, while snorkeling around the islet we saw vestiges of a life that was now submerged: planks, sheeting, pullies, doors; a whole environment that now had joined the world of silence.

And in the middle of those ruins, multicolored fish, starfish, shellfish, and sea cucumbers, that Gregory – in his omnipresent delicacy – called underwater turds. I had to agree though that those curious-looking brown animals, with their oblong and soft bodies, didn't look like much.

When we got back onboard, an hour later, lunch

was ready, and the table had been set. Jean-Pierre's assistant had grilled Colombo chicken while we were diving and lazing about on Caret Islet Beach.

What a treat it was to enjoy that Creole dish, while being gently rocked on the boat floating on turquois-colored waters, with a cool wind. Everyone was relaxed during the meal. We all were joking, laughing, but equivocally it felt like the end of our vacation. The dessert, a banana that was flambéed with rum, topped with whipped cream, was able to shake that nostalgia from us, perhaps helped by the glass of rum-laced punch accompanying it.

In the afternoon we all went scuba diving above the coral reef. I was quite astonished that the underwater landscape wasn't as sensational as I'd imagined it. I was hoping to see those images of multicolored coral, things that I'd seen in Commander Cousteau's documentaries. Instead of that I saw shapes that were varied, but their colors ran only from white to brown, and many shades of gray. The fish swimming around them however, had mind-boggling brilliant colors, and that was really what was worth seeing.

Jacques, with his submersible camera, kept filming them and Nathalie, when she got back onto the boat, had mentally recorded a sufficient number of images and was able to immediately begin sketching them.

The stand-up trio of Bruce-Naima-Gregory didn't disappoint.

As for Colombe and I, we took full advantage of the day, storing away images to bring back to France.

At the end of the day, Jean-Pierre took us back to Sainte-Rose Port, where we all said our goodbyes, and asked him for his email, so we could remain in touch when we got back.

WE WANTED to thank our hosts when we returned to Bougainvillea Domain for having lent us their van. Eusebius was nowhere to be found. Severine was sitting on a sunbed by the pool, looking out at nothing, a pen in her hand and a black notebook next to her. She hadn't heard us walk to the pool, though the sound of the gate opening wasn't really discreet.

"Severine?" called out Colombe softly.

She didn't budge, as if she was hypnotized.

I walked up to her, trying not to make any noise, so I wouldn't frighten her.

"Severine, is everything alright?" I asked.

Her head suddenly turned in my direction. She blinked several times, as if coming out of a deep sleep.

"Oh! You scared me! I didn't hear you coming, I

must have been sleeping with my eyes open, excuse me. How is everything? Have a nice time with Jean-Pierre?"

She sat up and I told her about our day.

"Sorry, I have to go now," she said.

She began walking out of the pool area.

"Wait a sec! You forgot your notebook!"

I picked it up and gave it to her.

"Thanks. See you soon."

I turned around and looked at Colombe.

"She doesn't seem like herself today."

~

WALKING AUTOMATICALLY AND FIRMLY, Severine went back to her bungalow, directly into her office, opening up her diary to the last page. As no one had been present in her resort that day, she'd taken advantage of that moment to continue writing. She reread what she'd written.

Right now, while I'm closing the loop, it's such a strange impression, like I'm putting an end to all this, like I'm settling old scores of a too painful past. Am I going to be able to go through with my decision? Do you need courage or cowardice in those moments?

Is actually doing it more difficult than being aware of it and deciding it?

So close to the point of no return, am I going to deflate?

Have I been illuding myself for all these years? Is this an error, a blind error?

I don't know anymore, I'm lost.

Am I really going to do this?

Sometimes, when you're on the edge of a precipice, your feet next to the edge, just a second before jumping, that is the very instant when you realize the futility of your resolution. So you slowly back your feet away, feet that were already half-way off, you go back to safety, passivity, voluntary renunciation...

At the poolside, after having written those words, she'd put her diary down next to the sunbed and had gotten lost in her thoughts, so far that she'd distanced herself from reality and hadn't even heard her guests arriving. They must have thought she was nuts!

Tough luck! No one's perfect all the time.

. . .

In such moments of indecision and doubt, all Severine had to do was to reread an old text, an excerpt where the young girl told all her terrible secrets and heartaches to her diary. Like this one:

Thursday, April 8, 2010

Am I cursed or what?

How could I have believed those illusions so easily?

They seemed so real, so sincere.

Just a week ago, I was on cloud nine, in the arms of one of the best-looking guys in high school, my Adonis, the one I'd always secretly admired without having imagined for even a second that it could be reciprocal.

That evening, as he'd walked me home, I had experienced a moment of grace, like I was starring in a romance movie, if I can put it like that.

The following days, in high school, I didn't believe my eyes either that I was still with him, being looked at, astonished, by other students, incapable of believing what they were seeing: Beauty kissing the Beast.

It was a romantically idyllic week, right before falling completely into an abject one.

Yesterday afternoon, he asked me over to his house, no one was home. We made out and he led me to his room. We petted, he undressed me and laid me down on the bed. There, while I was trying to hide my breasts with one hand and my sex with the other, – all that was so new to me – that was the moment he chose to crucify me.

"It's over between us!" he brutally said.

"What do you mean, over? I thought that..."

"That's enough! Look at yourself! What did you think? That I was going out with you because of your beauty?"

"That's disgusting what you're saying."

"But the truth. You know I can get any girl I want in high school, and you really believed that I'd want you in my harem?"

"Stop! Don't talk about girls like that! And don't talk about me like that either!"

"It's the truth. They'd fight to be a part of it, meaning ending up in my bed."

"You bastard! So if it's so easy for you to sleep with all the popular girls in high school,

why did you lower yourself to go out with me?"

"Because, thanks to you, I won a bet of twenty-four bottles of beer! You were so easy to catch, you couldn't wait till a guy like me spoke to you..."

"What are you talking about? I'm afraid to understand..."

"You understood me correctly. If I went out with you, it was just to win a bet with my friends. If I succeeded in overcoming my repulsion in going out with the High School Monster for a week, even if my reputation was tarnished, I'd win a twenty-four pack of Bud!"

"You're a scumbag!"

"Yeah, sure, so be nice, get dressed now, go back home and forget about me. I got better things to do."

I got dressed as quickly as possible and fled his ignominy. When I left his house, I saw in the window of the room I'd just left, a group of guys laughing their heads off.

I dried my tears with my sleeves before going home, where I locked myself into the bathroom and took a scorching hot shower, to try to wash all contact with my skin from *that asshole. I stayed in the shower until all the hot water was gone, my tears mixing in with it.*

Then I went into my room, locked that door and rushed to my bed, put my pillow over my head, trying to smother myself and my cries of hatred below the feathers, so no one would hear my soul suffering.

I miss my sister so much in cursed moments like this. She's no longer here to give me a helping hand, to listen to me, to comfort me when I need her.

More than ever now, I want to die.

After having read that, it was easier for Severine to rekindle the flames of her intensions. Doing what she'd planned, after having reread the horrors of the past, was now so evident for her.

She had to!

CHAPTER 28

Filled with disgust

It was surprisingly calm that day at Bougainvillea Domain. Something often the case on your last day of vacation. Some were trying to get that last site in, others were already busy packing, doing a last load of washing, or writing postcards. Most of the vacationers had decided to go to one of the nearby beaches, to enjoy the sun, iodine-filled air and the pleasure of following schools of fish or turtles. That sleepy day, Severine had to be careful while preparing their gala meal. She looked at her watch and decided to wait a few minutes. Just a few yards away she could hear Eusebius whistling at the poolside, already busy cleaning it.

Be with you in ten, honey, she said to herself.

But before, she needed to read another excerpt of her souvenirs in her black diary.

Saturday, October 16, 2010

Has luck finally changed? Will I be allowed to be happy? Today, my Dear Diary, that's what I'm hoping for.

My depression caused by that asshole Adonis, before summer vacation, is finally over.

For the whole summer things were bleak for me, I hardly even left my room, listening to songs by The Cure, reflecting my mood.

And then, like each time, probably because I'm used to it, I slowly bounced back.

In September when school started, I started taking in music lessons, haunted by Robert Smith's guitar chords. I thought that would do me good. I wasn't really wrong there.

My guitar instructor took good care of me. It was like I was the "teacher's pet," and he quickly told me I was really talented. All I wanted though was a minimum of attention and above all, consideration, something I'd never had in my life. Up until now, no one had really been interested in me. No one – except Scheherazade, but that didn't last – had tried to find out what was hidden behind my corporal envelope. No one had ever really tried to speak to my soul, my beautiful soul.

Each Saturday, after high school, I went to my guitar lesson.

Each Saturday I felt more and more at ease with my instrument and with my instructor, who so patiently explained the basics to me.

I loved those hours I spent with him, in his "studio" at home, where he gave his lessons. We would sit across from one another, on high stools, one foot on the wooden bar, and the other one on the ground. My guitar was on my thigh and its body against my stomach, sending its notes right to the deepest part of my soul.

He was teaching, I was learning. He was providing, I was enjoying. He was nourishing me by his knowledge, I was delighted.

And if he was judging me, it wasn't on the way I looked, it was on my musical skills.

He sometimes would go behind me, putting

his arms around me to reach my hands on the guitar. He would direct my movements on the chords, correcting the position of my fingers, guiding me for the right tempo.

I would feel his warmth against my back, his breath on my neck, his perfume that enveloped me... and intoxicated me.

I had to say, that guitar instructor, who I'll call Robert Smith here, troubled me but positively.

"You're gifted, never doubt that," he once said to me.

It's so rare that anyone compliments me. I'm not used to that at all, except in my family, especially my sister, so I blush each time. I nearly forget to thank him, so unsure I am that he's actually speaking like that to me. I know, my self-confidence is hovering around zero percent, but you gotta understand me!

I'm eighteen years old and I've never been happy!

I finally feel thought that maybe I can be.

Two weeks ago, Robert Smith surprised

me. While standing behind me, in that posture that overturned me so much, he whispered into my ear.

"You're beautiful, you know."

I fell off my stool, mentally of course. I gaped, paralyzed by those couple of words, words I'd never before heard.

The warmth of his breath infiltrated my ear. I didn't want to turn around, I knew he was there, right behind me, I was paralyzed.

Then he spun my stool around, so I was facing him.

He took my guitar from my hands and put it down on the adjacent table. Then he leaned down and put his lips on mine.

I was afraid to move.

Of course, it wasn't the first time someone had kissed me, but it was the first time that a real man, a mature man, did. I never asked him, it would have been impolite of course, but I'm sure he must be twice as old as I am. His graying temples, those little laugh lines around his eyes and mouth bear witness to his maturity.

What could interest him in a young lady

like me? Perhaps my youthfulness, that was all.

Since that day, the world seems brighter to me, though it's nearly fall, though the sky is full of clouds and it's getting chilly.

I count, impatiently, the days separating me from each Saturday. Today, I've just finished my lesson. Robert Smith gave me his last lesson of the day. I dare say that it was a long one...

Like before, he kissed my lips, he caressed me and this time he invited me to dinner. If you could only know, my Dear Diary, how precious I felt in his classy car. If you had only seen how he opened the door for me, how he took my arm at the restaurant, how he looked me in the eyes, with no shame, in the middle of the other customers. He couldn't have cared less about what those curious people thought of us. Nor could I! I was drowning in his eyes, I abandoned myself, blindly.

Then when we'd finished eating, he drove me back to his house. He proposed another drink, champagne, can you even imagine that? And I let myself be led to his bedroom...

He'd created an intimate atmosphere, with dimmed lights, music in the speakers, kissing me repeatedly while undressing me and delicately laying me down on his large satin covered bed.

When he was lying on me, skin against skin, warmth against moistness, I suddenly jumped, denying him, refusing him. I could only think of the shame that Adonis had inflicted on me that summer with his friends who'd been spying on us behind the window, to see how that asshole was going to humiliate me.

Smith noticed this and whispered tender words into my ear.

I thus gave myself for the very first time, to a real man!

I'm now a woman! Life is smiling at me and I'm smiling at life! A sideways smile, okay, but it's still a smile.

THIS WAS CERTAINLY one of the most beautiful episodes in that black diary, thought Severine, finishing her chapter. The most beautiful one. Had the story stopped there, you would have believed it had a happy ending. The life of that young lady nonetheless, – now a young woman – wasn't meant to finish in beauty.

I never should have turned the page, Severine thought. Because after that, I'd be filled with disgust... something inevitable.

CHAPTER 29

All in the same boat

MOMENTS no one wanted to see ending were now approaching quickly.

The last evening before your vacation is over, when you know that tomorrow you'll get up, put the last little things still on your bedside table or in the bathroom into your suitcase, your pajamas if you wear them, your toothbrush that you'll use again after one last cup of coffee, your passport that you'll be checking three times at least to make sure it's in your bag, your telephone battery that you charged at 100%... That's why you take advantage of every last moment on your last day of vacation.

. . .

Like when we arrived, there was a get-together at the bar by the pool, just like that welcome cocktail when we all got introduced to the others. Since then, we'd had intense experiences, magical moments, worrying events, even mysterious ones you could say, laughter, little secrets, and various desires. I wouldn't go as far to say that we'd become friends with the other tourists, even with our hosts, but all in all our vacation took place in a friendly and enjoyable atmosphere.

That evening, the music was booming, with Eusebius playing the double role of disc jockey and barman. He was standing behind the bar, shaking a cocktail, probably a rum-based one, when we walked into the pool area. Most of our fellow vacationers were already there, holding a glass, except for Bruce who sauntered in, wearing a T-shirt size 14-year-old, just a minute after us.

"Everyone's here!" exclaimed Severine. "Let the party begin!"

"I agree," continued Eusebius. "We're not here to complain that our vacation is over, right? Who wants a planteur?"

"My friends," continued the hostess, "I've concocted a couple of fun games for the party, hoping all of you will take part in my folly."

Everyone immediately agreed, without knowing

what she was talking about. We all trusted her, she'd taken such good care of us for the whole week. Earlier that day she'd told us to wear our swimsuits as a couple of games would be taking place in the pool. For some of the guests, it was easy to let go, whereas for others– and here I mean Jacques and Nathalie – they had to down a couple of glasses to relax.

Severine had imagined a type of contest composed of different games, with a ranking, classification and a champion.

"The winner tonight will leave with a trophy: a golden plantain banana!"

"What the hell?" Gregory asked, nearly spitting out his mouthful of caipirinha.

Behind the bar, Eusebius proudly held up a very phallic looking object, about ten inches long, an imitation gold plantain banana.

"Nice Johnson!" approved Gregory.

"Get your mind out of the gutter!" said Naima, ironically.

"Wanna come in with me?"

"I'm fine, thanks."

"Come on kids, recess is over!" scolded Severine. "First game: diving!"

Not surprisingly, Bruce won the first round, we'd

seen him dive at Acomat Falls and knew we didn't stand a chance.

Each time there was a new event, we stopped by the bar for another drink. Our heads were beginning to spin, our minds were turning too. The dance floor was occupied several times, in particular by our hosts. Colombe and I were in the same state, and I'd become sufficiently uninhibited by all the alcoholic beverages I'd downed that I also danced, me who had two left feet.

A bit later above the alcoholic vapor and watts of the music coming from the speakers, I could hear people talking loudly. At the edge of the dance floor, Naima and Gregory seemed to be having a disagreement. Greg was gripping the young lady's arm, as if trying to hold on to her so she wouldn't escape.

"Let go of me and I mean now!" she yelled right to his face.

"Come on, dance with me, don't be such a prude! I could see this whole week you wanted to get closer to me."

"You are completely crazy! You must need glasses!"

Gregory was trying to pull her towards him, to get up close and personal in an imitation of a sensual dance.

"Just leave!"

Bruce, hearing this, ran up to them, his pecs bulging. He got between those two, grabbing and squeezing Gregory's hand so he'd have to let go of Naima.

"You deaf or what? She asked you to let go."

"Just fuck off! It's none of your business, you big blond guy with a black thong. You think I didn't see you two? You fucked her, is that it?"

"Greg, you've had too much to drink. Stop it now, everyone's looking at you."

"Who are you to give me orders?"

Gregory tried to get out of Bruce's hold, threatening to clock him a good one. We all rushed to the two men who seemed ready to start a true barroom brawl. In the confusion, before Eusebius arrived to try to separate them, both of them fell into the pool, immediately followed by our host. Gregory was still trying to fight, but both men were holding onto his arms.

Luckily the now cooler water in the pool calmed Gregory down and sobered him up. Eusebius and Bruce took him to the side of the pool.

"What got into you?" asked Eusebius. "I think you had one too many of my cocktails."

"I'm sorry," Gregory articulated.

"Don't apologize to me, apologize to Naima.

Sometimes rum goes up to your head and you say things that you regret after that," said the Guadeloupean philosophically.

The young man agreed and apologized to her.

"Okay, let's forget that now and continue our party, okay with you guys? Vacations are to have fun, not to disagree."

And hour later, everyone had forgotten that incident and the games continued. There was an apnea contest that Colombe won, then a water basketball contest that much to my surprise I won.

And to conclude, Severine had imagined an original and fun game, one that everyone took part in, more or less willingly.

"No, I'm not going to make a fool of myself like that," Nathalie said.

"Come on Nat, everyone's taking part in the game," replied Eusebius, with a charmer's voice.

Severine explained that the game consisted of putting your head in a basin of water and planteur mixed together, with three slices of plantain banana on the bottom of it. The players had to keep their hands behind their backs, kneeling in front of the basin, and the goal of the game was to snare the pieces of banana with your teeth. After that you had to spit them out onto plates that were on the other side of the basin. It was a speed contest, where everyone participated at the same time. The first person who snared the three slices of banana and brought them to their plate would win. To do that, she had put seven basins side by side, we each had our own. We all kneeled down in front of our containers filled with a mixture of rum and water right up to the top, ready to dunk our heads in and snare a slice of banana with our teeth. Luckily absurdity doesn't kill anyone, otherwise we'd all be dead while I'm writing this.

But it was hilarious, we all were laughing. All in that same ridiculous boat, closely watched by our two judge-referees, we went to and fro between the container and the plate, a slice of banana in between our teeth. Not our proudest moments! And then very unexpectedly, the first person to bring the three slices was the winner of course, and it was Nathalie. And also surprisingly, when all of the points in the various games were added up, she was the overall winner of the golden plantain banana, which Eusebius gave her without forgetting to congratulate her and of course several innuendos followed. Just like when you win a Cesar, an Oscar, or whatever, we all insisted that she give a speech. With a tremulous voice, stemming from emotion and a bit too much alcohol in her blood, she stood up.

"I beat you all soundly! Wow! That's all I have to say! Thank you!"

And she raised her phallic trophy, making us all laugh hilariously.

WHAT HAD HAPPENED a while ago was forgotten and the party continued until the wee hours of the night. At that time, and for our great pleasure, Jacques surprised us. He saw a guitar hooked onto one of the walls of the bar and asked if he could take it down and play a few notes. And he played like a real pro, someone with real talent. We circled around him, just like a troop of young scouts around a campfire, belting out the songs he was playing for us. When he finished, everyone applauded to thank him for his impromptu concert.

"I just thought of something," he said, putting the guitar back down. "This week, we all took loads of photos and videos. Sometimes alone, sometimes of our group, like when we climbed up to the rock on top of Soufriere Hills volcano. Why don't we generate a shared file on the cloud, where everyone can upload their best pictures? That way we'd have more vacation souvenirs, what do you think?"

"A fantastic idea!" said Bruce enthusiastically.

"I can create the file for you. I do stuff like that regularly. I can even upload my videos of the Globicephala!"

This idea was validated unanimously. I also proposed exchanging our email addresses, also immediately validated.

In the meanwhile, the sun had set, and stars were twinkling in the sky. The clock on the wall of the bar displayed nearly three in the morning, and Eusebius poured us a last glass of rum before everyone went back to their cottages – or someone else's, who knows!

Our vacation was over.

YET JUST TWO WEEKS LATER, fate would bring us a more sinister vision of those events. But when we closed our eyes on the island for the last time, we still had no idea about it.

Part two

BACK TO GWADA

Biscarosse, March 2020

"Il faudra que tu apprennes
À perdre, à encaisser
Tout ce que le sort ne t'a pas donné
Tu le prendras toi-même.

Oh, rien ne sera jamais facile
Il y aura des moments maudits
Oui, mais chaque victoire ne sera que la tienne
Et toi seule en sauras le prix."

(Jean-Jacques Goldman, *C'est ta chance* [It's up to you]

CHAPTER 30

Victims of an ill-fated destiny

COLOMBE, now exhausted, closed the photo album one last time. We had spent over an hour together, examining each page, each of those hundred and twenty-eight photos, comparing them with the notes that Colombe had taken when we were there. Analyzing all that material now that we knew that three of our fellow vacationers had suspiciously died.

"I still don't understand," I admitted, disheartened. "Everything seems to be so normal, so commonplace. I have no idea when it could have screwed up, frankly."

Colombe shook her head from left to right, still dubitative.

"We had to have missed a detail. I'm still persuaded

that the key to those deaths in such a short time is there, right in front of our eyes."

"But sweetie, in what we've just looked at, day after day, event after event, I have no idea at all what could explain the death of several people. All I can see is an ordinary vacation, surrounded by ordinary people. There's nothing that could justify anything this tragic. That little spat between Naima, Gregory and Bruce? No big deal! Naima's diving accident? A technical incident, that was all. Of course, I do understand that you and I didn't witness everything that happened over there, among all the others, stuff that occurred when we weren't there. We weren't in their bungalows at night. So maybe the solution is there, in something that happened when we weren't present?"

"Could be. Or maybe... in what's irrational..."

I just looked at her.

"What the heck are you insinuating by that?"

Colombe changed positions on the couch, her legs benumbed by the way she'd been sitting, before answering.

"I was referring to that *quimbois* session... all of us participated in that."

In put my hands into the air, incredulous.

"No, no, no and no! You're not gonna bring that up again! I refuse to believe that you can think of something like that even for one second! Don't tell me that you actually believe in all that hocus pocus crap?"

"I don't know anymore. Back in the day I would have told you that I don't believe in the existence of Santa Claus or the tooth fairy. But I'm thinking that when you can't find a rational solution to a problem, what's left? And irrational one!"

"Are you trying to tell me that someone, during that witchdoctor's session in a cave would have tried to cast a spell on some of the participants – or on all of them?"

"And why not? Maybe it wasn't a mere game. And that also frightens me."

"Jesus Christ, you're afraid of what?" I nearly shouted.

"Afraid of being a victim, all of us, a victim of an evil spell, a victim of ancestral Guadeloupe, of their beliefs and their witchcraft. As far as we know, there already are three victims. Who knows if there won't be others? Who can assure me that we're not the next ones on the list? After all, we have no idea what each of them whispered into the ear of that *quimboiseur*, that night, at Hell's Gate..."

CHAPTER 31

Blindly abandoning myself

<u>Deshaies, March 15, 2020</u>

An undefinable malaise had taken over Severine's soul, despite the activity that was keeping her busy. For the past three weeks her resort had been full, and all the bungalows had been rented out. However, tourism could probably be taking a hit after the announcement of measures that would soon be taken concerning the health crisis, especially in metropolitan France. People were getting worried about some damned virus that was quickly making its way from Asia to Europe.

But that wasn't really what was bothering her. Ever since her group had left, the one that included five special guests plus the couple of young journalists, the young lady was no longer enjoying her job. She seemed to have lost her enthusiasm, her desires, her smiles. The adrenaline had fallen, she felt emptied out.

Trying to get back on track, trying to find a meaning for the past couple of weeks, she locked herself in her office – for the first time in the past two weeks – and opened up her black diary.

She'd opened it randomly to an entry that was hard to read.

Dijon, Friday December 31, 2010

My life is a series of roller coasters.

You think you've reached the top, but you fall even faster towards the bottom and its unbearable squalor.

I thought I was loved, but I was abused, duped, lied to, manipulated, degraded, soiled, raped. An unending list.

I was too credulous. Too naive. Stunned by the lights of an undoubtedly one-way passion.

Yet it had begun like a fairy tale. His guitar, the champagne, the sports cars with their sleek lines (not like my car), the sweet-

ness of my very own Robert Smith, blindly abandoning myself to his caresses, his loving words, his attention, his way of looking at me in the bottom of my soul rather than at me.

He'd kissed me on my mouth like I was normal! How could he have pretended for such a long time? Or was he actually sincere? Did his actions exceed his thoughts? Had his impulses, his tastes, his deviances taken control of him?

When it began, I considered it to be a game between two consenting adults. It was no big deal and was far from being unpleasant. Plus, what did I know about stuff like that? I had just begun in that field. Everything seemed normal to me, I wasn't shocked at all.

Except, the slope very quickly became slippery and each time I slid down a bit further towards the depths of despicability.

I'd become his toy, his whim, his sexual rejuvenation.

Never again, I can't stand suffering anymore, year after year, disillusion after disillusion... I've got no future.

. . .

Tears were running down Severine's cheeks, recalling that time, with each of the words slitting her soul open again. How could she have been so blind? Would she have been able to avoid the worst-case scenario had she been aware of that situation earlier?

December 31, 2010. A memorable date, a watershed date, including in her diary. There were now two distinct eras: the one before December 31, 2010 and the one after.

There was a duality, a bit like yin and yang, light and shade.

Just like those symbols, one could not exist without the other, both were a part of a complementary whole, an indivisible one.

December 31, 2010, the night when everything was overturned.

CHAPTER 32

Collector of useless things

<u>Biscarrosse, March 15, 2020</u>

Our herbal tea was already cold, and we didn't feel like drinking anymore, or even dipping our delicious Brittany biscuits into it. That mystery occupying our minds had paralyzed us. We'd just gone through each and every photo of Guadeloupe –both our album as well as the digital files on our computer – and with them, the image of our fellow vacationers still alive. Yet three had died in the interval. And we didn't have any news about the two others. And us? What would happen to us? Or were we just targeting evil with some unfortunate coincidences?

"What about calling Jean-Felix?" suggested Colombe.

"Jean-Felix?"

"You know, the *quimboiseur*! He gave me his card. You know how I collect useless things… It's not gonna be a big deal if we ask him a couple of questions. He'll undoubtedly reassure us."

I agreed that it was a good idea. Colombe dialed his number on her phone and was directed to his voicemail, a message that surprised us.

"JEAN-FELIX BOISJOLI, a quimboiseur and witchdoctor, a legatee of an ancestral Haitian gift, transmitted from father to son for the past ten generations. I am currently having a session. I can help you with fulfillments, spells, spell removal, love potions, and white or black magic. Tell me your most secret wishes and they will come true. Guaranteed results. Payment by credit card or wire transfer. Telephone consultations available. Leave me a message and I'll call you back. May the spirits be with you!

COLOMBE LEFT HIM A MESSAGE.

"All of a sudden, this is less frightening than when we were in that cave at Hell's Gate!" I exclaimed, almost busting my gut open laughing.

"I must admit it does sound like hocus pocus. I feel like I just read a flyer someone put under my windshield wipers in a parking lot. I hope he'll call back though to reassure us."

"In the meanwhile, what do you want to do?"

"I feel like sending a message to Nathalie and Gregory to see how they are. We haven't had any news from them yet."

"True, but we didn't check on internet or the networks. Maybe they're..."

"Stop! Don't say anymore, please," implored my dear girlfriend.

I didn't, and we searched the web for a moment, without finding any allusions of the death of either of them, which did reassure us a bit, I had to admit.

Then we wrote an email to both of them.

FROM: COLOMBE.DESCHAMPS@GMAIL.COM

To:nathaliewurtz@laposte.net greglabrousse007@yahoo.fr

. . .

Subject: Give us some news

Hi Nathalie and Gregory.

I hope both of you are doing well since our vacation in Deshaies. And believe me, I'm not just trying to be polite here!

I don't know if you know this, but I regret to have to tell you that some of our fellow vacationers have passed away: Bruce, Naima and Jacques.

That could seem improbable but it's the sad truth and reality. All three of them died within a couple of days, in three different cities. Don't you think that's strange and eerie?

If you're fine, please give us some news. Here, we're doing well, at least for now...

You can just respond to this mail or call us on 07. 24. 54. 40...

Hope to hear from you soon,

. . .

Colombe and Jerome.

The mail flew into the limbo of the web at the same time as our hopes of receiving some good news from them. Should that happen, we'd certainly end up by calming down, abandoning our apprehension.

A few minutes later, just as it was starting to get dark in our living room, Colombe's phone rang. She picked up, recognizing the number, and put it on the speakerphone.

"Thanks for calling me back, Mr. Boisjoli."

"My pleasure. How can I help you? Do you need a telephone session?"

"No, not at all, thanks. I don't know if you remember, just a couple of weeks ago we attended one of your sessions in a cave near Hell's Gate, with our hosts, Eusebius Sainte-Rose and Severine Rocamora, from Deshaies."

"Of course I remember. And? Did your wish come true? I hope so, because I don't do any after-sales service! Guaranteed success!"

"Well, actually that's what's worrying me."

"What do you mean?"

"Remember, we were in a small group."

"I remember. And?"

"Um... in that group, three of the members died since they came back."

"Jesus, Mary and Joseph!" exclaimed the witch-doctor (and I could imagine him crossing himself). "That's awful. How could that be possible?"

"That's exactly the question that's been eating away at me for the past couple of days. I'd hoped you could help me find a rational explanation."

"I would love to, but I don't see how."

I sent signs of encouragement to Colombe, to urge her to continue in that line of thought.

"Well, actually you're not going to be astonished, but I thought that maybe, one of the participants in our group could have asked you to do away with some other members of the group. And as you're the only one who heard those secrets whispered to you, you're the only one who can tell us if this is true."

"Miss Colombe," the witchdoctor burst out, "do you what professional secrecy means?"

Colombe made a face. "*Him a professional*?" she murmured to me. "*A quack, yes.*"

"Of course I do! I'm a journalist."

On the other end of the line, the other side of the ocean, we could detect a troubling hesitation in him.

"That doesn't give you all the rights though."

"I didn't say it did, don't worry. Yeah, I don't want to violate anyone's professional secrecy, Mr. Boisjoli, but could you just give me a yes or no answer if someone in our group asked you... to cause the death of some of us?"

There was a heavy silence on the line before the Guadeloupean witchdoctor replied.

"No one had that type of wish at all, I can swear it on my honor and on the spirits of my ancestors."

"Nor a type of serious disease or something like that?"

"Believe me Miss," continued Jean-Felix in a nearly bored voice, "the wishes your group told me were nothing special, you can believe me. Plus, with what I was paid, you couldn't have expected any miracles from me... You know that spirits are greedy."

"You were paid?"

"That's how I make my living!"

"I can't remember having paid anything though."

"You didn't."

"Who did then?"

"Your generous hosts, Eusebius and Severine. I gave them a discount though."

"Was this a 'planned event?'"

"You could say that, it was an authentic Guadeloupean experience. But be careful! *Quimbois* is serious. I have to go now, I've got a client. Take care of yourself, Miss."

WE HUNG up hoping that his last words were prophetic.

CHAPTER 33
Under pressure

Deshaies, March 15, 2020

His T-shirt open, a brush cutter hooked to his body by a harness, Eusebius walked out of the garden shed adjacent to their house. When he walked in front of the patio, he saw his wife sitting at their kitchen table, with sheets of paper in front of her. Severine was sitting straight up on the chair, the palms of her hands on the piles of sheets of paper, looking out over the horizon. Eusebius thought she hadn't even noticed that he was there, despite the noise that his safety shoes made on the gravel-covered path, shoes that he always wore when trimming the many weeds surrounding the paths.

"Hun?" he said.

No reaction.

"Hey hey! Anyone home?"

Severine gasped.

"What? Oh, it's you."

"Who were you expecting? Our clients are out and about. I'm going to trim the weeds. We're you supposed to go to the grocery store?"

"Maybe, but I have to finish studying first."

He opened his eyes wide, astonished.

"Studying what?"

His wife sighed.

"Are you crazy or what? Studying for final exams, they're in two weeks."

Had his brush cutter not been hooked to his hips and shoulders, it would have fallen from his hands.

"Final exams? You sure you don't got a sunstroke? What are you talking about?"

Severine closed her eyes and put her hands on her forehead, shaking her head.

"Jesus Christ, just leave me alone, will you? I'm not going to graduate if you don't let me study!"

Eusebius put the garden tool down and joined his wife on the patio, walking up to her to put his arms around her shoulders in an affectionate gesture.

"Calm down, honey. Maybe you didn't tell me

everything. Did you sign up for the exam on your own, is that it?"

His wife shook his hands from her shoulders.

"Of course not! We're already December 31st and the exam is for January 14th."

"Severine... Today is March 15... You're not making any sense. I think you had better rest a bit, these last few weeks have been exhausting for you.

Both for work as well as for emotions, thought Eusebius for himself, noting his wife's absent regard.

"I don't have time to rest, I still have to go over all my French literature notes, I've got fifty of them to study."

Severine's voice was now shrill, a sign that she was really under pressure.

"Why don't you just lie down for a moment in the hammock," he suggested softly to her.

"No time! Just look, it's right here on my calendar: final exams on January 14, 2011! You can read, can't you?"

"Excuse me for insisting, but... I think you're about ten years late for your exams. We're in 2020!"

Eusebius looked down at the sheets of paper spread around on the table. There were invoices, guidebooks for the island, posters, nothing at all on French literature notes nor the 2010-2011 academic year, like his wife had told him.

He discreetly sniffed his wife's breath to make sure it wasn't filled with rum, something that could possibly explain her spaciotemporal ravings and ramblings. Picking her up under her armpits, he took her inside their house, to their bedroom. She allowed herself to be taken there, without opposing any resistance. When he put her down on the bed, her pressure seemed to break and she began to sob.

"I'll never pass, I'll never pass those exams. I'm so exhausted. I just want 2010 to be over with. I can't do this anymore."

Then she closed her eyes and fell asleep. Eusebius put a sheet over her now peaceful body and then went back to the patio, again looking over the papers scattered on the table.

He didn't like that. Seeing her like that reminded him of too many bad memories. In the past, he'd known how to calm his wife down, how to reassure her, how to help her forget her past. How to distance the demons who populated her souvenirs.

That day he knew that another one of her attacks was imminent. Something he didn't like, not at all...

CHAPTER 34

And those rumors

Gueret, March 16, 2020

"We're at war!"

In bed, Nathalie, like most people in France, was watching President Macron's speech on television. Despite having a pounding headache, she had been trying to count the number of times the president used the "we're at war" formula. Three, four? She'd lost track of it, bothered by the President's slight lips and tiny space between his two front teeth, something that disturbed the harmony of his face. Nathalie had always been much more attentive to what was visible rather than its content, to appearance rather than a deep meaning. Something that had caused her a couple of problems in the past, but that was her personality, what could she do about it?

She loved Italian Renaissance painters, she had a cult for perfection and had trouble integrating the idea that such perfection could neither be human nor could it be natural. And she never bought into the trend that stated that differences, imperfections, and singularities were what created true beauty. For Nathalie, being good-looking meant being perfect.

She'd done several quick sketches of President Macron in her sketchbook that was on the bed next to her. She wasn't inspired that evening.

"We're at war!" repeated the President, bringing Nathalie back to the here and now.

She stopped watching the speech and picked up her phone which was on the bedside table, suddenly thinking of the email she'd received that afternoon from Colombe, that charming young lady she'd meet in Gwada.

She had trouble believing what she'd read. How could she imagine that three of their fellow vacationers had lost their lives so suddenly? She'd thought back on their vacation, remembering some of the details, but couldn't find a thing that could explain that triple tragedy.

"Hi Colombe, it's Nathalie. I'm glad to hear you're doing well. And Jerome?"

"We're both fine, thanks. What about you?"

"Actually I've been a bit under the weather for the past couple of days. I've got a sore throat, a runny nose and a slight fever too."

"Shoot... I hope you didn't catch that virus that seems to be all over," replied Colombe. "It's so scary."

"I hope not," whined Nathalie. "I've got a doctor's appointment tomorrow morning, I'll see what he says. The worst part is that I'm nauseous plus I've got such a headache, like a sledgehammer pounding in my head. Colombe, do you think that Naima, Jacques and Bruce could have caught the virus too?"

"You mean that they died from it?"

"It is a really anxiogenic situation. I should turn off the news completely, but it's so omnipresent that everyone's talking about it. So of course, you think of things, you imagine the worst-case scenario... And all these rumors about the virulence and transmissibility... Just imagine..."

She suddenly quit speaking.

"If what?" asked Colombe.

"Well, I mean we were in close contact with all three of them, like we were all together just a couple of days ago, And... we didn't take any precautions."

She suddenly thought of her nocturnal antics with Eusebius. And tried to mentally push them away.

At the other end of the line, Colombe's face suddenly turned ashen gray, frightened by Nathalie's alarming words. Perhaps the explanation is that simple, she wondered. Maybe they all caught that new virus going around.

"And when you take into account the incubation period that the experts all talk about, it could correspond," continued Nathalie, her eyes looking at the slightly too wide space between Macron's teeth.

She'd put the TV on mute and couldn't tell what he was saying. Anyway his speech was subtitled by some AI software.

"Those two weeks of incubation?" Colombe continued.

She did some mental math. Jerome and herself were right in the middle of the interval where symptoms could declare themselves.

"You should go get tested, you two," Nathalie warned. "At least, to reassure yourselves."

She hung up a few minutes later after talking about their recently departed fellow vacationers and said she certainly hoped that they both were staying well and promised to give her the results of her doctor's appointment.

THAT NIGHT, after Nathalie's call, neither of us could sleep. Like she'd instilled a deadly poison in us.

A poison that was running through our veins, our brains, one that couldn't be dissolved, coagulating our emotions. We now could think of nothing else than that horrible epidemic that was starting to spread throughout the world.

We hoped we'd be reassured tomorrow.

CHAPTER 35

I'm a monster

Deshaies, March 16, 2020

Severine seemed to be feverish. Closely watched over by her husband, for the past couple of hours she had been spitting incoherent words out. Eusebius had taken her temperature though and it seemed normal. The flames eating away at her came from elsewhere, much farther than the trivial present.

He'd brought her a weak grog, but she hadn't touched it.

"You're worrying me," he said to her. "You're worrying me."

"Why didn't you help me?" Severine moaned. She was lying on her left side, immobile, her eyes gazing at something in the distant. "Bring me my lit notes, now!"

"Right now you have to sleep. Tomorrow I'll bring you all your notes and I'll help you study," said Eusebius, entering into Severine's folly.

She turned around and was now on her right side, her back facing her husband, who was tenderly running his fingers through her hair.

"I didn't help you? Are you joking? I was always there for you, when you had the blues, you're unfair."

His voice was trembling, slightly higher than in his first sentence. Her head was rocking slowly and regularly, just like a metronome indicating whole notes.

She turned around again.

"You're right, excuse me. "You're the only *girl* who understands me."

"Severine?" murmured Eusebius, worried. "What is going on?"

He put his finger on her forehead. No fever. He looked into the whites of her eyes. As if no one was home. She continued her unsettling soliloquy.

"It's normal, you know that you and I are inseparable. You're everything for me, I told you that a million times! 'I'm you, you're me.'"

"I'm you, kill me."

"Why do you want me to kill you?

"Because I don't deserve to live, I'm a monster!"

"No! Don't say that. It hurts me too much."

"I'm a monster, I'm a monster."

"Stop! I'm suffering for you and as you're me, I'm you, I'm suffering for myself. Get that? So just stop..."

SEVERINE'S VOICE, distance, got softer and softer until she sighed, and her eyelids closed, something Eusebius welcomed with relief and her irregular breathing calmed down, her light snores seemed to be taking her towards a good sleep.

Eusebius laid down next to her, thinking, worrying. How long has it been since she'd been like that? Eight years? Ten years?

Whatever, he didn't want to go through hell again with her.

CHAPTER 36

May he rest in peace

Biscarrosse, March 17, 2020

We had to fill out the now unfortunately famous and omnipresent derogatory authorization to leave our home, checking the "doctor's appointment" reason. As of today at noon, France was on a strict lockdown, and any time you left your home you could be stopped by the cops and fined, if you didn't have that paper on you with a valid reason checked for being outside.

Dr. Vincent Beluche, our GP, quickly reassured us; we hadn't developed any clinical signs of that terrible virus everyone was talking about.

"I can understand that you're worried," he

concluded, behind his FFP2 mask, "if you'd been in contact like you said, with certain people during your vacation. Individuals who told you they had the typical symptoms of the coronavirus flu: fever, terrible headaches, sore throats, all that. You said you were in the tropics, is that right?"

"Yes, in Guadeloupe," I confirmed. "Why?"

"Because some of those symptoms you mentioned could also be infectious tropical diseases."

"Such as?"

"There are loads of them, caused by bacteria, viruses, or mosquitoes. Here I'm thinking of malaria, dengue, yellow fever, and leishmaniasis, just to mention a few."

"And they're mortal?"

"They can be of course, like any disease. In today's modern society, most people think that medicine can cure all, but believe me, that's false! Human beings are just vulnerable animals faced with nature. Luckily though, we've developed a host of vaccines and treatments."

Then I told our doctor that three of the people we were on vacation with had died since we'd returned.

"Ah! In that case, it is worrying. Either it's a huge coincidence, or you have to look elsewhere to explain it. But that's something I can't do."

"Should we do a Covid test?" asked Colombe, coming back to the reason she went to see him.

"There's a terrible shortage of tests. You don't have any clinical signs of the disease, so don't worry, I'm sure you're not carriers. Plus the incubation period is over, so it would be useless. Make sure you follow all the health recommendations, stay at home as much as possible, wait till this storm passes over, that'll be enough to protect you. Could I have your insurance card? That'll be fifty euros."

THE SAME DAY, to give us a break, we filled out a new authorization paper, this time to take advantage of the one-hour break allowing us to go outside within a half-mile radius of our home. We luckily lived near a forest, something that allowed us to enjoy fresh air and allowed us to take our masks off.

As we were walking hand-in-hand, Colombe's phone rang. It was Nathalie asking about us but also telling us she was feeling worse and worse. Her headaches were intensifying, her nausea also. Her doctor had prescribed a bunch of strong medication and ordered her to stay at home in bed as much as possible. As she was on speakerphone, I noted how weak her voice was, I could tell she was exhausted with each sentence she uttered. She was fatidic.

"I don't know if I'll make it this time," she moaned.

"Come on, Nathalie! Don't say foolish things like that," Colombe tried to reassure her.

"Foolish things? I'm sick as a dog, there's this fucking virus hanging over our heads like the sword of Damocles... And Naima's death, you think that's foolish too? And Jacques's? And Bruce's? Nonsense? No! That's sad reality, and I'll be the next one."

She burst into tears. It was hard to find words that were sufficiently comforting for her, especially so far away. She bizarrely tried to reassure us then.

"We did have a last fantastic vacation though, didn't we? Especially as it didn't cost much!"

I wondered where she was going with that remark, remembering all the expenses on my credit card, both for accommodations, the flight, and parking at the airport.

"It was a fantastic vacation," Colombe approved. "But what do you mean by 'it didn't cost much?'"

"I had a fantastic deal! All I had to pay for was the flight, and even then I had a deal so you can believe me when I say I hardly spent anything."

I suddenly remembered a brief conversation with Jacques, one afternoon at the poolside, where he'd also insinuated that the vacation hadn't cost him much either, some great deal. A curious coincidence, once again, that sparked a question.

"Natalie?" I said into Colombe's phone. "It's Jerome here. I've been listening in. What was that fantastic deal you were talking about? Who sponsored it?"

She tried to think.

"You know with this headache, it's not too clear, plus that dates back several months now. But I remember I received a letter."

"An email?"

"No, snail mail, something that arrived in my mailbox. A flyer on glossy paper, one that was full of photos of Gwada, a program of what we'd do there, and also details of their commercial offer. Something you couldn't resist."

"Man, too bad I didn't get one too. But I would have said to myself that it was a scam, you know they hook you in with a low price but sell you something expensive when you're there. A tourist trap."

"For sure, only paying three hundred euros for a great week's all-inclusive vacation in Guadeloupe, it was iffy. But you know, it made me think of the eighties. You're probably too young to have experienced that. But me, I was between ten and fifteen and my grandpa often took me with him on trips that were organized by bus, because my grandma didn't like traveling. We went to the mountains in Switzerland, to Costa Brava, to Germany, lots of other places and I can never thank him too much, may he rest in peace. He's the one who made me like traveling. Anyway, I'm getting off track here with my souvenirs. Turnkey trips like that were generally sponsored by companies, stores that sold wine or mattresses, stuff like that, and they paid for most of the expenses in exchange for sales presentations on-site, where they were hoping to sell a maximum of boxes of wine or their bedding, and they delivered that when you returned. Not such an idiotic economic model if you think of it."

"You're right, I've heard of it. So for Gwada, their flyer was a sponsored one like that?"

"Spot on!"

"And what company sponsored it?"

"If I remember correctly, it was a brand of diving equipment."

"But once we were there, we didn't have any demonstration meetings where they showed us their products, right?"

"Hmm! You're right, I didn't even think of that."

I remembered our activities in our Guadeloupean week.

"The only link we had with diving..."

"Was with Jean-Pierre..." said Natalie, completing my sentence pensively.

CHAPTER 37

Looking farther

Sainte-Rose, March 18, 2020

The electric catamaran tapped softly against the landing at Sainte-Rose. The port was nearly deserted, upsetting poor Jean-Pierre, whose sad eyes looked out over the sea, towards the coral reef. All the sea outings for tourists were finished, they'd all gone back home. The same was true for diving trips to Malendure. Adieu the cocktails well laced with rum on the boat anchored near Caret Islet. The official hour in which French people were allowed to leave their homes was just enough for him to go to the port, make sure his boat was fine and then return home.

His phone rang, pulling him out of his nostalgic contemplations.

“JP Excursions, how can I help you?”

“Hi Jean-Pierre, this is Jerome Bastaro, do you remember me?”

“Of course! One of Eusebius’s guests! The group with little Naima… How could I forget you?”

“That’s true,” nodded the journalist. “I hope you’re doing well, despite the circumstances.”

“It’s calm here,” sighed the diving instructor.

“Same here, it’s weird. But I didn’t call you to get news about the lockdown in Gwada, but because I had a question.”

“Fire away.”

“I wanted to know if you knew of any voyages that brands of diving equipment sponsored.”

Jean-Pierre, surprised by that question, didn’t answer immediately.

“What do you mean by that?”

Jerome explained the economic model that Nathalie had talked about the day before as well as the flyers she’d received and asked him if he knew of that on the island.

“Frankly, never heard of anything like that around here. At least not around me. That probably exists down by Saint-Francois, where there's much more mass tourism. But on Basse-Terre, no. How come?"

The journalist gave him his sources.

"Do you remember Nathalie?"

"That lady who never stopped drawing? The artist?"

"That's right. She apparently had the same fantastic deal as Jacques to go to Gwada. So I thought you might know something about it."

"I plead not guilty!" joked Jean-Pierre. "Speaking of which, how's she doing?"

"Not too well, poor lady. But when you compare her with the others..."

And what Bastaro then told him was enough to definitively sap his morale, which had already been pretty low.

"My friend, we're not out of the woods yet..."

~

As soon as he'd hung up from his conversation with Jerome Bastaro, Jean-Pierre scrolled down his list of contacts to find Eusebius Sainte-Rose's number. He didn't pick up when he called, but worried by the message his friend had left, Eusebius called him back ten minutes later.

"What's the rush, JP?"

"Strange news from metropolitan France. I thought you knew about it."

"Knew about what?"

"That three of your guests died! What did you do? You poisoning your vacationers now?"

"You're crazy JP! What the heck are you talking about?"

The diving instructor told him about the conversation he'd just had with Jerome.

"Jesus, Mary and Joseph! he exclaimed, crossing himself.

The two men talked about the news they'd just had, something that bothered both of them. Then Jean-Pierre told him why he had called him, about a possibly sponsored vacation.

"Did you know about that?" he asked, after having summed up what Bastaro had told him.

"I still have no idea what you're talking about JP."

"If I remember correctly, you're the one who asked me if I had any tips about printing out flyers. And I told you to contact one of my friends, Euclyde, who works in a printing shop in Pointe à Pitre. I think that was end of last year."

Eusebius thought back.

"You're right, I did. Now I remember. Severine

wanted to have some stuff printed professionally. You know, she's the one who takes care of all that stuff and all the paperwork. She's got the brains, I've got the muscles!"

"So she could have had a flyer like that printed?"

"It's possible, but I didn't hear anything about it. And I think it was just a new batch of advertising flyers for our resort. I knew that she was going to have some printed, I'm sure we must have talked about that. But I didn't take care of anything."

Jean-Pierre ironically cut him off.

"My friend, you wanna know what I think?"

"Tell me."

"I think there are things you better start taking care of."

CHAPTER 38

Vanished into thin air

Biscarrosse, March 19, 2020

Days went by, each as gray and sad as the others. We both of course were forced to work from home, not changing too much actually, though our hearts were no longer into what we were doing. Especially as we kept on thinking about the recent events that had affected our fellow vacationers. Their deaths, their illnesses, that too-good-to-be-true deal they'd had, all of that made a strange, tangled mess in our brains and demoralized us both.

"What link can there be between the victims?" asked Colombe for the umpteenth time.

"Now you're calling them victims? Meaning you think there's someone behind all that? A guilty party?"

"Right now I don't think anything at all. You can be a victim of lots of things: a victim of your success, an expiratory victim, victim of a disease..."

"Victim of luck or misfortune," I continued. "Why do you persist in wanting to link Naima's Jacques's and Bruce's deaths? They don't have the same profile, they don't live in the same place, we don't even know what they actually died from either. They probably don't have a thing in common."

"But they do. All three of them were on vacation at the same time in the same place. And what do you think of Natalie's health, she seems to be getting worse? Maybe she's the next one on the list?"

"What list? Jesus Christ, that makes no sense at all."

"There must be some sort of thing linking them together and that's what I want to find out. Who the heck sent out those flyers, what was in them and what could that mean?"

"We're not sure of anything at all. Natalie talked about them and Jacques just mentioned them. As for all the others, we have no idea if they got one too."

"Maybe we could ask that Adele lady, you know, Naima's partner, if she knows anything about that."

"Why not? But how are you going to contact her?"

"Using Naima's email."

"But she said it was obsolete now."

"That doesn't mean she disactivated it. Nothing ventured, nothing gained."

Putting her money where her mouth was, Colombe sent off an email to the attention of Adele, asking her if she'd heard anything about some vacation deal and asking her, if she read the message of course, to please call her on the phone number she'd given.

While she was online, she sent another email to Gregory, the person no one had heard from ever since they all returned from Guadeloupe. Up till now, he hadn't replied to any messages nor tried to reach anyone. We looked around on the web, but didn't see anything that had mentioned that the good-looking bad boy had either disappeared or had passed.

"Strange," I said. "He seems to have vanished into thin air, that Gregory."

"Your conclusions?"

"I've got two hypotheses, in the light of what we know now. Either he's dead, but that we don't know... or..."

Colombe didn't interrupt that heavy silence. But what she must have been thinking about didn't look rosy.

"Or?" I invited her to continue her line of thought.

"Or Gregory for some reason or the other, wants to be very discreet."

CHAPTER 39

The smell of blood

Gueret, December 2004

Though he wasn't consciously aware of it, what he like the best when he went to see his dad's laboratory in the back of the shop was the smell of blood.

Gregory had grown up in the middle of cadavers of animals, with blood dripping down from the cutting block into the gutters and finally ending up in aluminum pails. A good butcher, like his father was – and his butcher's shop was right in downtown Gueret – never liked to waste any merchandise. The blood he recovered found its way into spicy black blood pudding that he made himself, and that his customers lined up to buy every Sunday morning. Pork was the most profitable animal, from an economic point of view. Wasn't there an old saying: you can eat everything but the oink! And it was true, from its snout to its tail, from its feet to its ears, you could consume everything! And sometimes even its skeleton was used to make toys for children. Once the little bones in its feet, the ankle-bone and tarsi were cleaned, washed and scrubbed, little kids loved to play jacks with them.

Yet the butcher sometimes had to throw several pieces away - bones, fat, skins, some innards - in the huge dumpster next to the butcher's shop, in the alley. For a professional, it was heart-breaking to waste animals like that, as well as a terrible stench for the passersby on the sidewalk. In the summer when it was scorching hot, you either had to plug your nose or quit breathing when you walked by the dumpster where the waste was fermenting.

Young Gregory couldn't have cared less. A whiff of blood and rotten meat didn't bother him in the least, he'd grown up with those odors, like Moroccan kids who played in the courtyards of tanneries in Marrakesh. One day, he decided to play a joke on one of his classmates. The one he delicately had nicknamed the "Monster," that girl with that ugly scar under her nose that disfigured her. That day then, Greg went up to the dumpster, lifted the cover up without even pinching his nose and climbed up into it, amongst the plastic bags, to rip one of them open and pull a bloody rabbit's head out.

Perfect, he thought, proud of himself. That head with its glassy eyes would do the trick. He stuffed it into his schoolbag.

During the last course of the day, a math class, he succeeded in performing his own little magic trick, transferring the rabbit's head into the Monster's schoolbag.

What a surprise she'd have!

CHAPTER 40

A whole different kettle of fish

Biscarrosse, March 21, 2020

We had just gone from winter to spring, as seasons invariably changed every three months. Nothing new in the world. In our remote investigation though, we had an interesting new element that day.

Colombe's phone rang, displaying an unknown caller.

"Miss Dechamps?" asked a feminine voice. "This is Adele Petrus, I'm Naima's partner, you sent me a message two days ago."

"I did and thanks so much for calling me back. Let me start by telling you how sorry I am for your loss, it's terrible."

She sighed deeply and noisily.

“Thanks. I hesitated before calling. Then I said to myself that maybe we could pool our efforts to try to understand why Naima died. You must have elements that I don’t have, I mean after all, you were one of the last people with her over there.”

“But what did she die from?” Colombe asked respectfully.

“Everything went so fast...”

Then the dam broke, liberating a swell of hiccups and tears.

“Take your time,” Colombe said softly.

It took Adele a good minute before she was able to speak.

“When she got back from vacation, she was really tired. I knew that she had had a diving accident there, and that it had really impacted her. But I don’t think that could have explained her death. The day after she got back, she started to have a high fever and horrible headaches, ones that made her cry with pain. I took her to E.R... but she never came back from the hospital.”

Once again she sobbed, then paused.

“What did the doctors say?”

“They said it might be meningitis.

I made a face. If I remembered correctly, meningitis was a childhood disease. When I was little, one of my friends died from it.

"And how was it caused?" asked Colombe.

"They weren't categorical on that question but seeing as how she just got back from a tropical island, they thought it could be a meningitis infection. But not everyone agreed."

"Really?"

"Yeah, some of the professors, because of Naima's abdominal pains, thought that maybe she could have been poisoned."

That word was like an unexpected slap in the face.

"Poisoned?" exclaimed Colombe. "What poison?"

"They did tests, but they couldn't find anything."

We didn't know what to think. Had she died from poisoning, we had to find out what our two other fellow vacationers died from. But that would be a whole different kettle of fish, especially now as France was still on a very strict lockdown.

Colombe changed subjects.

"Miss Petrus? Would you still have that vacation deal flyer I talked about in my email? The one that Naima had received and answered to take advantage of that super price?"

"I found it, yes. I could scan it or send it to you as an MMS."

"Thanks."

"No problem. If that could help..."

"I'll let you know. Ah! One last thing. Perchance, can you remember anything that Naima told you about her vacation? Even if it seems idiotic, you never know. Every detail counts."

Adele thought for a moment before answering.

"Nothing really precise. We talked on the phone regularly, she sent me a postcard where she described a guy named Gregory who seemed to want to be very good friends with her, if you see what I'm getting at, but she pushed him away."

"True, he was pretty, what can I say? Persistent!" Colombe remembered. "Anything else?"

"Now that I think about it, she also talked about your host, a lady named Severine. Someone that impressed her apparently."

"How?"

"Because she vaguely made her think of someone. A girl she knew when she was a teen and lived in Strasbourg. Someone she was friends with but the year after she lost sight of. Just like Severine, that girl had an ugly scar on her upper lip. That why the resort owner in Guadeloupe troubled her. Naima even wondered if that Severine could be that girl she was friends with when she was in middle school."

"Was her friend also named Severine?"

"No, Naima couldn't recall her first name, but she was sure it wasn't Severine, that's what bothered her. She said it was something less common. Or maybe that friend changed names, changed her identity for some obscure reason."

More mystery for that unclear and bizarre story.

We thanked Adele for calling us in those trying moments, assured her once again of our profound sympathy and said we were looking forward to receiving that flyer.

"A SCAR ON HER LIPS, a change of identity?"

"This is getting curiouser and curiouser," I confirmed.

CHAPTER 41

The age of cruel abandonments

STRASBOURG, March 21, 2009

THAT DAY, March 21, 2009, all over in France people were dying, children were being born, people were falling in love while others were breaking up. Some were failing exams, others were signing contracts. Athletes were winning races, others were losing. Couples were being formed, friendships were budding, others were taking their distances, sometimes slowly, sometimes by slamming doors.

In one of the middle schools in Strasbourg, a young girl was sad because of a friendship she'd lost. And Naima felt guilty about being the one who had made her cry. But that was the sad truth about childhood and adolescence. The age of huge promises and cruel abandonments. The age of construction and destruction. The time of alliances and separations. But had she really had the choice in her decision? She wanted to persuade herself of the opposite, but deep down inside Naima knew that you always had a choice. You had free will in your convictions, the option of voluntary renunciation or loyalty.

The teen had thus chosen to abandon the girl who considered her as being her best friend, her Scheherazade, her fairy tale princess.

Scheherazade had closed the book of *One Thousand and One Nights* on the fragile fingers of her friend. She'd chosen the other side, the scoffers. She'd preferred to integrate the clan of mockery, those who got together to ostracize those who were weak, those who were different. In a group you always felt stronger. Without realizing that you also became idiotic, saying things, doing things, acts that would never take place had you been alone. That was the toxic effect of being in a group.

Naima had chosen that group. And she'd abandoned the Monster with her zigzagged mouth.

Without thinking of the consequences, without imagining the horrific psychological violence of her act.

Without realizing – at least not then – that her

choice would impact the future of that poor girl for the rest of her life. What Naima had put in motion by her decision was a mere stone that had fallen from that unstable building, one that just a few years later, would tumble down.

CHAPTER 42

A deeper neurosis

Deshaies, March 21, 2020

That March 21st, 2020, in a bungalow in a little town in Basse-Terre, Guadeloupe, a lady was delirious on her bed, surrounded by her husband and their friend, Dr. Lamblin, from Deshaies, whom he'd called, saying it was an emergency.

The doctor had just examined her and was getting ready to put his equipment back in his leather bag. He took Eusebius's arm and walked outside of the bedroom with him, as Severine peacefully had fallen asleep, with the help of the tranquilizers he'd given to her in an intravenous.

"Eusebius, I can't do anymore for her, I'm sorry."

Those words penetrated his heart just like poisoned arrows. His mouth immediately dried up, stifling the words bouncing around in his head. It took him a couple of seconds before he could speak.

"What do you mean, Alex? What's wrong with her? Don't tell me it's that fucking virus everyone is talking about?"

The doctor raised his hand to calm him.

"No! Don't worry about that. It was my fault, I wasn't clear. What I meant was that Severine's pathology is outside of my skills."

"Is it serious then?"

"I can't affirm anything, I'm just a GP. And what Severine is suffering from exceeds what us family doctors were trained for. Your wife seems to be delusional. I think you have to convince her to see a psychiatrist."

"A shrink?"

Another word that troubled his thoughts.

"Eusebius let's not lie to ourselves. We all know what happened to her. You haven't forgotten I'm sure how she was when you two first met. How long ago was it already?"

"Nearly ten years ago. In 2010, when Severine first came to Gwada. It's true that I sort of scraped her off the ground, like the saying goes."

"And at that time, shouldn't she have consulted one of my colleagues? Things were pretty confused in her little head. Did she ever tell you why?"

Eusebius sighed, showing his helplessness.

"No, she didn't. She was always really vague about her life in France but it's true that it must have been tough for her."

Dr. Lamblin nodded, understanding.

"Had she consulted a professional at that time, maybe we could have avoided her hospitalization. And potentially avoided her suicide attempt. But what's done can't be undone," said the doctor, philosophically. "Anyway, thanks to your love for her and your project of a resort, you can be proud of yourself for having helped her get better. Till today. Until this sudden relapse. Eusebius, what could have happened that could have made her delirious again?"

"I have no idea. Do you think it could have stemmed by this unprecedented and unnerving lockdown, everyone's fear of the virus and of death?"

"Of course, all of that impacts the morale people have. We'll soon be having a wave of depressions, that's for sure. But here, I'm not seeing a mere depression she's having, but a deeper neurosis, as if it had recently been triggered by something. She was perfectly fine when you called me here to examine your renter, that young lady who had a diving accident in Malendure."

"Naima," confirmed Eusebius. "And you're right, Severine was fine then. It was only after that she started acting strangely. Like she'd be absent, she would lock herself for hours in her office."

"Anything abnormal happen that you remember?"

Eusebius thought back to his souvenirs of that week.

"Frankly, that week was nearly like all the other weeks when we have guests here, and I would even say that Severine outdid herself in organizing all sorts of outings and activities for our guests. Sort of like she'd known them before, old school friends, something like that. I'd never seen her so exhilarated as then."

"Maybe it's biting her in the ass now," Dr. Lamblin said.

"I hope she'll be better soon."

"Eusebius? Listen, here's the number of one of the doctors I know in Pointe à Pitre, a psychiatrist. Call him and tell him it's an emergency. Friendly advice."

CHAPTER 43

Too good to be true

Biscarrosse, March 22, 2020

The weather could have sucked! On the contrary though, the imposed French lockdown began with nice weather, a small consolation that helped us endure that unprecedented ordeal. Work went on for Colombe and I: each of us worked on feature articles and analyses for magazines that employed us both as freelance service providers. Having something to do allowed us to forget while working the apprehension we had about those mysterious deaths amongst our fellow vacationers.

Yet the message that Colombe received on her

phone that afternoon placed us in the heart of the subject.

Adele Petrus, Naima Bentallah's partner, had sent us an attachment. It was that flyer that Naima had received in the mail. Her name was mentioned in the body of the ad, in a very attractive tagline:

"Miss Bentallah, how about a dream week in one of the most beautiful islands in the Caribbean?"

I wasn't at all astonished here, it was just an IT merger between a source document and a database, a file of leads that probably came from some rented or purchased mailing list.

After that tempting formula, the document had a series of high-definition photos, probably from some free image bank – and we also used them sometimes in our magazine articles – to amplify and generate a desire to travel.

Between the pictures there was a list of not-to-be-missed sites: of course, Soufriere Hills volcano, the mangrove, Caret Islet, and Malendure and Bois-Jolan beaches.

On the back page of the flyer they had listed the conditions of that exceptional offer, one you couldn't pass by, according to them. The price included: accommodations in a bungalow, a category B car rental at the airport, activities during the week including a morning of diving that was sponsored by a certain brand of equipment. The only thing that the traveler had to pay was the flight to and from Guadeloupe, and even then there was a price that had been negotiated.

In a nutshell, the chance of a lifetime… but was it? That was the question that the recipients of that flyer were undoubtedly asking themselves, especially as there was a tiny asterisk referring to a text written in a little font on the bottom of the page:

"THIS EXCEPTIONAL OFFER is only valid FOR ONE person per coupon."

THAT WAS QUITE A STRANGE CLAUSE, probably flying close to the wind in terms of legality and commercial practices. Nevertheless, the discount was so huge – the document summed up the total of services with a 90% discount – that it must have seemed impossible not to buy into it.

To do that, there was just an email that was given and all you had to do was to send the complete document back to reserve your place (and there didn't seem to be many of them) as soon as possible and obtain the information for that stay. The email address bougainvil lea-violette.travel@hotmail.fr, also invited recipients to come, as it was visually spun off as a logo, that represented the violet flower of the Bougainvillea, a plant that originated in the tropics.

"THAT REALLY MAKES you want to sign right away," I concluded. "Hard to resist."

"Frankly, don't you think that's a little too good to be true?" asked Colombe. "I wouldn't trust it. I personally never would have answered an ad like that."

"Cuz you're not a businesswoman! Except when you go window shopping," I joked.

"Very funny, I'm laughing my head off! Seriously though, I wonder where this offer came from. Who's hiding behind that email?

"Bougainvillea violet? That makes me think of something right away, not you?"

"You're right, Bougainvillea Domain, Severine and Eusebius's resort. Except for here, it seems to be some sort of travel agency. There's the word *travel* in the address."

"Okay. But that's not complicated, you can create any email address you want to. And anyway, did you notice that it's not a professional email? Just a simple Hotmail! Behind it maybe there's not even any legal entity, or any website. Had it been done be a pro, they would have given us the name of the domain, something like @bouainvillea.travel.fr. But that's not the case. Plus there would be a URL, a secure https... Serious stuff."

"A lack of seriousness that visibly didn't scare Naima or even Nathalie away. And I bet it was the same for the three others."

We both examined the document when suddenly Colombe leaned down to have a closer look at one of the photos.

"Take a look!" she exclaimed. "Here, on this photo, right behind the palm trees, what do you see?"

"Sand?"

"And?"

"Wooden buildings."

"Behind the red building."

"A white vehicle?"

"That doesn't ring a bell?"

I didn't need to answer that question because I mentally had followed Colombe's line of thought. But I did, in a slow and serious voice, just like a hero in an American thriller.

"Oh, Good Lord, Eusebius's van..."

CHAPTER 44

Below the sparkling varnish

<u>Biscarrosse - Dijon, March 22, 2020</u>

One more coincidence, or was it actually one? Wasn't an accumulation of coincidences evidence?

Each time we made a bit of progress in our research and testimonials, everything seemed to come back to Eusebius and Severine, our two hosts at Bougainvillea Domain in Deshaies. That white van on one of the photos of that attractive flyer with the reference to bougainvillea trees in their contact email made us think that there was some sort of involvement, or at least some probable link with the Guadeloupean couple.

Yet, what could that link be except that they rented bungalows at their resort? That was the question bothering us. We didn't want to think that such a nice and friendly couple could somehow be involved in the death of three vacationers who stayed at their place just a couple of days before. Seriously, we also stayed at their resort, a pleasant one, one that wasn't exactly the Red Inn!

"What about sending a message to the email on the flyer?" proposed Colombe.

"To say what? Is that offer still on the table? Eusebius and Severine, are you the ones hiding behind that underhanded deal for tourists? And by the way, did you have anything to do with Naima, Bruce and Jacques's deaths? Or Nathalie's serious health issues?"

"We can at least see if the email address is still up and running. Nothing ventured, nothing gained."

We thus threw that bottle into the sea, for the want of anything better.

"And if we simply called them?" I suggested. "Rather than imagining who knows what with our outlandish theories, we could just talk to them. And who knows, maybe they could give us a couple of clues or tips."

We only had Severine's phone number, not her husband's. We dialed the ten figures, but it went directly to voicemail. Colombe asked them to call us back.

In the meanwhile, before going outside for our one-hour authorized outing, I wanted to look more closely into Jacques's death, as I'd read that the investigation was ongoing ever since his body had been found at his home, two weeks ago.

What I was to discover though bordered on indecency.

I called Pierre, one of my fellow journalists who lived in Burgundy. He loved fine wines and lived in Dijon.

"Hello old friend, it's Jerome Bastaro. How you doing?"

After having exchanged a few words about the current health crisis, the impossibility of being out and about and our respective conditions, I got down to business about why I'd called him.

"Jacques Damiens's death?" Pierre reformulated. "Funny you're asking me about it, just two days ago I spoke to one of my sources, a cop, an old friend of mine. And let me tell you that his file stinks..."

"Interesting," I said, inviting him to continue.

"Yeah, wait a sec. Your Jacques, with his appearance of a successful businessman, three-piece suit, good-looking old guy, graying hair all combed right in place, nice sports cars and all that... Well, when you scratch that sparkling varnish a bit, you discover an inconceivable darkness, you can believe me."

"Gimme some details, Pierre! This is getting juicy!"

"I'm getting there. The investigators, who by the way still don't know the cause of his death – they'll probably conclude that it was just his time to die, there weren't any traces of any external interventions there – so anyway, the investigators examined his apartment, I'm sure you know that."

"And rightly so. So what did they find?"

"Between the four walls, not too much. But in his computer it was a whole different kettle of fish..."

"Dirty files?"

"You can say that again! That guy, who was a trader in his day job and a guitar instructor during the weekends, had pulled the wool over everyone's eyes. Or at least he presented two very distinct facets, his secret world, very secret, if you see where I'm going."

"Probably. But spit it out Pierre! What did they find?"

"Well, in his browsing history, the investigators found that he often consulted porn sites, up till then, nothing reprehensible, that was his business. The guy lived alone, didn't seem to have any girlfriends and I suppose that every once in a while he felt like getting off in front of his screen."

"Not the first, not the last."

"Right, it's no big deal as long as you watch traditional videos, meaning where two consenting adults are at it."

"But that wasn't all then?"

"It wasn't. That Jacques Damiens we're talking about must have gotten off watching child porn too, and let me tell you, if you're caught you get sent to the pokey for a long while. He luckily died before they caught him."

"If you can call it luck."

"But it fortunately wasn't stuff with little kids. Rather with young adults, see what I mean, though they weren't eighteen. And other videos or sites that proved he was attracted to... monsters."

"Monsters? What do you mean by that?"

"Not the monsters in horror flicks. Just what specialists call 'freaks'. This is the category of sexual videos involving all sorts of abnormal I could say, people, different ones, extraordinary ones. For example, midgets, hunchbacks, guys hung like horses, or the opposite, those with mini penises, legless cripples, harelips, web-footed people, those with spina bifida, girls with dicks, albinos, and I'm sure I'm forgetting a lot of others, believe me."

While Pierre was listing all this, I became more and

more disgusted. I was seeing mental images of Jacques, someone who was so prim and proper in Deshaies, in front of his screen drooling over videos like that.

"Okay Pierre, I get it, you can stop now! In a nutshell, Jacques had sexual penchant for deviants. But only virtually, right?"

"Not so sure of that. In one of his files, well hidden away in the tree structure of his computer, we found some really explicit photos."

"Of him?"

"Well, for that, we'll have to identity the owner of the ding-dong on the pictures. Find out whether it was an image that was uploaded from the web or if it came from a camera or a phone. The investigators are working on that now, especially on one of the images, a close-up of a mouth hard at work..."

CHAPTER 45

A minefield

Dijon, December 2010

The fog-covered evenings in December, something not at all unusual in Dijon, saw many passersby walking down Rue de la Liberté. Groups of high school students, couples, and people leaving their offices strolled down the street with its luminous Christmas decorations. Amongst that urban fauna, there were two lovebirds walking arm in arm, wrapped up in their winter coats. The tall, slim, gray-haired man was proud to have one of his recent conquests on his arm. Yet, she did not quite match the popular beauty standards. The very young lady stood out, compared with the other women he'd seduced.

This time he dared be seen in public with an ordinary girl… ordinary though special. It wasn't their age difference – an ostensible one – that made them stand out, but rather the gap between the way both of them looked. If beauty can actually be judged and measured, that is.

Jacques had proudly been out and about with the high school girl, taking her from shop to shop, buying clothes for her, covering her with gifts. They'd had a whipped cream covered waffle and a glass of mulled wine that burned their hands, but felt so nice in the bitterly cold weather.

After they'd had dinner in one of Dijon's finest restaurants, he brought her back to his house. Something they'd been doing for the past couple of weeks.

On each of these new evenings, he took her a bit further into the discovery of new sensations. He was initiating her on how to let go, inviting her to follow him in his most extreme fantasies. She, who had always doubted someone would be attracted to her, was now a man's center of attention. A mature, experienced, fierce man, one who she was ready to do anything for. Believing he couldn't have cared less about her monstruous appearance, she'd agreed to become his *thing*, as long as he never judged her, never made fun of her, as had so many before him.

That evening in December, he would go a bit farther in the expression of his erotic whims.

The young lady's eyes opened wide when they went into Jacques's room. The man had visibly spiced it up while she was in the bathroom. He'd given an undeniable romantic atmosphere to the bedroom: scented candles giving off dim light, incense that was consuming slowly, and music coming from the speakers that were incorporated into the headboard.

Jacques though had his personal conception of romance, and it wasn't the one that most people would have chosen. He was aware of the influence he had over the young lady, he recognized her weaknesses, her docility, her appetite to give in to each and every one of his desires. She needed to be loved so very much, whatever way love was shown to her!

They went to the edge of the bed. She allowed him to kiss her, to caress her cheek, let the man put his hand around her slender neck, shivering at the idea that he could squeeze it even harder. Jacques then surprised her with his next words.

"Now I'm going to blindfold you. You'll see, it's so exciting."

He continued while doing it.

"When your eyes can't see, you'll have to use your other senses. You'll enter deeply into yourself, you'll feel each of my caresses a hundredfold, each kiss, my teeth nibbling on you, my fingers exploring you, my tongue penetrating you, my breath on your skin, the sweetness of my nectar."

The young, blindfolded lady let herself be carried away by his words.

"Each pore of your skin, each nerve ending will become a cord in the instrument of your pleasure. Remember my fingers when I was playing your guitar. Tonight, you'll be my guitar, I'll make you sing, believe me! Your cords will vibrate under my fingers, with each note I play. Tonight, you'll be my instrument and I'm going to play my whole range of songs."

While he was kissing her neck, she felt the palms of his hands descending her arms. He took her hands and put them behind her back. Then he sat her back up, suddenly spinning her around. She now had her back towards him, her hands joined behind her back, hands he was firmly holding. She heard a clicking sound immediately followed by the contact of cold metal around her wrists.

"What are you..." she began, realizing she was now at his mercy, handcuffed.

"Shhh! Otherwise I'm going to have to gag you. And that's something that I'm not interested in, because I need your mouth... Your unique mouth..."

Now the young lady was visibly shaking, though she didn't say anything else.

"There you go, you're going to be a good girl now, right?"

She nodded, a tamed pet.

Now that she was deprived of her sight, her other senses were waking up. She heard the characteristic noise of a zipper being unzipped, a belt being unbuckled, a snap being opened. Then a softer sound of pants that were falling down over hairy legs, immediately followed by the metallic noise of a belt buckle on the hardwood floor. After that, it was the musky odor of mucosa approaching her face, a masculine smell of bushy hair. The young lady quickly understood what he wanted her to do.

Docile, she opened her mouth.

She first felt the thickness of his member, then the warmth of its thin skin, after that the slightly acrid taste of an intimate tear pearling on its tip.

How can he like doing this with me? she thought to herself, while allowing Jacques's expert hands behind her head guide her, giving her his desired tempo. How can't he be disgusted with my deformed mouth? That upper lip that was split in two and had been poorly sewn back together. That buccal orifice that looked like a minefield or a trench that had been destroyed in a

WWI battle. That was the poor image she had of herself. Comparing herself to a monster. But could someone actually love and desire a monster? Did that person's spirit have to be twisted too to love a girl like her?

Throaty panting drew her from her thoughts. The man visibly appreciated this. He then confirmed it, out of breath.

"Oh! Your mouth, your mouth, it's unique, I love it! Keep on, I've got the impression of penetrating into a monstruous cave."

She had no other choice than to accept those ignoble words. She'd suffered so much, she'd been rejected so much in the past. So to have someone tell her, whatever their motivation was, that she was attractive sufficed for now.

"Come on, yes, pump me my little bunny," Jacques encouraged her.

She suddenly felt him swell with impatience. She wanted to sit up, but the man's hands forced her to accept his last thrusts as he emptied himself into her. She felt nauseous, her mouth twisted itself a bit more, in repulsion.

When he took her blindfold off, she saw that he was holding his phone in one of his hands and that its flash was still activated.

CHAPTER 46

Offline

Biscarrosse, March 22, 2020

We were completely shocked by what our colleague Pierre told us about Jacques Damiens and the photos on his computer. Lightyears away from imagining him like that between the sheets. But then who could boast that they understood their peers in that same situation? When we read the paper it proved that the most innocent, innocuous people could be surprising, once the polish of their appearances was scratched.

I thanked Pierre and asked him to keep me in the loop of any progress in the investigation, if there was any.

"Do you think that his death and those porn photos could be linked? Such a strange underworld," sighed Colombe.

"Unless he died because of a too athletic blow job, I don't know! The investigations seem to be leaning towards a natural death, with no external intervention. Time will tell."

"Do you think that Naima's and Bruce's deaths are linked? Maybe he also received one of those flyers inviting him to Gwada."

"We don't know, and we probably never will, unfortunately."

"Unless the investigators get their hands on that ad at his home. Maybe you could ask Pierre to suggest looking for it."

"You're right, we could," I nodded, texting Pierre.

NIGHT WAS FALLING. We were starving. While continuing to think about all this, we prepared a salad of sautéed potatoes and chicken gizzards, with raspberry vinaigrette. One of our favorite go-to dishes.

"What about Bruce in all that? Like we forgot about him. What did he die from? Did he also get that flyer? And how is he linked to the others, outside of that week of vacation?"

Colombe took out her phone, clicked on the Facebook app, looking for the post mentioning the death of the young surfer, something that a guy named Mehdi Chafik had published.

"I'm going to contact that Mehdi via Messager, hoping he's got something to tell us."

In a couple of lines she resumed how we'd met his friend Bruce and why we wanted to know more about how he died.

The friend in question must have been on his phone as just a few minutes later we got an answer, while we were enjoying our dinner. There was one answer that undeniably did disturb us. He'd written a few polite lines followed by:

"The doctors said that my friend Bruce died because of a type of sudden and acute meningitis."

"Shit!" Colombe swore. "Meningitis, did you see that?"

Of course I did, that wasn't the issue. The problem lied in the fact that Adele, Naima's partner, had also mentioned that very same diagnostic, though the doctors hadn't been able to determine the exact causes for her death.

"You could say that it's another coincidence, but I think we're starting to have a lot of them, don't you?

Could you ask him if Bruce also received one of those fantastic deals for a vacation in Guadeloupe?"

Mehdi replied right away.

"He sure did! He was overjoyed to have received a flyer like that and told me about it. He thought it was some sort of scam though. But I told him to try, you never know. All he had to do was mail the response coupon, nothing difficult. The only constraint though was that it was only a one-person deal. I thought that was a pretty strange clause. And it was too bad because I would have loved to have gone with him. We could have gone surfing together in the West Indies!"

"Let's sum this all up," said Colombe after having hung up. "Naima: receives a flyer, goes to Deshaies, returns, dies with a suspicion of meningitis. Bruce: same thing. Jacques: no idea about the flyer, goes to Deshaies, returns, dies at home of a natural death. Natalie: receives a flyer, goes to Deshaies, returns and gets sick."

"We should call her."

"I'll do it. All that's left is Gregory and we don't have any news of him, like he's gone AWOL ever since coming back to France."

"All of that adds up to quite a few commonalities.

And what to say about Eusebius's van on one of the photos of the flyer and the email address where the word 'bougainvillea' was a part of it?"

We tried to call Severine's cell phone again, no answer, not even a ring tone preceding her voicemail, as if her phone had been cut off, was offline or the battery was dead. In a nutshell, radio silence in Gwada.

"This silence is worrying me," confirmed Colombe.

"Are you worried about them? That they'll be the next victims?"

"No. What I'm afraid of is that they are both involved in these deaths..."

CHAPTER 47

Invaluable sesame

<u>Deshaies, March 22, 2020</u>

The only thing you could hear that night at Bougainvillea Domain was the chirping of the nocturnal birds. In her bedroom, Severine had finally fallen asleep, after hours of feverishly tossing and turning on the bed and an inexhaustible and nearly unintelligible logorrhea. In the midst of that mishmash of words, Eusebius was able to make out a few snippets, thought he recognized names of cities and first names, including that of Nathalie, Jacques and perhaps Gregory. Final exams had also resurfaced with the same date: December 31st.

The Guadeloupean had not left her bedside, holding her hand, running his fingers thought her hair, humidifying her forehead to try to cool the lava burning in her skull.

When he was sure that she'd finally fallen asleep, with the help of a few tranquilizers that the doctor had prescribed, he left the bedroom and pulled the mosquito net around the bed.

He was nibbling on a few accras that were in the fridge when he had an idea. Inspired by a vague intuition, he went into their office, a room that his wife occupied much more than he did. This room was Severine's sanctuary whereas he'd always said he was an outside guy.

Eusebius was wondering about his wife's sudden crisis. What could have triggered it? She hadn't had an acute and strong crisis like that for nearly ten years and he'd imagined that her demons had finally disappeared. Sitting down at the desk, he started to glance at a few papers scattered on it. A couple of invoices, maps for tourists, business cards. Then he opened the drawers, one by one, rummaging around without any plan. That was when he discovered there was one drawer that seemed to be locked. And he had no idea where the key was, especially as he'd never even known that there was a locked drawer. He picked up the files, looked behind the photo frames, without finding a key. Suddenly he had an eureka flash: Severine's breasts.

Not that he was obsessed by his wife's cleavage, though it was nice to look at, but now he was visualizing the necklace she always wore. It was a thick one, shaped like a heart, that looked like it had been made from a polished amethyst, and it opened up like a tiny chest with hinges on it. And in it was a key.

He tiptoed in and unlocked it and with that precious sesame, went back into the office to try to open up that locked drawer. The tiny key penetrated easily into the lock, and he turned it. Inside there was only one object: a black notebook with a hundred or so pages.

Eusebius picked it up, curious, though he had the feeling he was violating his wife's intimacy.

When he opened the thick leather cover, it was as if his brain had fogged up. The front page, with whole sentences crossed out, revealed an undefinable something that curiously concorded with Severine's confused state.

While she was finally sleeping in the adjoining room, Eusebius began to read the dozens of pages of that notebook he'd never seen before.

He recognized Severine's handwriting, though it of course had changed as years had gone by. That being, he'd only known her for ten years and the young lady hadn't told him much about her past. She had hinted though that she'd had a difficult childhood, but now she had the intention of making progress, trying to see the glass half full, forgetting her past and rebuilding her life in Gwada. That was plenty for him, he hadn't tried to pry secrets out of her. For him, the most important thing was to help her reconstruct herself, both physically and morally.

The words that shot up from that notebook, just as black as its cover, unsettled him and took him aback. He read the story of those exams back in 2010, the one that the author of those lines feared so much. He discovered a whole facet of Severine's personality that he'd totally ignored. Who really was that woman, his wife, the person he shared his life with? Who had she been as a child, as a teen, before becoming the adult he'd fallen in love with?

He realized he didn't recognize her... he didn't even *know* her! Did her past determine her present? Was that crisis she was currently undergoing rooted in the issues oozing from that notebook? Eusebius shivered, afraid that this was true.

There was a long groan coming from the bedroom,

followed by footsteps. Eusebius quickly closed the notebook and put it back in the drawer, locking it.

Now he would have to be vigilant, now he'd have to protect her. Protect her from herself as well as from the dark shadows of her past.

CHAPTER 48

With your heart

AUXERRE, March 23, 2020

IN THE AMBULANCE rushing her to the hospital, Nathalie was screaming out in agony, her head pounding, her sinuses ready to implode. How could she possibly bear pain like that?

Before falling into the coma that her brain needed, she saw a flash of another series of images. Can we decide what the last images of our life will be? Some people say that when you're about to die, it's like a feature length film of your whole existence that races by in high speed in your thoughts. For Natalie though, it just was a quick video with a couple of shots.

She had enough time to remember some of the

sketches she did in Guadeloupe, especially the portrait of the owner, that Severine with her scarred lips that had reminded her of a much more ancient image. An image that dated back to her days in school, where one of the students had the same kind of unsightly scar on her upper lip. That scar that had triggered so many jibes and insults from the other students, things that she now regretted to have exacerbated.

Why had she always been so concerned with beauty? Why had she attached so much importance to physical perfection, whereas true beauty always lies elsewhere, someplace in the heart? Now she understood that, though it was too late: you only see things clearly with your heart, not with your eyes.

With her last glints of lucidity, the face of that little schoolgirl in Auxerre and that of her host in Deshaies were superposed one on top of the other, melting into one same person in her ill and foggy brain.

Just a few seconds before she closed her eyes for the very last time, the EMT next to her thought he heard these three last words escaping from her half-closed lips.

"Violet, I'm sorry."

CHAPTER 49

Exasperated

Biscarrosse, March 25, 2020

We were having breakfast when Colombe's phone, next to the baguette on the kitchen table, rang. It was Nathalie's number.

"Is this Colombe Deschamps?" asked a voice that wasn't hers.

"Speaking. Who's calling?"

"This is Jean-Francois Magnin and I'm a nurse in Auxerre Hospital. I'm calling... unfortunately to announce some bad news to you."

"Natalie?"

"Yes, Ms. Nathalie Wurtz just passed away here. I was part of the team that transferred her here from her home, she was nearly in a coma. We put her in the intensive care unit, but we couldn't do anything for her. And as she was alone and no one called to ask about her, I took the liberty of consulting her recent calls on her cell phone, which luckily wasn't password locked, and I found your number. I'm sorry to tell you that you were the last person to have spoken to her. I'm really sorry for your loss. Are you a family member?"

"Thanks for calling. No, we just know each other, we spent a week together during our last vacation. I called her a couple of days ago and she wasn't feeling well at all. What did she die from Mr. Magnin?"

"The doctors are suspecting meningitis, but I don't know any more than that. You'd have to contact Dr. Maillard, who tried to save her in the ICU. But I sort of doubt he'll have time to talk to you now..."

The epidemic that was overloading the pneumology and ICU services all over France wasn't going to help me get any info. In circumstances like those, it had become nearly impossible to talk about any other cases than those suffering from Covid 19, and all hospitals were exploding with cases, saturating both their infrastructures as well as their their staff members. Everyone was on edge, exhausted and exasperated.

"I understand. Thanks again for having called."

"No problem. Ah! One last thing. In the ambulance going to the hospital, Nathalie uttered a few words."

"What did she say?" Colombe asked.

"From the little I understood, she was apologizing to someone named Violet, but I'm not even sure of that, she was just whispering."

DESPITE WHAT THE EMT had advised us, we tried to call that Dr. Maillard. Not the best idea, as the mass of secretaries, also overwhelmed, wouldn't put us through.

"We have other fish to fry," was what one of them said. "Goodbye."

And then she hung up.

That was understandable though.

WHAT TO DO THOUGH? We were expecting it, fearing it, and the jury had given its harsh verdict: Natalie was also dead. She'd caught meningitis, probably as the other unlucky victims had. That was the last drop, our morale was now completely down in the dumps.

But what about Gregory in all that? We hadn't

been able to obtain any news about him. We were fearing the worst, after that terrible news that we got about one after the other of our fellow vacationers. It was a grim and totally despondent day for both of us. Despite that, we took advantage of our daily authorized outing to go walking, our heads down, in the forest behind our house.

In that anxiogenic and demoralizing climate, Colombe seemed to have a stroke of genius when her eyes happened upon the plants bordering the path.

She suddenly ground to a halt, let go of my hand, bent down and put her hands out to the ground covered with spring flowers.

"Look," she said, as if I knew what she was talking about. "Violets..."

"That's right. So what?"

"Strange, isn't it?"

"That violets bloom in spring? That's something that seems extremely logical to me, on the contrary."

"Don't be an idiot, Jerome. You know how much I believe in coincidences. Just a couple of hours ago, that EMT guy told us that one of the last words Natalie had pronounced before dying was 'violet,' and here we are in front of a carpet of 'violets.'"

"Like we could have seen a carpet of hyacinths, or daisies or tulips..."

"Are you being dumb on purpose or what?"

"Okay. Sorry, I'll shut up now."

"Listen, I think I just understood something, and I have to check it now. Let's go back home."

"Understood what?

"That we were unable to see what was right in front of our eyes back in Gwada."

CHAPTER 50

A withered flower

Pointe à Pitre, March 25, 2020

The tranquilizers that Dr. Lamblin had prescribed for Severine allowed Eusebius to drive her to downtown Pointe à Pitre. She was able to get up from her bed, where she'd been vegetating and ranting, rambling on about who knows what for the past several days. The medication had sufficiently calmed her so that her husband could walk her to his van. It was there, in the middle of Guadeloupe's largest town, after having duly filled out their authorization to leave their house for a medical motive, that Dr. Damien Michelin, a psychiatrist who'd studied in France, had agreed to see them.

"Dr. Lamblin, who I know well, insisted that I see you as soon as possible, Mrs. Rocamora. And with this lockdown, I don't have too many patients. So, tell me, why are you here?"

Severine didn't open her mouth, looking absently at the bald head of the shrink.

Eusebius was forced to explain the situation, telling him about what had taken place over the past few weeks and then going back to when he first met Severine, in 2010 when she came to Gwada for the first time, in a pitiful condition.

"I see, I see," kept repeating the doctor, his hands joined under his chin, nodding his head from top to bottom, just as regularly as a metronome or one of those plastic little doggies you put on the back window of your car. "Dear Sir, could you please leave us alone now? I have to hear what your wife has to say."

"I'm afraid she won't say much," Eusebius sighed.

"Trust me, I'm used to this," the psychiatrist said reassuringly. "I'll come to the waiting room when I'm finished. Thank you!"

Eusebius went into the waiting room and Dr. Michelin sat down across from the comfortable armchair where Severine was sitting.

"Mrs. Rocamora, how are you feeling?"

She gave a vague groan as a response.

"What do you mean by that?" joked the doctor. "I'm sorry, but I don't understand you."

Radio silence.

"Mrs. Rocamora, can you hear me? Severine?"

"My name isn't Severine!" she suddenly shouted. "Severine doesn't exist!"

The psychiatrist, used to reactions from his patients that were often surprising, continued calmly.

"I understand, don't get angry with me. What is your name then?"

"My name is Violet! That's not too complicated, is it? Violet, like the flower, like the color of an amethyst. An amethyst is beautiful."

"Yes it is," agreed the shrink. "So is the flower. And so are you, Violet."

"No! I'm ugly, I'm a withered flower, one with wrinkled petals!"

"Why are you saying that?"

"Just look at me! Look at my face! Look at my mouth! Do I look beautiful to you?"

"All ladies are beautiful, like Franck Michael, the singer, said."

"Never heard of him," grumbled Severine-Violet.

"No big deal, you're too young to have known him, excuse me. What I'm trying to say to you is that beauty is purely subjective. What some people like, others don't, each person has their own criteria. And if I understand correctly, your husband thinks your beautiful, doesn't he?"

"I don't have a husband! I don't want any men, never again! Men always reject me, they use me, they abuse me and then throw me away like an old sock with a hole in it."

"You've gone through hardships in your life, is that right? Failures in your love life?"

"Not even failures. We you fail at something, it means you succeeded before. I never succeeded in anything. Not even dying!"

"Dying?"

"That's right. I couldn't stand being me anymore, being like I was, being everyone's whipping boy! I suffered my whole fucking life!"

The doctor, paying close attention, was taking notes in a notebook placed on his crossed legs. His therapeutic strategy consisted in agreeing with her.

"Violet, when did you think you wanted to die?"

"Not too long ago, after my latest humiliation."

"What humiliation?"

"When my guitar teacher dragged me into his perverted games. When I understood that he was getting off on my deformity. He came when he was taking a video of my mouth while I was pleasuring him. I don't know what happened to that video. I hope he didn't show it to anyone."

"When did that all happen?"

"Easy to remember, just a couple of days before our big French exam."

"Which was?"

"In January, 2011. But I never took the exam."

"Why not?"

"Because I was dead..."

"And when did you die?"

"On New Year's Eve, December 31, 2010!"

CHAPTER 51

We didn't see a thing

Biscarrosse, March 25, 2020

We rushed back home, not because we thought we might be exceeding our authorized hour's outing, but because Colombe was marching as if she had a mission, excited by the idea she'd had when she saw that patch of violets on the side of the path.

"Wanna jog?" she asked.

Though we were both wearing sneakers, I hated jogging, but she just loved it, for some unfathomable reason, especially trail running.

"Go ahead, I'll join you!"

"Okay!"

And she disappeared at the corner of the path in an

airy and graceful stride. I merely took slightly larger steps. When I got back home, she was sitting cross-legged on the couch, her laptop on her thighs.

"So?" I wanted to know.

Her Windows file of our vacation was opened, and in it Colombe had grouped all the photos of our stay in Guadeloupe day by day in subfiles. She was looking at the Soufriere Hills file, scrolling through the various photos.

"Look!" she said excitedly. "That's what I thought. It was the word 'violet' that triggered something back in the forest."

"Sure. But what? There were some violets along the path up to the volcano?"

Colombe displayed successively five jpegs, that the lined up on the computer desktop in five distinct windows, that she'd reduced so we could see all five of them together as a whole.

"You remember that treasure hunt that Severine had organized?"

"Of course, I'm not senile."

"Read all the clues she gave us."

Colombe, who loved things like that, had taken pictures of the clues she'd written on pieces of paper that we discovered while climbing. Similarly she also loved taking pictures of road signs, posters, graffiti, or other manifestations of the human spirit that she then would mix in with our more personal photos. And luckily she'd done that.

I reread the five sentences that had led us up to the peak.

"In order to begin, you must go to the natural border..."
"In the savanna, you will run across mules..."
"Faujas thought he would die when he heard the explosion in 1798..."
"There are no flaws for the next clue..."
"Look below the large violet rock to find Gwada's yellow treasure..."

"See anything, Jerome?"

"Of course, I did see one word."

"Violet?"

"And?"

"Yellow? She was playing with colors?"

"Nope. Keep on looking."

It was crazy how she could irritate me, surprise me

and impress me at the same time when she was playing the role of a language detective. That suddenly reminded me of the way she'd solved part of the mystery surrounding the Lacassagne family in Nice, just by playing word games*.

I thus tried a few different research strategies, counting the number of words in each sentence, adding, or multiplying to see if that led me to a specific date or some other significant numbers.

"Come on, gimme a break. Is it linked to some number?"

"Not really, try to concentrate on the letters and words."

That gal was really irritating me now! I examined the words used, where they were placed. I was thinking of an acrostic, a type of poem where the beginning letter of each line spells out a new word. I reread each line, isolating the first letter, hoping to find a new word.

"T. I. I. M. B.?" was what I obtained. "That doesn't mean anything. Even when I inverted the letters, it still didn't give me anything coherent."

"You're right, that's not where you should be looking," taunted Colombe.

---

* *French Riviera - One Too Many Brothers*, Nino S. Theveny, 2019.

"I give up. Explain your idea to me".

"Okay! Take a close look".

She opened an Excel file where she'd copied each sentence one below the other with one word per cell. For example, the sentence "In order to begin, you must go to the natural border" filled the cells A1 to M1. The next sentence was A2 to J2, etc. up till line five.

"What about now? What do you see?"

"The same five sentences."

"Right, if you read line after line. Now, take a look vertically."

Which I did, column after column, but still didn't understand.

Yet when I reached the fifth column, I thought I was going crazy.

"Holy shit!" I exclaimed. "You were right: it was right in front of us, and we didn't see a thing..."

CHAPTER 52

A severe syndrome

Pointe à Pitre, March 25, 2020

Dr. Michelin led Severine– or maybe it was Violet, how could he know? – back to the waiting room which excepting Eusebius, was deserted.

"Could you please wait here for a moment ma'am?"

"Sure," she said, obediently sitting down.

"And sir, if you could follow me then."

Eusebius followed the psychiatrist into his office. He sat down behind his handsome Empire style desk in his comfortable stuffed armchair, put his hands together, palm against palm, with his index fingers against his lips and gave Eusebius his diagnostic.

"I'm afraid that your wife is suffering from a severe syndrome of a multiple personality disorder. Were you aware of that, I mean in your daily lives?"

It was true that Eusebius sometimes thought that his wife was a bit confused at times. That was the case when they'd first met, then as time went by, things got much better as he'd always paid very close and loving attention to her. Their project of opening a resort for tourists had also occupied Severine full time and because of that, she'd forgotten her demons, at least for a while. That was the short version that he told the doctor. The doctor continued.

"Also, outside of a multiple personality disorder I think your wife is also suffering from a spatial-temporal imbalance. She's mixing up dates, times, and characters that she's embodying. Sometimes she says she's a certain Violet who's dead, then she says that she's Violet who's alive and Severine who's dead. Do you have any idea who Violet could be? And is Severine her real name?"

"I wouldn't have the faintest idea, Doc. Maybe she's inventing her own world? People that don't exist?"

"That could be possible," the psychiatrist said, thinking aloud. "In cases like that, to escape from a painful past, sometimes patients build their own universe and become someone else. In that world, they believe they're a new person, someone they know or not, a real or a fictional one, someone they admire and who they want to resemble. Tell me, what do you know about Severine's or Violet's childhood?"

Eusebius squirmed on his chair, uncomfortable.

"Not too much, actually. She was never too talkative about her past. When we met, back in 2011, she had just arrived in Gwada, and she wanted to turn the page. I had the impression that something had happened before but... but she always occulted that part of her past."

"Does she have a family back in France? Parents who are still alive, brothers or sisters? What do you know about them?"

"Same thing, not much at all. She told me she was an only child."

"Are you two married?"

"We are. But we got married here, a little wedding. She didn't want a big wedding, she hated family get-togethers. We got married on Bananier Beach, just with one witness for each of us. It was so romantic," Eusebius said, dreaming.

"She must have told you a little bit about her family?"

"She told me she'd been adopted. And that she

didn't have any ties with her adoptive family anymore. That was it. Doc, do you think I should have insisted more on her origins?"

"Generally speaking, I don't encourage things like that. Plus, here we're talking about a bygone era. What I'm more worried about is what's happening to her now. Does that name 'Violet' make you think of someone or something?"

"Nothing and no one, I'm sorry. But, and here I'm a little ashamed to tell the truth, but the other evening, when she started talking crazy stuff, I rummaged around in her office and I found a diary, something she'd apparently been writing for quite a while. Since she was a kid, I mean."

"Really? Did you learn anything?"

"The confirmation of how unhappy she'd been. But also the presence of a little sister who loved her, the only person she could count on at that time."

"Which contradicts what she told you, that she was an only child."

"It's a real headache, Doc."

"I think we'll be seeing each other in the future, unfortunately. We're going to have to get to work to discover who your wife really is..."

CHAPTER 53

Completely intelligible

Biscarrosse, March 25, 2020

"You will die for Violet"

That's what the five clues of the Soufriere treasure hunt revealed when zigzagging down the Excel file Colombe had made.

"That's completely crazy!" I murmured after having read what was actually a completely intelligible sentence.

Terribly intelligible!

"And after that you're going to tell me that I'm inventing things? Seems pretty clear to me, no?"

"I can't believe that Severine wrote that and especially wanted that!"

"Who else could it be? She was the one who organized that surprise treasure hunt. I think it was the day we went diving in Malendure. And just to think that we looked at those clues, one by one, without even thinking there was a threat."

"It was impossible though at that time. We were considering the papers individually for that game. Not globally."

"And visibly it wasn't just a game," Colombe said, cutting me off. "At least from Severine's point of view."

I nodded, contrite.

"Wait a sec. We can't accuse her like that without any proof. Those are just words."

"They're not just words, they're also deaths, it's not the same thing!"

"Okay, there's a clear warning: *You will die for Violet*. And we know that Nathalie, Jacques, Bruce, and Naima died after coming back from Guadeloupe. But we can't make any concrete and irrefutable correlation between them and her. For that, we have to find out how Severine was linked to those people she targeted. Discover some shared past between them all. Understand what Severine's motive could have been. Why did she want to kill her guests?"

"Remember what we just learned. It's evident that they all came specifically to Bougainvillea because of that super deal in the flyer. Someone wanted them in Gwada to eliminate them!"

"But eliminate them how?" I asked. "While you were there, did you feel any animosity, any danger? As far as I know, no one was killed there."

"No, of course I never felt endangered. And you're right, no one died there."

"You're right! That's evident. No one died in Guadeloupe. You think you can kill someone remotely and using a timer? No traces, tic tac toe, a perfect crime?"

Colombe thought that over.

"There are certainly some types of poison that don't kill you right away."

"Honey, you've been reading too many Agatha Christies. All that's gone up to your head. In real life, it's not that easy to kill someone. To boot remotely. And even less, several people nearly simultaneously."

"Not that easy but not impossible either I'm afraid when I see all that accumulation of cadavers gravitating around us. All I can think of is poisoning."

"We don't know everything about killing people."

"Maybe we'll discover something new pretty soon," said Colombe prophetically, convinced she was right.

"Maybe we will. I really want to untangle all the ins and outs of this crazy story. I think one of the key questions we have to answer is this one: *Who was that Violet in the message?*"

CHAPTER 54

A bile point pen

<u>Deshaies, March 25, 2020</u>

Severine, who are you? wondered Eusebius while he helped his wife back to bed, exhausted as she was after the appointment with the psychiatrist and all the tranquilizers she'd ingurgitated.

Severine? Violet? Who did I marry? Are they the same person? Which is her real name, which is a pseudonym?

Why is she lying to me?

Eusebius could have written a whole page of similar questions, his mind was filled with so many of them. But rather than torturing himself with useless interrogations, he had an idea: back to that black notebook.

He was hoping to find some of the answers to the questions tormenting him. He'd only read through the notebook superficially the other evening, globally, trying to find things out. But now, with what he'd recently learned, he'd have to read it through again and this time thoroughly and carefully to quench a new thirst, to detect clues to understand!

In the neighboring room, as Severine's peaceful snores were allowing him to give free rein to his curiosity, Eusebius picked up that black notebook once again.

This time he interpreted those lines differently, as if they'd been written by blood rather than ink, by a *bile point pen*. Such omnipresent pain, year after year. From the little girl in grade school up to the young lady who was abused by her guitar instructor, someone who got off on her deformed and imperfect face.

Yet, what surprised him the most was to see that the author of those pages mentioned two or three times the presence of a sister, the only person who was there for her, who listened to her complaints and understood her pain.

Had Severine always lied to him when she'd told him she was an only child?

CHAPTER 55

A foul temper

Biscarrosse, March 25, 2020

"We really have to talk to Severine or Eusebius," insisted Colombe. "At least to make sure they don't have anything to do with this."

"We already tried. Emails, calling the only number we actually have, Severine's. No results."

"And? That silence doesn't seem strange to you? As if it were a confession of guilt?"

"Not necessarily. Let's not take any easy shortcuts here. Maybe we can bypass that problem. I sort of feel like calling Jean-Pierre. We know he has Eusebius's phone number, they called each other when we were there."

I called our diving instructor's number.

He was completely despondent. He told us about how he took his lockdown one hour of liberty per day to walk on the beach, look out to sea, impatiently waiting to be able to take his boat out, to go to Caret Islet or into the mangrove. All those little now forbidden pleasures of life.

We told him about the progress we'd made in our investigation and about the death of several people he'd been with just a few days before. We didn't even have to insist on getting Eusebius's phone number; he was just as eager to understand what had happened as we were.

When I asked him if he could conceive that Severine was guilty, Jean-Pierre's answer took me by surprise.

"Nothing's impossible. You know Jerome, I've known Eusebius for about fifteen years and Severine ever since she moved to Gwada, about ten years ago. What I can tell you is that right away she impressed me, when she moved in with my old friend."

"How?"

"Well, you know, already... physically. Her scar, the one over her lip, it's impressive, don't you agree?"

"I must say it's hard to miss. But she's far from

being the only person who's had an accident in their lives. Jean-Pierre, perfection doesn't exist."

"Oh! That's not what I meant. What I meant there is that she's someone you don't forget, because she's a little bit different. But that wasn't necessarily what bothered me. Rather it was the way she had some sort of psychotic nostalgia, or even a bipolar disorder, I don't really know how to define it. I'm not a doctor."

"Can you tell me more?"

"Sometimes it was like there were two people inside her... One of them who was always joyful, laughing, hyperactive. And then another one who was depressive, pouting, anxious and withdrawn. Severine could go in the snap of your fingers from being euphoric to a completely foul temper."

"Foul," I repeated evasively, not liking what I'd heard. "More precisely, do you think she'd be able to attack someone in one of her depressive phases?"

"There's a big gap between having a depression and killing people, you know."

Then I told him about the clues she'd written for our treasure hunt and how Colombe thought she'd found evidence about her involvement.

"YOU WILL DIE FOR VIOLET"

. . .

"HOLY SHIT, well I guess that is pretty explicit, even if I have no idea who she's talking about with that Violet," Jean-Pierre admitted with reticence. "Unless..."

"Unless what?"

"Unless, I don't know, I'm maybe talking like a wannabe shrink, but it's easy to imagine that her bipolar disorders express themselves like that, by the embodiment of a second person in Severine's mind."

"You mean she thinks she's Violet when she's depressed and Severine when she's euphoric?"

"Yeah, something like that. Even if that could seem pretty far-fetched, to me Severine seems to suffer psychologically from some sort of multiple personality disorder. But from that to killing people... I can't and I don't want to believe it. Why would she want to do something like that?"

"That's exactly what we're trying to find out and that's why we have to talk to Eusebius, as we can't get through to Severine."

CHAPTER 56

Logical connections

<u>Deshaies, March 25, 2020</u>

Eusebius's phone vibrated in his pocket, interrupting him in his umpteenth reading of that black notebook belonging to the lady he'd married. A lady whose past he'd had no idea of up till now, but one he discovered page after page, with incomprehension. He swallowed painfully and cleared this throat before picking up, trying to mask his emotion.

"Hello."

"Eusebius? This is Colombe Deschamps, do you remember me?"

"Ah! Colombe. Of course, such a beautiful name, how could I forget it. What can I do for you?"

"Jerome and I are really worried. Did you hear about Nathalie, Bruce, Jacques, and Naima?"

"Shit!" Eusebius swore. "Nathalie too? I knew about the three others, Jean-Pierre told me. What is going on? This is completely crazy!"

His voice broke while he was speaking.

"I know, that's what we wanted to talk to you about. Is Severine with you?"

"She's sleeping, why?"

"Because we're more precisely worried about her."

"What do you mean?"

His voice was now trembling.

"Eusebius, this is hard for me to say... And hard for me to believe too."

"Believe what for goodness' sake?"

"How is Severine?"

"To be honest, she'd not doing too well right now. I'm worried too. She's been delusional for the past couple of days, I don't even recognize her."

Colombe nibbled on her bottom lip, hesitating on what words to employ so she wouldn't hurt the husband of the person she thought was guilty of murder.

"Delusional, you said?"

"That's right, she's confused, incoherent."

"Eusebius, is she saying that her name is Violet, per chance?"

There was a long silence on the line, a silence as large as the Atlantic that separated us two.

"How did you know that?" he sighed.

That formulation equaled a positive response for Colombe.

"By a series of deductions and cross-checks. But we're still missing the most important part, meaning concrete elements, and proof."

On the other side of the ocean the silence persisted. Eusebius remained slumped in his armchair, his phone on one ear and Severine's notebook opened facing him.

"Eusebius?" said Colombe.

"Sorry, I'm here. You're right, Colombe. Sometimes she thinks she's someone else. She already pronounced that name, Violet, this morning, when she was talking to a psychiatrist that we were able to have an emergency appointment with. He said she was suffering from a multiple personality disorder."

His voice got weaker with each of those sentences he ripped from his heart.

"I'm so sorry, Eusebius, really," Colombe said, trying to console him. "And even sorrier to be having to ask you these questions bothering me. We learned that Severine had concocted a stratagem to attract five tourists who were on vacation at the same time we were, by using a flyer with a fantastic vacation deal on it. They all came. Did you know anything about this?"

"Sort of," he admitted. "But at that time I didn't pay any attention to it."

"Okay. But do you think it's possible that Severine had some specific reason to want them to come to Guadeloupe and do you think that she wanted to harm them?"

Eusebius kept on staring at the open notebook. Logical connections were putting themselves in place, more and more clearly.

"I discovered her diary," he whispered.

"A black notebook?" asked Colombe, who remembered having seen her writing in it one day. And that day, she was really distant, like something was bothering her. Probably a "Violet" day.

"Yes, a black notebook. I'm looking at it right now. I just discovered it very recently. It was her own secret world, she kept it in a locked drawer in her desk."

"What's in it?"

"Souvenirs spanning several decades. Ever since grade school. I now can realize how much she'd suffered when she was young. Before I met her."

"And does she mention the names of Nathalie, Gregory, Naima, Bruce, and Jacques?"

Eusebius thought that open, flipping through the pages.

"Not explicitly, but she wrote about someone she called the Bitch, someone she called the Sucker, a Scheherazade, an Adonis and a guy named Robert Smith. Five individuals who really hurt her, if I can believe what she wrote."

"Maybe five nicknames that could match them, do you think that's possible?"

"They could... one of them was an art teacher, like Natalie and her sketches, another one played the guitar like Jacques on your last day at Bougainvillea."

"That's pretty unsettling. Tell me Eusebius, when was the first page written?"

"On December 15, 2003," he said, opening it up.

"And the last?"

"Well, the week you all were here! Wait a sec, let me reread that."

Colombe heard pages being turned, then there was silence while he reread Severine's diary entrances. Then she heard him swear.

"Jesus fucking Christ!"

"What is it?"

"I've got the feeling that everything was written there, black on white. Now that we know what we know, I'm afraid it's a confession."

"Can you read it to us now?"

Eusebius read the last paragraphs of Severine's diary out loud, the ones dating back just a few days.

Right now, when I'm closing the loop, it's such a strange impression, like I'm putting an end to all this, like I'm settling old scores of a too painful past. Am I going to be able to go through with my decision? Do you need courage or cowardice in those moments?

Is actually doing it more difficult than being aware of it and deciding it?

So close to the point of no return, am I going to deflate?

Have I been illuding myself for all these years? Is this an error, a blind error?

I don't know anymore, I'm lost.

Am I really going to do this?

Sometimes, when you're on the edge of a precipice, your feet next to the edge, just a second before jumping, that is the very instant when you realize the futility of your resolution. So you slowly back your feet away, feet that were already half-way off, you go back to safety, passivity, voluntary renunciation...

"That can't be true..." Colombe lamented.

Right then, Eusebius heard the sound of a foot dragging along on the floor. When he turned around, Severine was at the office door, holding an iron bar in her hand.

Colombe heard the sound of his phone being dropped on the floor.

"Eusebius? Eusebius? Are you still there?"

CHAPTER 57

Biscarrosse, March 25, 2020

We weren't able to reach Eusebius on the phone after that. We quickly called Jean-Pierre, the person who lived closest to them and described what had just happened, and why we were so worried. Despite the government-imposed lockdown, the diving instructor said he'd leave now, and tough luck for the cops if they fined him.

While we were waiting, we received a voicemail that both relieved us and worried us even more. It was from Gregory, someone we hadn't heard a word from ever since we got back from Guadeloupe. In a tiny weak voice, he asked us to call him back as soon as possible, before it was too late.

Our remote lockdown investigation seemed to be a race against the clock. Who would win? Was there actually something to win or to lose? Or was it anyway too late for everyone?

"Gregory? Hi, this is Jerome Bastaro, we got your message. How are you?"

"Hi Jerome. Sorry I didn't contact you earlier. To tell you the truth, during and since our vacation in the tropics, I've been feeling like the fifth wheel in your group. I had the feeling I was bothering everyone, so I kept a low profile, including answering emails. And then, I learned about the others... It's horrible. And now I'm freaking out too."

"What's wrong?"

"I'll give you the short version, I'm in ER and waiting to be transferred to neurology, in their ICU."

"How come?"

"The doctors are thinking it's meningitis. My face is as big as a watermelon. Plus they hooked me up all over, in the arms, up my nose. What the hell is happening to all of us? What did she do to us?"

I was startled.

"Who, she?"

"Severine, who else?"

"Greg, what do you know about her?"

He was now having problems articulating. It took him ages to spit it out, but I let him speak at his own rhythm.

"I noticed something when I was there. I realized that it hadn't been pure luck that I got that deal. When I saw Severine with that god-awful scar on her lip, she reminded me of a girl I went to school with, who had the same scar. I'm embarrassed to admit this –but you know how kids are – I always made fun of her. I harassed that poor kid, with her ugly harelip. Once I even put a bloody hare's head that I'd taken out of my dad's dumpster into her schoolbag. Get it – a hare's head for a harelip. Not proud of that... Anyway, I understood that Severine was the adult version of my middle school scapegoat."

"Was her name Severine then?"

"No, not at all, that's why I wasn't sure of myself. The little girl that was in our 6D class had a much rarer first name, one you don't forget. Her name was Violet."

"Holy shit! You're sure of that?"

"I am, in spite of this headache that's driving me crazy. I even checked."

"How'd you do that?"

"Ever heard of Classmates.com?"

"Just the name."

"You can check it out for yourself. Marouzeau College in Gueret. Academic year 2004-2005, class 6D. You'll find a girl named Violet de Beaulieu in the photo that was published. She wasn't just a country hick, she was the Prefect's daughter, the well-known Herve de Beaulieu. Just goes to say that though you might have noble ancestors, you're not always a top model."

A coughing spell interrupted his speech.

"Greg? You okay?"

"Fit as a fiddle!" he joked, between two coughs. "My dad's here. If I croak, he'll call you..."

I rebuffed him and after I told him to hang on and get well soon – though I didn't believe that, not even for a second – I hung up and logged into the site he'd just mentioned, looking for that class photo.

In just a few clicks I found that photo and easily recognized Gregory's face, at that time a little pimple-faced kid who must have deserved the nickname of Sucker, two rows above a girl whose facial features were immediately recognizable.

When I scrolled above that face distorted by her harelip, there was the name of Violet de Beaulieu.

It was easy to see a vague and troubling family resemblance with the Severine we'd met in Gwada...

CHAPTER 58

Without scars

Deshaies, March 25, 2020

Turning towards the door leading to the office, Eusebius's eyes popped wide open when he saw the metallic bar that his wife was holding.

He dropped his phone.

"Severine, what the...?"

"Stop it! I don't know anyone named Severine, you deaf or what?"

It was easy for him to see that his wife was still delusional, delirious, her black eyes sending violent bolts of lightning to him. Eusebius had to buy into her folie.

"Excuse me, Violet, I didn't recognize you. Please,

just calm down, put that bar down and we'll talk, you and me."

"I don't have anything to say to muckrakers who put their noses in what's mine. Why did you steal the key in my necklace? What are you looking for? You don't have any right to, those are my intimate secrets."

"We have to talk about this, on the contrary, Sev... Violet. I'm your husband, I can help. You can trust me."

Severine-Violet slowly walked into the room towards Eusebius, her arm raised with the iron bar. She saw her diary in the middle of the room, open.

"You know everything then?"

Her husband nodded.

"I'd like you to explain a couple of things to me, will you do that?" he asked calmly. "We'll talk, just you and me."

Violet paused in the middle of the dimly lit room. It was dark outside already. The nocturnal birds had begun singing their intoxicating, repetitive melodies.

The iron rod was lowered vertically, along the sarouel that Severine-Violet had quickly put on after getting out of bed.

"What do you want to know exactly?" she asked, with poorly contained impatience.

"What you wrote in that notebook... did all that really happen? Were you really humiliated like that?"

Violet snorted through her nose, a short contempt filled snort.

"Of course! What do you imagine? That I'm a pathological liar and I invented all that? That I want you to feel sorry for me? No, Eusebius, what I went through during all those years I wouldn't wish that on my worst enemy."

Her husband picked up on that word immediately.

"And you had enemies, didn't you? That's how you saw those five people who psychologically wounded you when you were young?"

"You understand quickly, great! What would you have done in my shoes? Each of them, in their own way, tortured me, day after day, year after year. Is it a crime to be born with a harelip? What did I do wrong? Am I guilty of being ugly?"

"You're being foolish," he consoled her. "I think you're beautiful and you know it. Come here, put that down, come on."

"Eusebius, you've always been nice to me, I can't take that away from you. But now, things have changed. I can't backtrack anymore."

Eusebius was also convinced of that. In the past few weeks, events had been precipitated.

“Violet, what did you do? The five vacationers we hosted here that week that the two journalists were there, were those people the ones who hurt you? What did you do to them? Do you have any idea what happened to them since they left?”

“I don’t know, but I can imagine it. So what? Now I should feel sorry for them? They got what they deserved.”

“But... Colombe and Jerome... please reassure me, you didn’t hurt them too?”

“No, those two were nice. I’d never met them.”

Eusebius started to get up.

“What did you do to the others? How come they’re dying, one after the other, since they left here? Did you poison them?”

“Sit down!” barked Violet, raising the iron bar again. “Sit down or I’ll bust your head open like a coconut! It doesn’t matter how I offed them, understand? What counts is that I got revenge for what they did to me in the past. And without any traces! Any scars, see what I mean...”

“I do. You think you pulled off a perfect crime?”

Violet laughed, a frightening laugh that Eusebius had never heard before. Like a hyena hurling at night.

“What I can guarantee you is that none of them are

going to live!" she gloated when she'd stopped laughing.

Shaking his head with incomprehension, Eusebius clenched his fists, bit his lips and had to force himself not to pounce on his wife, who visibly was possessed by the demons of her past.

"If you did commit those crimes, you understand that they'll be punished, are you aware of that? One day or another, justice will be done."

"Are you going to turn me in? You, my husband, you're going to the cops?"

"But Jesus Christ, you can't take the law into your own hands in this country!"

Without even giving him time to say another word, she rushed up to him, the iron rod raised above his head.

CHAPTER 59

Ad patres

<u>Sainte Rose, March 25, 2020</u>

For once he didn't have his phone on him! *What a waste of time*! grumbled Jean-Pierre when he finally heard the message from France. He had just gotten out of the shower and was getting ready for bed, not without having tried to read a couple of pages of a novel, though that night he hadn't really felt like reading. He heard Jerome Bastaro's panicked voice on the voicemail loudspeaker:

"Jean-Pierre, you're the closest one. I know that it's difficult with the lockdown and everything, but you have to go to Deshaies. I've got a really bad feeling here and I've got my reasons to think that something bad has happened in Bougainvillea. We just called Eusebius and..."

All the rest was details in Jean-Pierre's brain. He immediately put his jeans on, without even thinking of filling out his authorization paper to leave his home. On that official document, there wasn't a box to check to help a person in danger.

The diving instructor grabbed the keys for his car and ran down to the parking lot. He'd downed a couple of glasses of rum that evening but felt he was capable of driving. He had no other choice.

He didn't often use his old rusted out car, with its moss-green joints around the windows, its salt-eaten exterior, its odometer that must have been reinitialized at least twice, but it still worked. Four tires, an engine, a steering wheel, and three pedals would do the trick for him. As he lived right next to the port and less than 500 feet from the shops, Jean-Pierre started up his catamaran much more often than his ancient Peugeot.

Which, probably miffed, refused to obey when he turned the key. It coughed, sneezed, groaned. Finally though it accepted to start, probably because of its owner's perseverance and intimidated by his loud swear words.

In just a couple of minutes, Jean-Pierre was out of the little town of Sainte-Rose, heading to Deshaies, by the unique twisting and turning coastal road.

Though tourists loved that road, it of course was deserted. It was a peculiar and nearly unsettling feeling to be on that quasi-deserted road, one that usually was packed.

Nighttime had shed its dark veil over the island, and the sides of the road, excepting when he was in the villages, were dark, poorly lit up by the tired headlights of his Peugeot 205 clunker. Jean-Pierre just missed hitting a cow, who though attached by a chain, was chomping away next to the road. Its sudden apparition in the car's headlights had destabilized him and nearly sent him up *ad patres*, to his fathers. He judiciously had the reflex to turn the steering wheel. Nonetheless, he continued, holding on to the wheel with two trembling hands. He stepped on the gas and the vehicle responded to its best, considering its venerable age.

Jean-Pierre lived a mere twelve miles from Severine and Eusebius, in the south of Deshaies, right near the discrete Petite Anse Beach. About a half hour drive to reach Bougainvillea. The road was sometimes dangerous, and you couldn't speed all the time. Anyway, his Peugeot wouldn't have been able to.

He actually could have arrived in time at his friends' house, but bad luck invited itself to the party.

Something foreseeable: at Perle Beach, halfway there, there were cops blocking the road, systematically controlling the few cars on the road at that time of the night.

CHAPTER 60

The humiliated people

<u>Deshaies, March 25, 2020</u>

He succeeded in dodging the first swing of the iron rod with his forearm. The second one though, executed without delay, hit him on the top of his head that was barely protected by his thick dreadlocks. Before he even had time to blink his eyes, Eusebius collapsed on the floor in his wife's office, knocked out like a boxer after a right-handed punch on the temple.

Before he passed out, he was able to distinguish the last words Violet said to him.

"I'm so sorry my love. I didn't have any choice. I have to finish what I started years ago."

These words came out of the woman's mouth,

with her crazy eyes darting, and sobs she couldn't restrain. Tears coming from afar, from the depths of her personal history. Tears that were both hers as well as those of all the humiliated people in her life, those who had been left behind, pariahs, those who Others rejected without trying to understand them.

"I love you, I love you, I'll still love you when all of this is finished. Adieu."

Violet unclenched her fingers and the heavy iron rod with which she'd just knocked her husband out fell to the floor. She stayed there, hesitating for a moment, contemplating the scene she'd written with her own determination. She watched, as if absent, the iron rod as it slowly dropped down next to Eusebius's head, from which a trail of blood could be seen between his locks.

She finally shook herself mentally and left the office, without even thinking of taking her black diary that had remained open to the last page that Eusebius had read to Colombe on the phone.

However, she took the keys to their SUV, which were on the rattan sideboard next to the door and ran from the bungalow towards the private parking lot in Bougainvillea. The vehicle started up immediately, its powerful motor purring in the dark.

Its tires squealed on the gravel, for an instant not

finding purchase between the maneuvers she'd made to leave their resort. Violet took the road that snaked around the steep slopes up to the coastal road. She didn't stop at the intersection, ignoring the sign. At that time of the night though and with the exceptional lockdown circumstances, there was no one on the road.

She was free to go wherever she wanted.

CHAPTER 61

Cornered

<u>Pearl Beach, March 25, 2020</u>

"Driver's license and insurance please!"

Jean-Pierre had no other choice than to stop at the cops' roadblock. He couldn't have avoided it though: there was only one road going to Deshaies, unless he went through the mountains. But the roadblock was before that turnoff.

"Excuse me, Officer, but it's a question of life or death."

"That's all?" asked the policeman ironically.

Then he turned to his colleague.

"Hear that, Olivier? No one's told us that one yet.

Ever since lockdown began, we've heard 'I forgot my paper,' 'I didn't take my phone,' 'my grandma's sick,' 'my dog sprained its ankle...' but that one takes the cake!"

"Please, just listen to me," implored Jean-Pierre.

"One minute. To start with, can you give me your ID, plus the registration card for your vehicle, your insurance attestation and above all, your paper to justify why you're out this late at night. You must know the whole island is on lockdown here. Maybe you saw the news? You must have enough time, especially now."

"I've got friends that potentially are in danger. They live near Deshaies. You can escort me. After that, you'll have all the time in the world to check my papers!"

"Listen, we see people like you every day, enlightened ones with shiny eyes because they've had a couple too many glasses of rum, spouting off all sorts of nonsense. I'm going to ask you to take this breathalyzer test now. Your breath seems a bit full."

"I'll take any test that you want, but please, I'm begging you, come with me! It would be too long to explain all the details to you, but please, you gotta trust me on this one!"

"We'll trust you when we've checked what we have to check. Understand?"

Jean-Pierre had no other choice than to obey. He reluctantly took that breathalyzer test – which was positive – and showed them all the documents they asked for. Luckily the gendarmes didn't say anything about the deplorable state of the car. Only after he'd done all that could he explain the situation to them, the ins and outs, since the week of vacation the tourists had spent in Bougainvillea, to the phone calls with the two journalists in France and then Colombe's deductions as well as his own.

All of this took at least another fifteen minutes, making their trip to Deshaies even later. Then they couldn't leave their roadblock control post before another team of gendarmes came to take their place. The captain had agreed to escort Jean-Pierre to Bougainvillea Resort but was forced to wait until the second team came to replace them.

"I can't rob Peter to pay Paul," he said philosophically and stoically.

With all that administrative crap, Jean-Pierre and the gendarmes accompanying him only left an hour later on the deserted road.

"My friends' bungalow is that one, right above," he said, pointing to it.

They all rushed to the house, which was calm. They heard a soft groan coming from one of the rooms inside.

Opening the door of the office, they discovered Eusebius's imposing silhouette, on the floor, like a worm that a shovel had unfortunately cut in half.

"What did I tell you?" railed Jean-Pierre, leaning down to his friend.

"Move over," the gendarme ordered him.

Then he kneeled down to the Guadeloupean's body, trying to find a pulse. There was a large pool of blood drying on the man's hair and on the floor.

"Boss! There's an iron rod here."

"Shit," muttered the boss. "Someone really had it in for him. Can you hear me?" he asked the wounded man. "Can you hear my voice?"

Eusebius moaned, his eyes still closed, then moved his members weakly.

"Looks like he's just knocked out. I don't think it's too serious. Vincent, call an ambulance anyway," he told his teammate.

He pivoted towards Jean-Pierre, who was kneeling at the head of his unconscious friend.

"Do you know him well? What do you think happened?"

"From what I've learned in the past couple of

hours, I'm persuaded that his wife, Severine Rocamora, was the one who did this to him. And visibly she took off. Fuck, why did you have to be there at the Pearl? I could have arrived in time..."

"Calm down. We've got this taken care of. We'll find her and we'll get this figured out."

The captain left his assistant with Eusebius while he went outside with Jean-Pierre.

"Are you familiar with the resort?"

"Yeah, I know it pretty well."

"Do you think that Severine could be hiding someplace here? In one of the bungalows maybe?"

Jean-Pierre thought that it might be possible, until he saw that the owners' SUV was missing from their private parking lot, and that the white van was still there. He could see ruts in the gravel. He pointed them out to the gendarme.

"Looks to me like she took to her heels, after having hit a home run. Maybe that little lady thinks she's up to bat for the Red Sox!"

Though Jean-Pierre also loved baseball, as did most of those living in the Caribbean, he didn't continue with the gendarme's metaphors, preferring to think about where Severine could have driven to. But to tell the truth, he had no idea!

"I'm going to put roadblocks on all the roads leaving from here. In Basse-Terre, there's not that many of them. That little lady's gonna find herself cornered" predicted the gendarme. "She can't escape us."

CHAPTER 62

Other fish to fry

Biscarrosse, March 26, 2020

Early in the morning, after a difficult restless night full of harrowing thoughts, and a couple of hours of sleep, we got a phone call that unfortunately didn't surprise us.

"Mr. Bastaro? This is Gerard Labrousse, my son Gregory begged me to contact you if..."

The sentence that Greg's father, a butcher, was trying to say was lost in an irrepressible but totally understandable sob.

"I'm so sorry for your loss, Mr. Labrousse. That's just awful, I don't know what to say."

"I don't either," replied Gregory's father, after having cried for a long moment. "It was so quick."

"What did the doctors say?"

"It was viral meningoencephalitis, something like that. He died in just a couple of hours and got much worse right after he called you. They put him in a coma, transferred him to the ICU, and then... the curtain closed."

Just like the steel curtain in front of your shop, I thought, imagining the butcher shop in Gueret closed for the next couple of days.

"I understand, that's terrible. But, Mr. Labrousse, did your son tell you anything about his recent vacation in Guadeloupe?"

"Vaguely, why?"

I didn't know where to start unveiling my thoughts to Greg's poor father, especially right now, but I felt that I had no other choice than to seize that opportunity before it was too late.

"This is really delicate to talk about, and I know it's not the moment," I began. "But my girlfriend and I were on vacation at the same time your son, and both of us are nearly convinced that your son's death is linked to his vacation in Guadeloupe."

In my opinion, that was vague enough not to

shock him but clear enough so that he'd positively respond to the idea that I just had.

"You think he caught that shit in the tropics?"

"I'm almost sure that the problem came from there. But I wouldn't be able to say if he caught something or if something caught him..."

Of course, now wasn't the best time to talk about the suspicions we had about Severine Rocamora, but nothing was preventing me from giving him a few hints, setting off a couple of alarm bells. Which might help him take the direction that would help us in our line of thought.

"If I can do anything to help you, I will," consented Mr. Labrousse.

That was when I told him about the death of the others on vacation with us, hinting at the most enigmatic point, trying to make Gregory's father see that there must be some cause-and-effect relationship here. But what, and how to prove it? I carefully chose my words.

"If it's not too difficult Mr. Labrousse, what would be very useful would be... to have an autopsy done on your son."

There was a long and heavy silence, one I imagined painful for Gerard Labrousse, and it lasted so long that I thought that we had been cut off. I could have understood that he wanted to end that difficult conversation, just a few moments after his son had died. Time though was working against us. And during this lockdown period, people got buried immediately. And once the burial had taken place, it would be extremely difficult to legally demand an exhumation. And were he to be cremated...

"Cut my son up?" Labrousse spit out, reactivating the conversation. "That's not human!"

I thought that coming from a professional butcher, that was quite an unsettling and ironic remark.

"That unfortunately is the only solution that will allow us to understand why he died, and believe me, I'm really sorry."

Labrousse sighed noisily.

"With what's going on now, I'm not so sure that the doctors will want to do it. They got other fish to fry, don't you agree?"

"I do. Except here we've got five deaths in such a short time, people who had a vacation at the same place and same time together, who died more or less in the same way, and for me that's not at all something natural!"

"That's true, it isn't clear at all."

"I'll let you think it over with your wife. But this is really an emergency situation. You are the only ones who still can react, influence the course of action for these events, help us solve our investigation and find out the truth."

"I'll talk to my wife and get back to you. But I'm not promising anything."

"I understand, thank you, Mr. Labrousse. And once again, our deepest sympathy for you and your wife."

AFTER HAVING HUNG UP, still overwhelmed by the pain Gregory's parents had, we tried to find a way to urge the hospital to proceed with an autopsy on his body. Only the immediate family could request that, or of course, a judge. But no official investigation had yet been opened.

While mentally going through the list of our professional contacts, I remembered that I'd met a retired professor of medicine, a man named Jacques Siethbüller*. Perhaps I could convince him to intercede with his peers in favor of Gregory Labrousse's autopsy?

I texted him. He called me back an hour later, and after a long conversation, he agreed to help us. At the

---

* Cf. *True Blood Never Lies*, Nino S. Theveny, self-published, 2020.

same time, he left us with a ton of new and unsettling questions.

D

UNDERMINING

Slowly, making sure they wouldn't touch the clayish sides of the burial place, the four undertakers had to use their muscles to lower the coffin into its final resting place. The heavy hemp cords descended, inch after inch, in their powerful fists, luckily enveloped with leather gloves. They'd clenched both their fists and their jaws, their muscles were tense, but as always during each ceremony, the four men tried to make this look easy. It was essentially a physical pain for them, thought they were not insensitive to the morale pain of the grieving families.

That day though, while the drizzle continued to undermine everyone's mood, freezing both bodies and souls, not too many people were surrounding the gaping hole where the lacquered wood of the coffin had just hit the bottom.

When the priest invited those present to toss a flower, a handful of earth, or any other object of their choice, the coffin didn't even have five impacts on its riveted top.

A few minutes later, everyone there had left to go back to their regular lives – the priest to his flock– family members to their bereavement – except for the undertakers who had to work hard for yet another hour, in the rain, to fill that hole back up.

A ton of earth later, a layer of crushed stone on the top, all that was left to do was to leave all that settle for a couple of days, before putting a concrete slab on it and a nice marble tombstone.

CHAPTER 63

Not that far

<u>Guadeloupe, March 26, 2020</u>

The black sky barely lit up by a lazy new moon wasn't helping the police force trying to find Severine Rocamora, alias Violet de Beaulieu.

Captain Maxime Servant, the highest-ranking officer, took charge of the investigation.

"Vincent, what the hell are you doing? There's not fifty thousand roads leaving from here! How could she have escaped? Where did you set up roadblocks?"

His teammate spread a map of the island, which was shaped like a butterfly, out on the hood of the police car, pointing at the places where there were police.

"We posted guys in Pointe-Noire, Caféière, and Sainte-Rose. Also on National 1, at the intersection where Route de la Traversée comes in. And if she'd already gone farther than that, we also have people at Bouillante, Vieux-Forts and Trois-Rivières. Same thing on the Atlantic coast, at Capesterre and Goyave. Of course downtown Pointe à Pitre is also blocked at the intersections."

"What about Grand-Terre?"

"In Sainte-Anne, Saint-François, Port-Louis, Anse-Bertrand and Le Moule."

"Okay, but that's not sufficient there. They've got roads all over, not like in Basse-Terre. If she left over an hour ago, she's a goner. At this time of night, she could be anywhere."

"Including where we're not expecting her?"

The captain didn't understand his teammate's question.

"What are you thinking of?"

"Well, Cap, sometimes we go looking real far to find what's right below our eyes almost."

"Continue."

"She could very well have started up her car, gone two or three miles and then come back by foot. Hiding in a place that's not too far, who knows?"

“That’s right, who knows? Anyway I sure don’t and that’s starting to piss me off!”

“We should mobilize more people, explore the whole island...” his subordinate suggested, as he’d been taught at National Gendarmerie School in Chaumont, where he was born.

“Yeah, that’s theory. To mobilize as many people as that – and they’ve probably got other stuff to do – we’d have to be looking for Public Enemy Number 1. And I don’t think we are. As far as I know, that little lady didn’t kill anyone. She just knocked her husband out with an iron bar. No one died.”

“Maybe Cap! But if we believe what Jean-Pierre and that poor husband told us after he woke up, without considering what we read in that lady’s little diary, she really wanted to harm some of her vacation renters.”

“And some of them died after getting back from Gwada, I know. But still, that doesn’t prove a thing. For the moment, it’s just fiction. A police mystery story. Except that we’re not in a novel, we’re in real life! You’ll soon learn that generally speaking, events don’t always take place in the same way. And in books, investigators usually are luckier.”

At that moment, the radio crackled in the captain’s pocket.

"I'm listening!" he barked into it.

"Captain, this is Corporal Letourneur. We just found that SUV that you put the BOLO out on."

"Jesus Christ. Where is it?"

"At the end of a cul-de-sac, in Pointe-Noire."

"That's vast. Can you be more precise?"

"Grand-Case Road, a road that goes up to the hills, not too far from Baille-Argent Port."

"Fuck! You were right, Vincent, she wasn't very far..."

"Excuse me Captain?"

"Nothing. I was talking to my teammate. And our little lady, you found her too?"

"Negative, Cap!"

"Any traces of her?"

"Nothing concrete for now, we're still looking. But for the moment, that little lady has vanished into thin air."

CHAPTER 64

A little sex party at the poolside

Biscarrosse, March 26, 2020

The morning dragged by gloomily. Gregory's death, the last one in the long list of Gwada's victims, that was what I was now calling them, had sapped our morale.

In addition to that, increasing our emotional wanderings, Jean-Pierre told us about what had happened that night in Deshaies: the iron rod, the black diary, and Severine's disappearance, or whatever her real name actually was.

We were cooling our heels, immobilized by a nationwide decree, at home. For us – as it was for nearly the whole population in the entire world – this was something we'd never experienced. Usually when we were doing our investigations, we were free to go where we wanted to, could meet anyone, anytime, anywhere. Luckily for us though, modern communication made up for the restrictions in traveling. However, immobility forced us to think, and that probably was a good thing.

We had time to think about what we'd just learned from Professor Siethbüller's mouth. He'd asked Gregory's parents to proceed with the autopsy, and they had finally accepted. Now we had to wait for a couple of days to receive the preliminary results from the coroner in charge of the procedure.

In the meanwhile, our conversation with Siethbüller was both instructive and unsettling, leaving us with yet a new enigma.

"In reality, meningitis can have several causes. To make it short, it could be either viral or bacterial. For most people it's bacterial, with a very high mortality rate. It more rarely can be caused by eating mushrooms, for example."

"I don't think we had any while we were there," I thought out loud.

"Good, because that type is mortal. Anyway. No, the most frequent form is meningitis is meningococcal meningitis, and it comes from the streptococcal bacteria, you heard of that?"

"Of course. But how do you catch it?"

"Just like a strep throat."

"Specifically?"

"By droplets, for example, if someone coughs or sneezes on you, but also if you were to touch an object that has been contaminated. Or by saliva, when you kiss, for example. Maybe the victims contaminated each other? I wonder which of them was the first one to have caught that bacterium? Maybe you can help me here, Jerome."

"Yes?"

"We know how things can sometimes happen on vacation. There's promiscuity, exchanges, all that... Maybe there were intimate relations between some of them? A little sex party at the poolside?"

"As far as I know, not at all!" I said ironically. "Or else we missed it or weren't invited!"

"If it was to end up like them, maybe it's better to have missed it!"

"You're right there. All of that is fine and dandy, but first of all, I don't think anyone was sick over there and contaminated all the others, and then if this all was caused by some bacteria or virus, an external element, that totally excludes any human intervention. And it also means that our host, Severine, couldn't be guilty."

"I agree. After that, we know that there are a few forms of bacteriological threats that some people know how to manipulate to harm others. A bacteriological war isn't a mere myth. Remember, in the United States, that affair of the envelopes that were contaminated by anthrax..."

"I doubt that it's true in our affair here, but you can't exclude anything I suppose."

"I totally agree, and the autopsy should give us more precise indications. Nonetheless, it's rare that you die nowadays from meningitis. There are antibiotics and cortisone treatments that usually do the trick. When you've got five people that died and all of them presented similar symptoms and shared the same environment, that's starting to be a lot."

"And? What direction should we be looking in then?"

Professor Siethbüller hesitated for a moment, as if he was gathering his thoughts.

"I've perhaps got something we could explore."

"What?"

"If the cerebral biopsy performed on Gregory Labrousse's cadaver showed a PAM..."

"What the heck is a PAM?"

"Primary amoebic meningoencephalitis. An extremely rare but particularly dangerous pathology caused having inhaled the amoeboid excavate *Naegleria fowleri.*"

"Never heard of that."

"That's not surprising, Jerome. And that's why I told you it was just an idea. This pathology was identified over a century ago, but there's only been a few more than two hundred verified cases of it in the entire world! Meaning at a global and human scale, a very rare exception. On the other hand, when it hits, you die! I did some research on the question and in medical literature, there are only seven cases of survivors in all of history. Meaning that the survival rate is much, much lower than for the Ebola virus."

"Oh!" I shivered. "And is it the same means of contamination?"

"Not at all. But the being in the tropics is conducive to the presence of amoeba like that, and they generally appear in stagnant water about 75°F. Jerome, did those five people go swimming in any ponds, or were they in swamps or any stagnant water when you were in Guadeloupe?"

I mentally went through all the places where we'd gone swimming, but each time it was either in the sea or in rivers. Meaning water that was always in movement, not stagnant. Also, both Colombe and I did what the others did, and we were still alive! That's what I told the professor.

"In that case, I have no idea," he said apologetically.

I thanked him warmly for his help and hung up, troubled.

"Where the hell is the fault in this logic?"

"Maybe the others went swimming someplace without us, and without us knowing about it?" suggested Colombe.

"It's possible, but I doubt it."

Suddenly, as quick as a Jack-in-the-Box, Colombe jumped up from the couch and rushed to her laptop.

"I've got an idea! But it's so strange I don't really think it's possible. Plus, I can't see how..."

"How what?"

"How she could have done it?"

"Who?"

"Violet!"

CHAPTER 65

Broke in

BAILLE-ARGENT, March 26, 2020

THE GENDARMES WORKING under the orders of Captain Maxime Servant were doing overtime. He'd been on the bridge since last night, when he took over from the patrol group who had roadblocked Pearl Beach.

Since then everything had picked up speed and that didn't include the latest development that his deputy had just announced.

"Cap! You gotta come see this, please."

"Now what?" grumbled Captain Servant.

"This man wants to tell us something."

There was an old man, dry as a stick, with black skin that was wrinkled by decades of sun and sea salt, and curly hair that was so white it was nearly translucent, standing at the Baille-Argent Port landing dock, not far from Severine Rocamora's abandoned vehicle, though she was still missing.

"Hello," greeted the captain. "Who are you?"

"My respect, Mr. Policeman," he stammered. "I'm the guardian of this little port, I've worked here since 1976."

"Congratulations! It seems you have something you want to tell me," the gendarme encouraged him, seeing how shy and impressed he was.

"Um, yes. When I arrived this morning, I saw something didn't add up here. I have to tell you that at night, there's no one here, this is an itty-bitty port, you understand."

"Of course, that's normal. You can't pay someone to keep an eye on every landing dock in the island! What did you see then?"

"We were missing a boat."

"You're sure of that?"

"That I am. When I left last night, there were five boats. And this morning there's only four. Maybe I didn't go to school like you, Captain, but I still know how to count to five, you know," the old man said apologetically while nervously scratching his chin.

The sound of his yellowed nails was like someone grating a coconut.

"I don't want to offend you. Here, you're the boss," Servant said. "Do you know who the missing boat belongs to?"

"Sure do! It's Toussaint's little boat. I mean that Toussaint is the pilot, but it belongs to one of those associations that organizes outings for whale watching."

"Perfect. And this Toussaint, maybe he took his boat himself really early this morning, like before you arrived?"

"Well, it is possible, of course, but you know like me that normally we're on lockdown here."

"You're right there. Speaking of which, what are you doing here?" asked the gendarme, tired by his sleepless night.

"It's not the same thing for me, I live about two hundred feet from here, see that house over there? That's mine. Every morning, lockdown or no lockdown, I come to my little hut here. And I've got my official paper authorizing me to be out, if you want to see it."

"No, that's fine. Finish your story, that's much more interesting. So you don't think that it could be that Toussaint who took his boat out? Why not?"

"Follow me."

The old guardian led him to his hut. He pointed at a panel on the left side of it.

"There you go. This is the panel with spare keys for each boat."

"And you're going to tell me that one is missing?"

"I am! Ah! Now I know why you're the captain!" the guardian sneered.

"In respect for your age, ancestor, I won't pay attention to that insult of government official" grumbled Servant. "Just tell me who's got access to this room, that, I imagine is locked at night."

"Theoretically, only me. But each owner of a boat that's docked here also has a key to the hut, you never know. But that's not what's bothering me."

"What is bothering you then? Gimme the facts old man! You could have written mysteries, you know how to string things out."

The old man burst out laughing and turned around, pointing at the door.

"You see? Someone broke in! Someone broke in last night".

The gendarme rushed out of the little hut on the landing dock, where he looked out to sea, the blue immensity of the Caribbean, and swore, grabbing his radio.

"Shit! She's gone! I sure hope it's not too late."

CHAPTER 66

Putting your finger on it

Biscarrosse, March 26, 2020

"So what was your crazy idea?" I insisted, knowing that Colombe was capable of hatching the most extravagant theories.

She fired up her laptop. We'd just had a light lunch, neither of us were hungry, too bogged down in trying to solve this apparently unsolvable enigma. How could five people have contracted primary amoebic meningoencephalitis without – at least without us knowing about it, of course, – having swum in some contaminated stagnant water?

The subsidiary question, and not the least important one, resided in trying to find out if there was any link between their pathology and Severine-Violet Rocamora-de Beaulieu's murderous intensions.

"I know you're going to think I'm crazy Jerome, but I'm still going to explain my idea to you."

"You trying to make me beg for it? Go ahead!"

Colombe sat down and began to do some web research on the *Naegleria fowleri* ameba, also called "the brain eater" by Professor Siethbüller just a few minutes ago. She googled several sites.

"See, they were able to detect the presence of those bacteria mainly in stagnant water, but not just that. Also in drinking water pipelines, cooling water, and in poorly maintained swimming pools."

"Pools? Isn't there water always mixed and filtered?" I asked, astonished.

"It normally is. But just imagine that someone intentionally contaminated the water in the pool, knowing that some other people were going to swim in it."

I nodded, incredulously.

"Are you insinuating that Severine polluted her own pool to contaminate those using it?"

"Why not? Maybe it's technically feasible."

"It probably is. But in that case, she'd be putting herself in danger, and Eusebius too!"

"Do you remember having seen them swimming while we were there?"

That was a legitimate question, and I thought back on it. I remember having seen Severine lying down on a sunbed at the poolside, but never in the water. As for Eusebius, I'd instinctively say that he probably went in but couldn't guarantee it.

"But still, even if we didn't see them swimming, both of us did swim in that pool. And as far as I know, we're not sick."

"Did you put your head under water?" asked Colombe.

"What the heck do I know? I can't remember tiny details like that. I'm not crazy like you are."

"That's nice, thanks a lot."

"Sorry. But frankly, I'm nearly certain that I dove in, that I swum under water, and probably drank some too, like each time I try to dive. Sincerely, your theory just doesn't add up."

"Nothing proves that everyone is systematically contaminated either. Otherwise I'd imagine that there would be thousands of cases each year, and the professor told us that there weren't even two hundred people that died from it in a whole century. Okay, I admit, my idea is a bit farfetched. But if you've got another one, I'm all ears."

I sighed.

"No, I don't know, I don't know anymore, I'm completely lost."

"Yeah, okay, be like a blackbird..."

"What?"

"No, nothing, I thought you were going to sing the Beatle's song there. Forget it."

"It's true, I'm lost. I feel like this problem is unsolvable. Like I'm feeling that we're missing a detail here and I can't seem to put my finger on it. And that is royally pissing me off! Anyway, that won't make those five people come back, so why insist?"

"Lest we not forget. So they didn't die for nothing. And if there really was a crime, I don't want it to remain unpunished. We owe it to them, we owe it to them as victims."

"We do. We'll keep on trying to solve this. Speaking of which, I wonder what's going on in Gwada."

To try to find out, we called Eusebius, Severine and then Jean-Pierre, but no one answered.

"Why don't we go for a walk, think of something else?"

We filled in our mandatory permits to leave our homes, went into the forest, admiring the violets on both sides of the path that had tipped us off a couple of days ago.

"Maybe we should try to track down that famous prefect, Violet's father. Herve de Beaulieu, I think his name was..."

"Maybe he's still working someplace."

I scrolled down my phone after having entered his name and profession. The most recent articles mentioned that he was now in Noumea.

"Should we try to call him?"

"And the time difference with New Caledonia, you forgot maybe?" Colombe reminded me.

"Shoot. How much do you think?"

"I'd say nine or ten hours. Ahead of us."

"Okay. So it must be about one in the morning over there. I'll call anyway, you never know, it's a public service and there's probably someone available 24/7."

I clicked on the number displayed on the site and got their voice-mail message.

BECAUSE OF THE sanitary measures linked to the Covid 19 pandemic, and to protect the general public, the prefecture, including the department of motor vehicles is not accepting any visitors. Please call back during our exceptional opening hours, on Tuesdays and Thursdays from ten twenty-five to one pm. Thank you. Take care. Bip.

. . .

"SHIT!" I yelled. "The whole world is against us".

CHAPTER 67

Almost there

<u>Guadeloupe, March 27, 2020</u>

At the very end of the day, the gendarmerie received a call that would finally give them hope.

Ever since Severine Rocamora had left her home, they hadn't been able to find her. She'd apparently taken to the sea, but who knows where! Plus it was at night.

In other circumstances, the territorial waters surrounding the island would have been sufficiently crisscrossed by many boaters and yachtsmen, fishermen, or cargos. But because of the lockdown measures, the sea was also deserted. Chances were slim to nothing that someone had seen that stolen boat. And what direction had she taken? Had she landed on a tiny islet? On another island in the Caribbean arch? How much gas did the boat have in its tanks and how far could she have gone with it? Or maybe she was being clever and wasn't far from Deshaies, waiting to weather the storm? It was like the gendarmes were trying to hunt down a ghost.

As Captain Maxime Servant's morale was in the dumps, he was glad when his assistant rushed into his office.

"Cap? Someone walking just reported a boat that was run aground in a little crick in Grand-Terre. And the description of the boat corresponds to the one that was stolen in Baille-Argent!"

Servant smiled, suddenly interested.

"Where exactly?"

"In Hell's Gate Bay."

"Let's go!" the captain said.

It was an hour's drive from the Pointe à Pitre police station to Hell's Gate, but as there was hardly any traffic and they'd put their flashing lights on, they made it there in forty-five minutes, despite a tropical rainstorm. They parked in Chez Coco's lot, where a gendarme was waiting for them.

The boat, attached to a tree on the bank, where the waters were calm, was swaying. A bit farther on, after the rocky arch, the Atlantic's furious waves were beating against the ragged rocks torn apart from centuries of their incessant backwash. The captain stopped, his cap soaked, sweating in his raincoat, in front of the boat.

"Empty, I imagine?"

"Yes, and the witness didn't see anyone."

"Can you pull it in a bit? I don't feel like stepping in the mud."

The gendarme pulled on the chain. As soon as he was close enough, Servant jumped in. He, who didn't have sea legs, was destabilized by the pitch.

"Have you examined the boat?"

"Yes, Captain. We didn't find much. Except for this," he added, pulling out a plastic bag from his own raincoat. "It fell in the boat, below one of the seats."

Servant took the transparent bag that had some keys inside.

"Car keys," confirmed the gendarme.

And they were car keys, the old-fashioned kind you put into a slot to start the car. A black plastic magnetic key accompanied by two smaller ones, all held together by a metallic ring with a silicone keyring, representing Guadeloupe.

On one side, the captain could read, with a glint of satisfaction in his eyes:

"Bougainvillea Resort, Deshaies"

"Ah! All right! We're almost there. All that's left to do is to find her now," he shouted out to his men.

CHAPTER 68

Strong probabilities

Biscarrosse, March 28, 2020

We both felt a huge void inside our heads, lost in cogitations that were going around in a loop, when the phone rang that evening, fanning even more the mental inferno burning us.

It was Professor Jacques Siethbüller getting back to us about Gregory Labrousse.

"Jerome? My coroner colleague gave me his preliminary findings from the cerebral biopsy he carried out on Gregory. Your hypotheses seem to be confirmed."

"Meaning that the analyses show..."

"The presence of brain eating amoeba, that's right!" confirmed the professor.

"That was the cause of death?"

"No doubt about it. That bacterium is responsible for the primary amoebic meningoencephalitis that the young man had."

"Shit! This is completely crazy! Professor, do you think the others died from the same cause?"

"If they had the same clinical signs, like you told me last time we talked, it's a very strong possibility that they did."

"But we still can't see how or when they were contaminated. A real unsolvable riddle."

"A brain eating riddle?" said the doctor, who was used to laughing at death as many of his colleagues were: black humor as an outlet for death that was omnipresent in their daily lives.

I sighed loudly while thinking quickly.

"It's true, we're racking our brains to try to understand. We thought about the water in the pool, but that doesn't cut it. And we tried to remember where they could have gone swimming in infected waters, but unsuccessfully."

"Maybe you don't know everything they did while they were there?" said Siethbüller.

"We've got the impression that we were nearly always together, for the whole week. Except at night of course, everyone was in their own cabin."

"And what went on at night is none of my business, Jerome! Try to think back on the most minute details, probably something will pop up at one moment or the other."

Colombe was gesturing towards me, in front of her computer, all excited about another sudden idea she'd had. She came closer to the phone, which was in speaker mode.

"Professor, this is Colombe Deschamps. I've got a question."

"Go ahead."

"So, maybe this is nothing, but do you think that technically it would be possible to, um, transport those bacteria, those amoebae, from point A to point B?"

"Ah! That is a pertinent question, and it requires a detailed response. Technically it would be possible to transport contaminated water from a point A to a point B, using a pipeline or some sort of containers. But specific conditions would have to be respected to provoke a PAM."

"Which ones?"

"The first one would be that the amoeba would have to penetrate the encephalon through the nasal cavities, by going through the olfactory epithelium."

"Which means?"

"That ingestion of that amoeba takes place only by

the nose and not by the mouth. That your head would be under water, but you wouldn't necessarily have to had swallowed any of it."

"And any other conditions?"

"The second condition, and it is a very important one, is that the water temperature must never fall below 77°F, otherwise the amoeba would return to its vegetative form."

Colombe turned ashen gray.

She pointed at one of the photos she'd taken when going up to Soufriere Hills volcano.

"I understand now... It's completely mind-boggling!"

CHAPTER 69

Furious waves

<u>Hell's Gate, March 28, 2020</u>

Night always fell quickly in the tropical latitudes. In merely fifteen minutes, the sun had totally disappeared behind the horizon, plunging Guadeloupe into total darkness, which was accentuated by the absence of the moon that night and any artificial lights here at Hell's Gate, with its cliffs overlooking the Atlantic. The rainy weather wasn't helping the gendarmes who had been looking for Severine Rocamora either, since they'd discovered the boat she'd stolen at Baille-Argent Port.

In his impermeable pea jacket, Captain Maxime Servant was going around in circles, walking from one group to another, encouraging them with a few words, a gesture, or simple shared silence.

The masked gendarmes using their flashlights, were examining the shore. And that wasn't easy in that part of the island with its cricks that were battered by furious waves and freezing froth. They were wearing reinforced safety shoes, but they certainly needed them walking on the sharp rocks, like slivered lace that had been cut out by thousands of years of unbridled waves. Some of them though were complaining about being out in that weather, trying to find that "lady on the run," as their captain liked to say.

"Boss! Can you come here?" shouted one of the gendarmes, examining a cranny along a sandy path.

Servant rushed up to him.

"Well? You found her?"

"Not exactly, Cap, but this could interest you."

He pointed at a piece of brightly colored cloth that was hanging on one of the rocks with its shear asperities. The captain kneeled down at the foot of the rock and took the multicolored cloth, looking closely at it.

"It looks like a piece of boubou or sarouel, one of those loose things women wear and that could have been ripped off when she touched that rock here. Her husband said that she wore outfits like that nearly all the time."

"You think maybe it's her then?"

"No idea, it could have been there for days, maybe it belongs to someone else. To be sure we'd have to analyze it, but we don't have enough time. So let's just assume then that it belongs to her and hope that we'll find other identical pieces of fabric a bit further on... up till we find her."

As if a hypothetical god of the police force had heard his voice, a couple of hundred feet farther on, another gendarme shouted out to the captain.

That gendarme was standing on the edge of a spray covered cliff, one that was whipped by furious winds destabilizing the men's balance.

"Over there, Cap, down at the bottom," he said when the captain joined him.

Maxime Servant put his forearm in front of his eyes, to protect them from the pouring rain and looked down at the tiny creek at the foot of the cliff. The waves were incessantly pounding against the rocky walls, hitting them furiously in a muffled roar and watery spray.

In the midst of that natural turmoil, there was a swaying body, floating on its stomach. Long hair was spread out like a bride's wedding veil on a wide back covered with a multicolored sarouel.

CHAPTER 70

Without imagining for even a second

Biscarrosse, March 28, 2020

After having spoken with Professor Siethbüller, I leaned over one of Colombe's shoulders to see what she was pointing at on one of the photos taken while we were climbing up to Soufriere Hills volcano.

She loved taking pictures of things that I thought – and I was often wrong – were useless. There were road signs, maps, graffiti, lots of apparently insignificant junk that would find a place, or not, one day or another in a photo album.

On the photo she was pointing at, there was a sign in front of the pond called Bains Jaunes, or Yellow Baths, at the foot of the ascension.

. . .

"Amoeba present. Do not put your head under water."

Then after that a few sentences explaining the danger of doing that. I nonetheless remembered that during our outing up to the top of the volcano, there were several people in those Baths, including kids. And I hadn't paid any attention to the warning on the sign. But there was no way I would sit in that Bath, much too risky in my humble opinion. I just dipped my toes in that hot water with a slight scent of sulfur, just like the air around the volcano.

"But none of us went in that day!" I said to Colombe.

"You're right."

"So?"

Colombe was excited about her theory. It was getting late, and I was exhausted from having spent my whole day trying to figure out what could have happened. But she knew how to get me to listen.

"We already talked about that, remember that day we went diving in Malendure?"

"Of course."

"Severine wasn't with us that day."

"True."

"And we learned later that she spent that morning putting in place that treasure hunt for when we'd climb the Soufriere. So she was alone then, at the volcano."

"I'm still with you there."

"In your opinion, would she have made the round trip just to hide some pieces of paper for a dumb little game for kids?"

"Why not? She wanted to make sure we'd have a good day there."

"I don't think that was all she did at Soufriere. Remember that afternoon after we went diving in Malendure, we helped her unload her car?"

"Yeah, now that you mention it. She had tons of stuff. Full shopping bags and heavy cases."

"And inside those heavy cases?"

"There were isothermal flasks."

And that scene came back to me in a flash, just as if I were in Deshaies again:

We saw Severine who was unloading her trunk, and seeing as it was full, we offered to give her a hand.

"Thanks, but it'll be okay," she replied.

"But we really want to," Colombe insisted.

She hesitated politely, then accepted.

"After all, that way I won't have to do so many round trips."

I took a large PVC crate, filled with isotherm flasks, that weighed a ton, making sure I didn't fall over from its weight.

"What the heck is in there Severine? Quarts of macerated rum for the whole week or what?"

"Don't be so curious! You need plenty of energy to keep up a steady pace, don't you?" she said with a smile and her arms full of bags. "Looks like you all appreciate it!"

"We never say no to good stuff, especially when we're on vacation," I confirmed, putting the crate down on the table on their patio.

After two other trips to her car, all the groceries were unloaded. Severine thanked us and we left.

"JEROME, THAT WASN'T MACERATED RUM," Colombe whispered.

"Are you insinuating that..."

"What I mean is that she could have transported contaminated water inside those isothermal flasks."

"Oh! Fuck! When I think that I carried that crate...

without imagining one single second… But, after that, what could she have done with the water in those flasks? How could she have transmitted that horrible disease to five victims?"

"That's what we've still got to find out. I got my little idea there too, even though it seems crazy. I only see one possibility."

"You either said too much or not enough."

"Remember our last night at the resort?"

"Of course!

"I'm persuaded that it all happened there, right under our eyes! We didn't see a thing, Jerome. We didn't see it coming…"

CHAPTER 71

Cross-checks

<u>Hell's Gate, March 28, 2020</u>

After the diving team fished out the lifeless body of the lady and brought it back up to the top of the cliffs, Captain Maxime Servant approached it to identity if.

Despite a few bruises on her face and arms, probably caused by hitting those rugged rocks, the woman's features perfectly matched the description they'd been given of her. There was one detail which also betrayed her identity: that scar that deformed her upper lip, that resulted from what most people called, though improperly, a harelip. Severine Rocamora had had it ever since she was a baby, according to her friends.

Severine Rocamora or Violet de Beaulieu? wondered the captain. On her official papers, it was the first name that appeared, but for the past few hours, he now doubted its authenticity.

The investigation, which officially was now open, would probably untangle what was true and what was false in this troubling case. Up till now, there was nothing that could explain the woman's death. Was it an accident, a suicide, or a murder? The investigators would have to determine the cause. The attorney general in Pointe à Pitre, who had recently been nominated, was in charge of that case and had his work cut out for him.

Guadeloupe, an enchanting destination for tourists, seemingly calm, yet was a region where crime ran rampant. The latest figures published for Pointe à Pitre had a 8.2 homicide rate for one hundred thousand inhabitants, whereas a city like Paris only had 4.5... That meant people were twice as likely to be killed on the island than in the French capital! The police force thus didn't have time to take advantage of their island, and this new investigation was just making things worse.

The victim's husband, who had been admitted to the hospital for a contusion and subsequent tests, would have to officially identify his wife's body in the upcoming hours or days. As for now, he was considered as a victim of assault and battery.

Jean-Pierre Wilfried, the couple's friend who had alerted the gendarmes and led them to the victim's home, was giving his deposition at the station. Cross-checking all the contacts that he himself or the two owners of Bougainvillea Domain had had during the past couple of weeks, the investigators linked that case to that of five people who had died in France after they returned from their vacation. And they'd continue to cross-check, as they'd reached the two journalists who were also investigating the same case, as well as they could. With the time difference, it was the middle of the night in Biscarrosse.

CHAPTER 72

You are very much mistaken!

Biscarrosse-Noumea, March 29, 2020

It was an emotionally intense day for us, beginning right when we woke up.

Jean-Pierre had left us a message telling us about Eusebius's aggression by his wife, Severine or Violet, no one cared, as well as informing us that her dead body had been discovered in a creek near Hell's Gate.

"Not far from Man Coco Hole and the *quimboiseur's* cave," Colombe rightfully added.

"You think there's a message behind that?"

"Probably just another coincidence, one more."

While drinking my coffee, I looked up at the clock on our kitchen wall.

"Maybe we should try Noumea again, try to get through to Herve de Beaulieu."

Turning talk into action, I called the prefecture in New Caledonia, where apparently Violet de Beaulieu's father had been working for the past couple of years.

This time, instead of the recorded message on the phone, I got lucky, and a real human being replied.

"Noumea Prefecture, hello. How can I help you?"

I introduced myself as quickly and simply as possible, knowing how difficult a job that must be to answer calls that were sometimes ridiculous. And I had to say that my request was completely ridiculous. I tried to choose my words carefully.

"I'd like to speak to the prefect, Mr. de Beaulieu, in person. It's really important, even urgent."

"Mr. Prefect does not take any personal communication, I'm sorry," the lady said politely.

"I'm sorry I have to insist here, but is he in right now?"

"I'm sorry, Sir, but I'm not allowed to communicate that type of information to you. Why do you want to talk to him? I could eventually give him a message."

"That would already be nice," I tried to appease her. "But what I have to ask him is private."

"In that case, you must have a private way to join him?"

"Unfortunately, I don't. That's why I called the prefecture and I'm counting on your help. Please, I'm begging you. It concerns the safety of people that I know and this could be linked to Mr. de Beaulieu. People have died and I'm afraid that others could too. I'm sure that Mr. Prefect has essential elements that could help us avoid this. If he's in the building, could you simply ask him if he could give me a couple of minutes? It won't be long. Please."

The lady on the phone sighed, nearly resigned.

"Okay, hold on, I'll see what I can do, but I can't promise you anything."

"Thank you so very much!" I said while the music on hold, some obscure remix by Richard Clayderman, filled my left ear.

A few minutes later, a deep voice oozing with authority replaced the switchboard operator's melodious chant.

"Herve de Beaulieu here. I don't have much time. To whom am I speaking and why have you called me?"

The prefect's harsh voice impressed me, but I tried to be diplomatic and introduce myself as briefly as possible. On the other end of the line, on the other side of the world actually, all I could hear were a couple of repetitive "*hums*" when I summed up the tragic events of the past weeks, since Severine's body had been found at Hell's Gate and going back to our stay at Bougainvillea. Every once in a while there would be an absence of his "*hum*," which I didn't understand that would then destabilize me. The prefect's silences were stronger than his words. I finally finished.

"And what have I to do with all this, Mr. Bastaro? How, from New Caledonia, can I help you solve an enigma in the West Indies?"

"I mean... I've got strong presumptions about the fact that Severine Rocamora, who owns Bougainvillea Domain, has hidden her true identity from everyone, something I still don't understand."

"And what is her true identity then?" barked the prefect.

"Our hypothesis is that her real name is Violet de Beaulieu."

A silence that was vaster than the seas separating us went on for ages.

"Sir?" I asked, hearing his muted breathing. "Are you still there?"

"I can hear you, Mr. Bastaro," he replied, with a less authoritarian voice this time. "But I must tell you that your theory has neither head nor tail. You are very much mistaken!"

Shoot, now doubt was insidiously insinuating itself

into my mind. Yet I was nearly sure of myself. I tried to attack from another side.

"Mr. Prefect, you are the father of a girl named Violet de Beaulieu?"

A new silence, a new wave of noisy breathing.

"And how could you be concerned by my private life? I don't know you, I don't know what your intentions are. Why should I answer a question like that?"

"Because lives were taken, undoubtedly because of serious things that took place years ago. Please, Mr. de Beaulieu, I'm begging you, could you just answer this simple question: Is Violet your daughter?"

"Yes," he finally admitted, sighing tiredly. "But that doesn't change a thing in your far-fetched theory."

"Why not?"

"Because my poor daughter Violet died ten years ago, on December 31, 2010..."

AND HE HUNG UP.

CHAPTER 73

They didn't suspect a thing

<u>Hell's Gate, March 29, 2020</u>

The night was short for Captain Maxime Servant and his team.

Severine Rocamora's corpse had been transported to the Pointe à Pitre morgue to be autopsied.

A new team of gendarmes had been sent there to relieve the first one, who had worked through the night. The second team was in charge of sweeping the zone, the entire coastline surrounding the creek where the woman's body had been discovered, to try to find any other clues that would help them try to understand and explain the motive for her act and how it took place.

In the middle of the morning, the captain's phone rang. It was the non-commissioned officer he had sent to Hell's Gate.

"Captain? We just found a document that's gonna interest you! It's a handwritten letter that we found in a cave that had been used, not too far from Man Coco Hole."

"Used?" Servant asked. "You mean someone lives there?"

"Not, not that. Or at least I don't think so. For me it's one of those places where they do black magic, know what I'm talking about?"

Yes, Servant did. Those ancestral rites lived on in the island and they often turned a blind eye to them because they all knew that stuff was just smoke and mirrors, superstitions, hocus pocus. If a handful of pigeons were ready to spend a fortune to get... well, to get their fortunes told, he personally couldn't care less.

"Okay. A place where a *quimboiseur* works, is that it?

"That's right. With candles, a circle made with charcoal, a flashy junk altar, all sorts of stuff like that. Anyway, we found that letter I told you about on the alter."

"So what did the letter say? It's about our case?"

"No doubt about it. Want me to bring it to your office?"

"No way! You take a picture of it, and you send it right off to my email address, got it?"

"Got it boss!

A minute or two later the captain received an email with the attachment he'd been expecting, and he printed it out.

Hell's Gate, March 27, 2020.

My name is Violet de Beaulieu and I died on December 31, 2010.

"WHAT THE HELL IS THIS CRAP?" the captain swore, before continuing to read.

I'm already dead, so now my life is no longer important.

I suffered too much and for too long. Born under an unlucky star, I grew up with the mark of the demon on my face, something

I couldn't hide from my torturers. Some people say that that little dimple you have in the middle of your upper lip was formed the day you were born, when an angel came down and put her finger on your lips to tell you to be quiet. So that the child who was born wouldn't be able to reveal the secrets of the gods, the secrets of reincarnation. For me, I know it wasn't an angel who put her finger on my lip to hush me. When I see that ugly scar that distorts my mouth, I know that it was the Devil in person who forced me to remain silent.

But I didn't want to!

I no longer want to suffer without retaliating.

I don't want all the humiliations I've undergone for my entire life to go unpunished.

Everyone insisted that I was harboring Evil inside, stigmatized by that malefic print.

Did they want me to be Evil incarnate? Not a good idea.

I found them, all of them, one by one and got them together.

I attracted them, cast my nets out.

They didn't suspect a thing. They didn't

see it coming. How could they have?

And I took the law into my own two hands. They thought they were having fun, they were blinded by my ruse. They emptied the chalice right to the very dregs... I did though leave them with some clues that could have set off a couple of alarm bells. But no, they were too foolish.

My plan nearly failed though. I almost regretted to have accepted the reservation of those two young journalists during the same week as those five bastards. I could have eliminated them too, it wouldn't have been hard and that way I would have gotten rid of any embarrassing witnesses. But those two were so cute, so sweet. And they had never hurt me!

And incidentally I'm sure that little Colombe, so intelligent, will end up decrypting all the clues I sowed. I know she'll understand my intentions and she'll discover my stratagem. The investigators will just have to ask her!

Now that I've done my duty, there's no longer any reason for me to remain on Earth.

I'm leaving, serene, peaceful, avenged.

Like Man Coco, I'll be diving into the devasting ocean. Its powerful stormy waves will project me onto the sharp rocks. Should Death take it's time to hold me in its hands, should I suffer, that is not important. It will only be the very last time. One more time, one less time, that's not important now!

I died on December 31, 2010, and today I'm finally alive!

Violet

"WHY ME?" lamented Captain Servant, taking his head into both hands.

—E—

DEATH WAS NO LAUGHING MATTER!

A dark day, a day of grieving, an inconsolable bereavement.

The cemetery emptied out slowly as night was falling. No more passersby putting a wreath on the tomb of a friend or family member, nor no more wannabe genealogists looking for some long-gone ancestor.

No more undertakers either. They had all left, with the satisfaction of a job well done, ready to go back home after a new and hard day's work. The site supervisor was driving up the central path slowly, so that his team, on foot, holding their shovels, rakes, pails and trowels in their hands, could follow him. They'd just finished up the burial place that they'd dug out a few days ago. They'd installed concrete blocks, the marble tombstone and headstone, two tons of material that they'd laid out professionally and without visible emotion, as they did for each of their new tenants, giving their company an excellent reputation. Death was no laughing matter!

While the men were leaving the cemetery, a sudden gust of wind blew a pile of leaves that had been raked that very morning and piled together at the end of the path where they'd just finished working.

Such beautiful red, yellow, orange and brown leaves began to slowly rise and circle in the air, scattering themselves here and there, helter-skelter, on each side of the path, on the headstones, the chrysanthemum plants, Christmas wreaths and commemorative plaques. One of them, with warm shades of parm, deep red and purple, flew above a brand-new tomb. It turned, floated up and down, waved, and then delicately drifted down, as if it were modest, on a commemorative plaque with these engraved words:

For our dear daughter,
Violet de Beaulieu,
1992 – 2010

CHAPTER 74

Shedding light

<u>Pointe à Pitre, March 29, 2020</u>

This case was a never-ending brainteaser for Captain Maxime Servant. It was now up to him to cross-check all of the information, statements and other clues to try to shed light on a hoard of questions.

Who was that Severine Rocamora, who pretended she was Violet de Beaulieu, someone who'd died ten years ago?

And who was that Violet de Beaulieu?

How did she succeed in killing those five victims she mentioned in her manuscript? Who were they?

What did she have against them?

And how could she have done such a thing?

He rapidly found reliable answers to most of his questions, but for the others, it wasn't going to be easy.

He'd have to identify that Colombe lady, the one Severine mentioned. She apparently would be able to help him shed some light on part of those enigmas.

He thought about setting up some interviews, amongst them with Eusebius Saint-Rose, the martyred husband and Jean-Pierre Wilfried, the friend of the couple and person who had alerted them.

He'd also interview the psychiatrist who had briefly seen Severine a few days earlier.

All that would take time, energy, and lead to paperwork and red tape. But after all, that was his job. He'd signed on the dotted line to work like a mule, as he sometimes said to his teammates when they started moaning and groaning.

But for now, there were some new dates he had to integrate into the puzzle he was trying to finish, a file that one of his investigators had just brought in.

"Here's a few elements we gathered when we searched the office of the couple in Deshaies, boss."

"Thanks."

The captain opened the file and found a series of yellowed photos.

On several of them there was a teen about fifteen years old who vaguely looked like Severine Rocamora.

Yet there was something he couldn't pinpoint, something that bothered him without being able to put it into words.

He looked at the back of the photo.

Severine, Auxerre, 2003

But still, something was fishy here. One too many details, or one missing detail. Which one was it?

An image suddenly came to his mind while he was squinting, moving the photo closer to his eyes to make out the details.

The image of the cadaver fished out at Hell's Gate hit him. Her devastated face, ripped apart by the rocks, covered with hematomas, and right in the center, drawing in his look like a magnet, that scar that he'd mentally and instinctively associated with the stigmas of a reconstruction operation for a cleft palate, more commonly called a harelip.

On the yellowish photo of Severine as a young girl, a perfect and splendid smile, without any scars nor congenital malformations.

What if that body we recovered from the sea wasn't the one we thought it was? Captain Servant wondered.

CHAPTER 75

Our mill to grind brainpower

Biscarrosse, March 29, 2020

"Seriously!" I exclaimed as there was silence on the other end of the line. "I don't understand a thing anymore. "Who is Severine? Who is Violet?"

Calling Prefect Herve de Beaulieu, in Noumea, left us with more questions than answers. And I would have had loads of questions for him, but the way he'd hung up on me didn't encourage me to call him back. I figured though that it would be to no avail, as he'd certainly told the receptionist to block me.

To top it all, an unexpected element came to bring some water to our mill to grind brainpower. We got a call from Gwada, from the Pointe à Pitre gendarmerie.

"Captain Maxime Servant here. Is this Miss Colombe Deschamps?"

"Speaking, why?"

"Miss, I'm calling because your name came up in the framework of an ongoing investigation, as an ocular witness. I'd like to ask you a few questions."

"I see what you're talking about. How can I help you?"

The gendarme on the phone explained to Colombe the latest developments in the case, terminating by the confessions that Severine/Violet had made.

"In that handwritten letter, the victim – and potentially the guilty party – referred to a certain Colombe who had stayed at their resort. Mr. Jean-Pierre Wilfried, someone we also questioned as a witness, confirmed that it was you and gave us your number. It would seem that you could help us understand some of the things that occurred while you were on vacation in Deshaies."

"That's true, I think I now understand quite a few things that match what you said you read in her confessions. You must be wondering about how the five people who died recently were contaminated."

"That's right. In her letter she clearly says that you're 'so intelligent' and that you'd be able to '*decrypt all the clues, understand her intensions, and discover her stratagem.'* Could you tell me what you discovered?"

Colombe sat down comfortably, took a deep breath and started telling him the details of her theory.

"So, here we go... it might seem crazy, insane, impossible, whatever you want, yet captain, I'm nearly sure that this is how it took place."

"Go ahead, tell me everything, we'll try to figure it out later."

Colombe told the gendarme what seemed logical to us, thanks to the statements we'd obtained and cross-checks we'd proceeded with. How Severine had attracted her five preys to Guadeloupe using personal and targeted flyers, sent to them by email with an address that already had a clue in it about Violet, Bougainvillea.violet.travel@hotmail.fr. Then she described the treasure hunt that our hostess had concocted for the day that we were climbing up to the top of Soufriere Hills volcano, and the other clues, that were dissimulated amongst apparently innocuous sentences on the five pieces of paper. Severine thus had used five clues, five words, five victims, and you could take a word from each of them vertically to form the unequivocal sentence: "*You will die for Violet.*" She finished by telling him what we learned from a trustworthy source, after the brain biopsy had been performed on Gregory Labrousse's body, which was the presence of brain eating amoeba. And they were responsible for the primary amoebic meningoencephalitis that had killed him, just as it had the four other victims with similar symptoms.

"We'll have to autopsy the four others then," said the captain. "I'll contact the prosecutor. So, if I understand correctly, we now know the cause of death of those persons but what I still don't get is the 'how.' What us cops call the 'modus operandi' in our criminal jargon. Could you explain your theory, Miss Dechamps?"

"Well, we thought about that question, and I think we understood how Severine pulled this off. The day that we all went diving in Malendure, she didn't come with us. That day she went to Soufriere to hide clues for our upcoming treasure hunt and above all – at least, that's what I'm thinking – to fill quite a few isothermal flasks with contaminated water from the Yellow Baths located at the foot of the volcano. That afternoon Jerome and I helped her unload those very same flasks and take them to her bungalow. But I don't know where she hid them till the last night of our vacation. Probably in a place where she'd be sure that the water would remain at 77°F, which was the temperature required for the survival of the bacteria."

"What happened then that last night?" the gendarme asked.

"I'm nearly sure that that was when the contamination took place."

"But how?"

"That night, everyone had been drinking a lot and all we wanted to do was to have fun. Severine had organized another game, a ridiculous one, but one in which we all took part, including Jerome and I."

"What was that game?"

"Well, hard to describe, it was a goofy one. She'd put these basins on the ground that were filled with water and a little bit of rum, now that I think about it. And then at the bottom of each basin, there were three pieces of a plantain banana that we had to pick up with our teeth, I forgot to tell you, we had our hands behind our backs and then spit the pieces of banana out again in a saucer at the other end of the pool. Meaning our heads were under water. And during all that excitement, it was impossible not to have drunk any of that water or inhaled it. So for me, that's where the contamination took place, Captain!"

"That's crazy! But you two also participated, right? And you're both fine."

"I think that we could have easily died like the others," said Colombe unsteadily.

"Like she said in her confession letter, she could have eliminated you two also, but she liked you both. She didn't have any grudges against you, and she was only targeting the other five."

"I suppose then that she placed us all in front of the good or the bad basins. And now that I think of it, I can see her pointing at our places."

"She didn't leave anything to chance," confirmed Maxime Servant. "She had well thought out her plan and it was carefully executed. A perfect crime. But that's going to be hard to prove. Except that we now have various statements – including yours – plus her own written confession. Speaking of which, that letter seems extremely confused. She says her name is Violet de Beaulieu and that she died on December 31, 2010. Does that name ring a bell, Miss Dechamps?"

"It certainly does. We briefly talked to her father, a man named Herve de Beaulieu, who is the prefect in Noumea. And he confirmed that his daughter died on that date. But then he hung up on us. If you question him, I think he'll be more cooperative with someone in the police."

"If Violet died in 2010, why is that Severine

pretending to be her?" wondered Captain Servant out loud.

"In my humble opinion, you'll have to consult a psychiatrist to find the answer."

CHAPTER 76

Like two peas in a pod

<u>Pointe à Pitre / Noumea, March 30, 2020</u>

Captain Servant had to find the right time at each latitude to audition Prefect de Beaulieu.

It was thus early in the morning in the Antilles and late at night in Noumea. Seven in the morning for Captain Servant and ten at night for the Prefect.

"So, is this terrible story all true then?" asked Prefect Herve de Beaulieu wearily.

"Unfortunately it is, Mr. Prefect. That's why I need your full and entire cooperation. I have to hear your statement on a couple of precise points. Lives were stolen here, and if I understand correctly, the roots of this sad case go back many years. And, according to our sources, you witnessed those years and events. Violet de Beaulieu was your daughter, is that correct?"

"She was, yes. And will always be in my heart."

The prefect's voice warbled.

"And your daughter was the one who died on December 31, 2010, in Dijon?"

"That's also correct."

"How then can I explain that another person assumed her identity? Did you ever hear of Severine Rocamora?

"Should I have?"

"I assume so, yes. Remember, Mr. Prefect, you accepted to cooperate with us," Servant reminded him.

"I did know someone named Severine Rocamora."

"Please tell me where and when."

There was an instant of silence between New Caledonia and Guadeloupe. Herve de Beaulieu finally began to speak.

"In 1989, I met an adorable woman. Her married name was Victoire Rocamora. But she was a widow. That marvelous lady was still grieving when I met her. Her husband was felled by a type of very aggressive cancer. Victoire had just turned twenty-five and was already a widow, with a daughter who was two years old. Severine, who of course had her father's last name. I fell in love with both of them and immediately adopted the child. Officially recognizing Severine Rocamora. Two years later Victoire got pregnant and had our daughter, Violet."

"So, Violet de Beaulieu and Severine Rocamora were step-sisters then," the captain summarized. "They grew up together, right?"

"Despite the difference in their ages, five years, yes, they did grow up together. They were very close to each other. And God is my witness here, Violet needed her big sister, something that I now regret not having understood earlier."

"Why are you saying that?"

"I'm sure you'll understand me, Captain, because both of us are in the same boat."

"What do you mean?" asked the gendarme, astonished.

"Our civil servant status, as officers. You know, like I do, how difficult it can be to have high-responsibility jobs where you are forced to move every two or three years, sometimes even after only a year, according to transfers that your hierarchy imposes on you, or your ambition to climb the rungs in the administrative ladder."

"I certainly do," sighed Servant, who was still single

because of his professional instability. "But where are you going with that?"

"I just meant that because of my very intense professional life, one where I kept on moving around, I didn't really worry about our two daughters. We dragged them with us wherever I was transferred to: Auxerre, Gueret, Strasbourg, Dijon. Each time the girls had to change schools, leave their friend and try to make new ones – and that is if they had time to make friends. Which was even more difficult for Violet because of her congenital infirmity.

"The operation she had to reconstruct her cleft palate?"

"Exactly. You can call it a harelip, everyone does," the prefect said sadly. "Violet grew up with that. Except that us, her parents, we didn't know, we didn't see her internal suffering. She never complained to us about the bullying and harassment she was a victim of at school. Just imagine, the prefect's daughter who was a monster... Kids are so mean between themselves. And the monsters aren't always the ones that you think they are. She only told Severine, her big sister, about this. She's the one who told us after 2010. But it was too late. Those two were like two peas in a pod..."

"To the point that Severine wanted to identify herself as her sister after she died?"

"Probably. That tragic event completely destroyed our family. My wife just withered away, she couldn't stand the fact that her daughter had died, and just three years later, she joined her. As for Severine, she fled France and disappeared without giving us any news. I learned later that she'd found stability in Guadeloupe. But I was far from imagining that insanity that was smoldering inside her, if what we just discovered is true. As for me, I asked for and obtained posts on the other side of the world, in Reunion Island, Polynesia, and now in New Caledonia. I wanted to put as much distance as possible between my past and my shame for having been so blind. Shame also to have been ashamed to have been the father of a daughter with a face like that. It's idiotic," the prefect said, sobbing, touched by his own confessions.

"But it's human," replied Captain Servant philosophically. "No one's perfect in this world, something we both see in our professional activities... Oh, one more detail."

"Yes?"

"Severine didn't have a scar on her lip when she was a child, did she?"

"Not a one, I can affirm that. Why?"

"Because she has one now. She must have had an accident..."

CHAPTER 77

The twists and turns of the human mind

Pointe à Pitre, April 15, 2020

Doctor Damien Michelin, the psychiatrist, had filled out his authorization to leave his home with the motive of an "administrative or legal convocation" checked, and was now in Captain Maxime Servant's office.

"Doctor, now do you understand?"

"Let's just say that with all the statements and data gathered, I was able to establish quite a complete anamnesis."

"An ana-what?" Servant cut him off.

"Oh! Excuse my jargon. An anamnesis is a Greek word coming from '*ana*' and '*nmesis*' which literally means 'raising souvenirs.' Or in other words, all the antecedents of a person. Medical antecedents, interviews, results of exams carried out, etc. In the case we're interested in, I used the declaration of witnesses, meaning the victim's husband, that couple of journalists, the friend of the couple, the father, all those people you communicated to me. Of course I also used the consultation that I had with Mrs. Rocamora in my cabinet as a firsthand source. Lastly, reading and analyzing her diary and her testament-letter to complete the picture. A very dark and bleak picture, believe me."

"Tell me your conclusions, Doctor."

The doctor cleared this throat and picked up his notes before beginning to give him technical explanations that would give a picture of Severine Rocamora's psychological portrait and perhaps explain why she killed five people before taking her own life.

"Severine Rocamora suffered from a syndrome called 'hyper-empathy.'"

"You're starting to speak Greek again, Doctor! You're going to lose me."

"Don't worry, I'll explain it in plain terms. I'm sure you've heard of the buzzword, 'empathy?'"

"Of course, everyone uses that word now. Tell me about it."

"Empathy is a very positive, useful and desirable quality. It is the aptitude to *put yourself in another person's position*. That means that you are able to think like them, you feel their emotions to understand their heartaches, their feelings, their apprehensions, everything. In a nutshell, '*I feel what you feel*,'' or '*I understand what's happening to you*.' All of that is very good! But as always in life, an excess of anything isn't good, what's ideal is to be balanced. And here, hyper-empathy is an excess of empathy. Too much is too much! A normally empathic person will feel the emotions of another person whereas a person suffering from a hyper-empathy syndrome will become a *mirror* and a *sponge*. You see where I'm going here?"

"I do, thanks. So you're going to tell me about Severine and her step-sister, Violet?"

"Exactly. When they were young, the two step-sisters were always very close to one another. The younger one, Violet, only told her big sister about how she suffered day in and day out, permanently, at school and probably elsewhere. She was a victim of being mocked, made fun of, rejected, and betrayal, in particular by those five people that Severine consequently became obsessed with. Severine felt not only what Violet herself felt, but she also suffered from that. It was like a type of physical and visceral pain, something that generated anxiety. But what was the worst was the Severine could no longer discriminate where she ended and where her sister began. She '*became*' Violet."

"Which explains the beginning of her letter. *'My name is Violet de Beaulieu and I died on December 31, 2010,'* the captain remembered, as that introductory sentence had shocked him.

The doctor nodded his head.

"That's an incontestable proof of her mental disorder. And that date is the turning point in their story. On one hand, the younger daughter effectively dies, and on the other hand, the psychological death of the older one. From that day on, the day that Violet killed herself – and we now know that she also committed suicide – Severine mentally *became* Violet. From that moment, her hyper-empathy turned into a personality disorder, a duality. Severine Rocamora showed evident signs of the deterioration of her own identity, as we can see in many passages of her diary. The way she uses 'I' becomes confused. She can no longer distinguish '*I Severine*' from '*I Violet*.' And that diary has something else that's unique."

"Oh? What?"

"Something which is glaringly obvious, in the light of what we now know of Severine's pathology. In reality, that diary is not really Violet's nor is it really Severine's."

"Whose is it then?" asked Servant.

"Both of theirs! It's Violet's diary *then* Severine's. It has confessions that Violet made up until December 31, 2010 and after that Severine's beginning on January 1st, 2011. Making their handwriting a bit different, before and after that turning point. Severine, in her delusion of identification, nearly copied the way her sister who killed herself wrote. I had one of my colleagues who's a graphologist analyze their writing and he was astonished: the differences were really minute."

Dr. Michelin took the diary and opened it to a page where he'd put a bookmark.

"Here are the last words the real Violet wrote before killing herself. You'll see, they're eloquent:

> *Never again, I can't stand suffering anymore, year after year, disillusion after disillusion... I've got no future.*

"No future," repeated the gendarme.

"And as of the next day, it was Severine Rocamora's hand that wrote the following pages. Severine snitched her younger sister's diary as of the very next day, continuing in her vivid souvenir. That's how she made herself think that her sister was still alive, she gave herself that illusion, she was living through her sister. A psychotic type of behavior. A huge obsession that lasted ten years, up until she also committed suicide, after having taken revenge on the outrages her sister had been a victim of. A person suffering from hyper-empathic syndrome, someone who's overprotective only has one obsession: solving all the problems the others have. For ten years Severine's excessive compassion had grown, up to the point where she felt guilty and responsible for Violet's hardships and suffering. A poisoned cocktail, composed of an identity disorder, obsession and suffering. All this led her to feel like she was responsible for her death and that it was thus a legitimate reason to eliminate the five people that Violet had designated as the one's who'd tortured her during her youth. *'You will die for Violet!'* Severine had warned them during the treasure hunt at the volcano."

"Had they understood then, perhaps they would have been able to escape death," Servant sighed.

"It's possible. So, anyway, those are my conclusions."

He began to get up.

"Doctor, there's still one little detail that's niggling in my mind."

"Which is?"

"The scar Severine had on her upper lip. She didn't have one when she was younger."

"Ah! You're right, I had forgotten to mention that aspect of her psychotic disorder. I was able to access Mrs. Rocamora's medical file when she was admitted to the Pointe à Pitre Hospital in 2011, in the Reconstructive Surgery Unit . Not surprisingly, it wasn't a case of reconstruction of a cleft palate, like Violet had. It was a multiple and large wound that had been caused by a cutter."

"An aggression?"

"I'd say a mutilation! A voluntary one. A symbolic scoring with the goal of being stitched up again, reconstructed you could say, like her sister had been. Remember, as of 2011, she'd *become* Violet! This is a syllogism."

"What's that?"

"It's a three-part argument, based on logic. I *am* Violet. *But*, Violet is disfigured by a scar on her upper lip. *So*, I must also be disfigured by a scar on my lip too."

"This concludes the demonstration," confirmed the gendarme. "But still, self-mutilation like that, she must have been completely nuts!"

"It's true and yet so logical. Inflicting physical pain

on yourself to better identify yourself with the other person, the one who is psychologically suffering. The twists and turns of the human mind. It's something I see every day, unfortunately, that's my bread and butter."

"The darkness of the human soul," agreed Servant, "that's also what pays the bills for me."

CHAPTER 78

A perfect crime?

Biscarrosse, April 30, 2020

On the other side of the Atlantic, the Rocamora case had been closed. We'd signed our declarations as witnesses and would be sending them to Captain Servant. The day before, he'd given us his conclusions – the case hadn't gone to trial as the verified guilty party had committed suicide – with six deaths, not including Violet's death, an expiratory victim of the other five. All of that was like a terrible chain reaction, an avalanche of dominoes, falling one after the other because of the lowest and darkest human instincts.

No one would be judged, as all the participants in that tragedy had perished.

"Could we call this a perfect crime?" I asked Colombe while we were enjoying our hour's outing in the forest, like every day since the beginning of the French lockdown.

"It could have been if Severine hadn't written her letter. She left too many clues, on purpose of course. She's guilty. When I think that we were there without realizing a thing, that's completely crazy! We didn't notice anything! And the clues were right in front of us: the Soufriere treasure hunt, that was written black on white! And all the rest could have been avoided..."

Colombe's voice began to break.

"Okay, stop that and stop it now! We can't blame ourselves. We couldn't have known. After the fact, alright, but when it was happening, no!"

"And the murder weapon that we both had in our hands? Huh? We helped Severine transport those isothermal flasks from her car to her bungalow. The murder weapon –that brain-eating bacteria – was in the flasks that we had in our own two hands."

"Once again, we learned that after the fact, not when we were carrying them."

"And the day the crime was committed? We were right there, next to the criminal and her five victims. We were laughing, playing, having fun in the pool when five people were joyfully dipping their heads into those contaminated basins. A five-fold crime that took place right under our eyes, in total euphoria! All that in that beautiful resort, with its lush vegetation, in that sweet country of Guadeloupe.

"Killing people while making a game out of it, that is something that's quite original. Nearly perfect, that's true. Plus the victims themselves contributed to their own deaths, if I can put it like that. All five of them plunged their heads several times in those contaminated basins. Drinking and breathing in their chalice to the dregs."

"Nearly consenting victims, though of course they had no idea. And just think that we did the exact same thing! But luckily not in the same basins," Colombe sighed.

We continued walking silently, both shook up by the memories of those few though enchanting days in Gwada.

"Maybe that's where Severine made a mistake," I said, summing it up. "Not eliminating us too. We became witnesses of her crimes, though they were well hidden."

"No. On the contrary, that was what she wanted, she wanted us to witness her crime, she wanted us to discover her intentions and see how her plan succeeded. That probably was what saved us."

We continued our walk, taking the same path, the one that led us to a bunch of wildflowers in the woods. Colombe kneeled, picked one of the flowers and brought it to her nose to smell its sweet fragrance.

A violet.

One of the most beautiful flowers in our undergrowth.

A BEAUTIFUL AND INTOXICATING VIOLET.

— Epilogue —

<u>Gwada, June 30, 2020</u>

The two men accosted on tiny Caret Islet. There, under a blue cloudless sky, cooled by a slight breeze from the sea, they were sitting side by side on the white sand beach, looking out over the immense calm sea which was just inches from their toes.

Soothed and at rest.

"Now I understand why Severine always hid those dark years of her past from me," declared Eusebius. "It was too hard to bear, especially for her, like a sponge, someone who absorbed all the pain others had. Especially her little sister, Violet, someone I didn't even know existed."

"Sometimes ignorance is much better than knowledge," Jean-Pierre replied laconically.

The diving instructor had taken Eusebius and himself on his electric catamaran to the tiny island that was slowly disappearing. After a much too long lockdown period and so many tragic events, finally freed, how they were trying to appease their souls. And that was a perfect place for it, making them the Robinson and Friday of modern times.

"I'm going to put Bougainvillea Domain up for sale," said the Guadeloupean. "I can't live there anymore."

"I totally understand. What are you gonna do now?"

"Hmm. With what I get from the sale, I'll see. After, I don't know, maybe I'll try to get a job in another resort, for lawncare and stuff like that. Or try my luck in France."

"Are you crazy? Stay here in Gwada! Why don't you come and work with me?" asked Jean-Pierre. "I'm thinking of purchasing another boat. You've got your boating license, haven't you? We could be associates!"

"Yup. I think that would be just fine."

The two men both nodded at the same time, without looking at each other, still looking out to sea. Pensive and optimistic.

Looking out towards a brighter future.

THE END

Acknowledgments

The novel you've just read germinated, then grew, like a virus, a bacterium, during our vacation in Guadeloupe, just a few days before the Covid 19 lockdown that struck France, closing it down as if a shroud had been tossed over it, as well as the entire world. A few more days and my wife, children and I, would have been "stuck" in the West Indies for two months. I must admit though that our prison could have been worse, we could have ended up in Cayenne.

And that was where, when we were climbing the Soufriere Hills volcano, I had the key idea for this new book. As yes, I do believe that it's possible, if you stick closely to the *modus operandi* I describe in this book, to commit a perfect crime. Perfect...

Of course, all this was only fiction and elucubrations in this author's brain.

Or was it? It's up to you to decide, I wash my hands of the matter...

As for Covid 19, I hesitated for quite a while before deciding to include it in the plot that took place during that complicated period. After all, this is a fiction book so why take all the trouble to have my characters developing during a restrained space and time?

I ended up deciding that the virus could play a key part in my plot and narrative tension by imprisoning my characters in a type of actions that took place behind closed doors.

I'd like to thank, as I often do, my wife, for being my very first reader and special co-author.

Also my team of beta-readers.

Thanks, Sophie Ruaud, who is my proofreader.

And thank you, Jacquie Bridonneau, my favorite French to English translator, without whom you wouldn't have read this book in English.

But above all, I wish to thank my loyal readers all throughout the world. Without you, an author is nothing. And without us, readers have nothing... to read! The circle is thus closed.

See you all soon then for some new adventures of Colombe and Jerome Bastaro, in my new book starring them, *Bloody Bonds, A Race against Death.*

Bibliography

THE KAREN BLACKSTONE SERIES

Into Thin Air (2022) *(Winner of the Cuxac d'Aude Favorite Novel, 2023 / Finalist in the Loiret Crime Award, 2023)*

I Want Mommy (2023) *(N°1 in Amazon Storyteller France sales 2023)*

The Lost Son (2023)

Alone (2024)

Volume 5 to be published in 2025

THE BASTERO SERIES

French Riviera (2017) *(Winner of the Indie Ilestbiencelivre Award 2017)*

Perfect crime (2020)

Bloody Bonds (2022)

OTHER NOVELS

True Blood Never Lies (2022)

Thirty Seconds Before Dying (2021)

Eight more Minutes of Sunshine (2020)

Who am I?

Nino S. Theveny is one of France's leading indie authors. He's married and has two children. In 2019 he was laid off from a multinational company and decided to make the most of his newly found liberty, turning to writing, his passion, which is now his day job.

With 15 books published to date, Nino S. Theveny, Sébastien Theveny's American pen name, has over 200,000 readers. Translated into English, Spanish, Italian, and German, his thrillers are appreciated throughout the entire world.

With his fourteen-year-old son, he has also co-authored a thriller for young adults which was published in March, 2024.

Printed in Dunstable, United Kingdom

65610081R00296